"Be advised: Taffy Cannon's A POCKETFUL OF KARMA dishes up far more than a pocketful of masterful suspense. Funny, tough, smart, moving, this is a mystery debut that should not be missed. Move over, Grafton and Paretsky—Taffy Cannon is here."

—WENDY NELSON HORNSBY
Author of *Bad Intent*

"Taffy Cannon creates a strong sense of place so that the reader can see, smell, hear and feel her Southern California settings. Her gently cynical depiction of the Southern California culture is amusing, sometimes affectionate, sometimes satirical, always entertaining. Her smooth clear prose, wry sense of humor and keen insight make her a new mystery writer to watch."

—*Grounds for Murder Newsletter*

"This very good first mystery is definitely worth acquiring. . . . A well-told, compassionate tale with an underlying theme of accepting responsibility."

—*Booknews from The Poisoned Pen*

"Taffy Cannon's A POCKETFUL OF KARMA treats Southern California as a culture, not just a region. . . . Cannon's sleuth has a good sense of humor, and her story line is strong. . . . Throughout, the author plays up her Southern California setting well, distinguishing its identity and particular brands of looniness from those bred elsewhere in our country of regions."

—*Wilson Library Journal*

By Taffy Cannon:

CONVICTIONS: A Novel of the Sixties
A POCKETFUL OF KARMA*

*Published by Fawcett Books

A POCKETFUL OF KARMA

Taffy Cannon

FAWCETT CREST • NEW YORK

For Bill and Melissa

A Fawcett Crest Book
Published by Ballantine Books
Copyright © 1993 by Taffy Cannon

Library of Congress Catalog Card Number: 92-43618

ISBN 0-449-22388-4

This edition published by arrangement with Carroll and Graf Publishers, Inc.

Manufactured in the United States of America

First Ballantine Books Edition: August 1995

10 9 8 7 6 5 4 3

PROLOGUE

There was an incredible surge, far beyond the familiar adrenaline rush, knowing you were about to kill, a soaring transcendancy over plebian rules and laws and conventions.

The killer.

It had an intriguing ring to it, a chilly toughness. *The killer.* And maybe it hadn't started out to be like this, but now there was no choice. There was simply too much at stake.

Deciding to do it, that had been the hard part. The planning went much more smoothly: possibilities explored, foundations laid, contingencies covered. And with the plans complete, there was a new feeling as well, a strange sense of calm.

But now it was necessary to move, and to move quickly. There were still too many things that could go wrong.

So the killer gazed down at the young woman slumped in the chair and smiled solicitously. "It's time to go home, Debra."

Debra raised her head slowly. Her eyes were dimmed, foggy. "Wha—"

"Time to go home. You're exhausted."

"I'm ... all right." The girl shook her head as if to clear it. "I'm just so ... so very tired." She gave a whisper of a smile, a vestigial apology, then flopped her head back again.

"You may be getting sick. There's a lot going around." To put it mildly. The killer smiled again.

So far, so good. The original plan would have been better, of course, but Debra's guard was raised and it would never work. That was why the planning had been so important, why the contingencies were so necessary. This substitute plan had a drawback or two, but it would yield the same ultimate result: a tidy solution to a potentially nasty problem.

The killer took Debra's elbow and helped the limp girl to her feet, walked her slowly and deliberately across the room. Debra's things were piled in a neat stack by the door. The girl started to reach down and momentarily lost her balance.

"Never mind, I'll come back for that."

They walked in tandem into the starless night, crossed the few short steps to the waiting car. It was much cooler now, with a hint of fog creeping into the nighttime air. The killer opened the passenger door and rolled down the window. Debra collapsed onto the seat, reached instinctively to fasten her seat belt.

"I'll be right back." The killer walked briskly away, pulling on thin cotton gloves.

Moments later, with Debra's things stashed in the trunk, the killer slipped behind the wheel and started the engine.

Debra looked over, confused, feeling perhaps the first glimmer that something was wrong. "I thought—"

"Just rest." The response was gentle, soothing, almost parental. "Don't worry about anything. I'll get you home."

Debra's shrug was almost imperceptible as she leaned back against the seat and closed her eyes. That was better.

When the car stopped later, everything was dark and eerily quiet. The killer turned off the engine, stepped out into the still night, and looked carefully in every direction. There remained only to select a weapon, and that was simple. The ground was littered with fist-sized rocks. One slipped easily into the old sweat sock, a perfect fit.

When the passenger door opened again, Debra didn't stir. She never noticed the glove on the hand that released her seat belt. It took a brisk shaking of her shoulders to rouse her at all.

"This way, come along now." The tone was gentle and firm, as if addressing a child. This part would have to be done quickly.

"Why are we . . . what are you . . . ?" The girl's words were slurred and hesitant as the killer helped her out of the car. Confused, she tried to turn, to get back into the car again.

"No, no, this way," the killer instructed her. "Here."

Debra looked up now, her eyes momentarily clearing. Fear filled them as they widened in sudden recognition and realization. The killer could tell that the girl was remembering, knew it was necessary to act swiftly.

"Home," Debra started to say, turning back toward the car. "Let me go—"

The killer swung a fist forward and smashed the rock into Debra's jaw. The girl gave a small gasp and cry as she sprawled backward.

After that, the rest was surprisingly easy.

CHAPTER 1

Nan Robinson frowned as she flipped through the file on her desk. She was not looking forward to the upcoming interview, yet another remorseful attempt to expiate an appalling list of legal sins and omissions. James Weston Richfield would slink in with his tail between his legs, an upbeat note from his substance abuse counselor, and a promise that he would never ever again betray the trust put in him by the State Bar of California.

They all did.

They were starting to run together in her mind, Nan realized, these fortyish fellows who flushed away promising legal careers as they frantically juggled the demands of creditors, ex-wives, office overhead, miscellaneous addictions, and the clients who invariably ended up on the bottom of the heap.

Richfield, for instance, had maintained a solo plaintiff's personal injury practice uneventfully for eleven years before his own downward slide began. Then he started missing appearances and stopped returning phone calls. He settled one case against his client's wishes and held the payment for six months before passing along the client's share. He blew the statute of limitations for another client, leaving the poor sap in financial limbo and setting himself up tidily for the inevitable malpractice charge. By the time he checked into Betty Ford, his practice was in shambles.

Nan raised her head at a tentative rap on her office door. "Nan?" Violet Thomas looked worried. "You have a minute?"

4

"Of course, Violet," Nan told her. "Come on in. What's up?"

The office manager for the State Bar Trial Division had been, for years, the spiritual center of the entire operation. Violet knew everything about "her" people—the attorneys and investigators and support staff. She remembered their birthdays and their children's birthdays, knew whose marriages were floundering and whose illnesses were truly serious. A widow with Missouri grandchildren, she worked far longer hours than she was expected or paid to. Violet was tall and angular, with the kind of posture that could only be called "good carriage." Her neatly permed white hair had just enough silver rinse to highlight the dark violet-blue eyes for which she'd been named.

A worry line deepened now between those eyes. "This letter came in the morning mail," Violet said, laying an envelope carefully on Nan's desk. "I'm not exactly sure what to do with it."

The address was handwritten to Mrs. Debra Fontaine at the State Bar Trial Division. The return address was on a tiny white sticker featuring an American flag: Mrs. Peter LaRoche on an unfamiliar street in South Bend, Indiana.

But Debra hadn't worked at the State Bar since she married Tony Fontaine and moved out to Canyon Country. What's more, she'd taken back her maiden name, LaRoche, the moment she filed for divorce. Her mother might have chosen to ignore the latter, but she certainly should have known the former. Why on earth would she send mail to her daughter in an office where Debra hadn't been employed in over three years?

"Very strange," Nan agreed.

"I was just going to forward it," Violet said, "but then I realized that I don't have a current address for Debra anymore. I thought you might know. . . ." Her voice trailed off delicately.

"Sure, I've got her address, assuming she hasn't moved again in the last three months." Not likely, since Debra was living in a Hollywood bungalow purchased with the first installment of an enormous insurance settlement. "I'll get it to her."

"Thanks," Violet said with some relief. "It just seemed, so . . . so . . . peculiar."

"Don't give it another thought," Nan told her.

After Violet left, Nan turned the envelope over and over in her hands, feeling guilty. She hadn't really even thought about Debra for months now, since that lunch they had after Debra's first meeting with her divorce lawyer back in May.

And she should have.

Debra had been through hell in the past year. Her eighteen-month-old son, her pride and joy, the glue she hoped would hold together an already faltering marriage, had been hit by a car. Timmy lingered in intensive care for seven horrible days before he died. Nan did what she could at the time—precious little, really—but didn't keep in touch afterward the way she could have.

Should have.

She owed Debra at least that much.

Nan had first know Debra LaRoche as a pigtailed border-line tomboy with perennially skinned knees, a peppy little girl who climbed trees and roller-skated backward and raced her two-wheeler fearlessly down the quiet streets of Spring Hill, Illinois. She was called Debbie then, a doted-on only child with limitless energy and a bright, cheerful smile. The LaRoches lived a few doors down from the Robinsons. The two families weren't exactly friends, but everyone in the neighborhood got along reasonably well, and Nan occasionally baby-sat for Debbie.

Debbie LaRoche was barely ten when Nan left Spring Hill for Stanford. At some point during Nan's college years, the LaRoche family moved to South Bend, and apart from her mother's sometime references, Nan never thought about them again. Then, when Nan was twenty-six, the midwestern old girls' network swung into action. Debra's mother wrote to Nan's mother, who called Nan, who said sure, have Debra get in touch when she got to LA.

Nan somehow expected a larger version of the little girl

she'd known in Spring Hill. Longer pigtails maybe, bigger Band-Aids. She was totally unprepared for the young woman who breezed into LA with an aspiring rock musician boyfriend and a recent degree from an Indianapolis secretarial school.

Debra as an adult was tiny, vivacious, and tough, in an oddly vulnerable way. She showed up at Nan's apartment on a Saturday afternoon in skintight jeans, a glittery silver tube top, and matching silver high heels. Her hair was spiked in a punk cut, and she wore a single earring that resembled a hotel chandelier and brushed her bare shoulder. There were no Band-Aids in sight.

She was nice enough, but there was none of the connection that sometimes happens when people who've known each other long ago come together again. They were polite strangers, essentially meeting for the first time. With definite misgivings, Nan arranged a meeting for Debra with the office manager at McSweeney Lane, the prestigious law firm where Nan was then a junior associate.

It came as a distinct shock, then, when Debra showed up at the firm—in a prim little dress with gold button earrings, hair demurely combed down—and demonstrated formidable secretarial skills. She was promptly snapped up as a "floater." During the next few months, Nan saw Debra around the office occasionally and they spoke politely.

Then Nan's secretary went on medical leave for gallbladder surgery, and Debra was offered as a substitute. The situation had great potential for embarrassing disaster. What if they didn't get along? Could Debra take instructions from somebody she'd first known when she was losing her baby teeth? Could Nan maintain a professionally detached relationship with someone she'd tucked into bed wearing pink footed pajamas?

Finally Nan reasoned that it would only be a few weeks, that Debra had to be competent or she wouldn't have been hired, that there was no way around it without hurting Debra's feelings. She gritted her teeth, smiled graciously, and agreed.

Afterward, she shuddered to think how close she had come to losing the secretary of a lifetime. Not only did Debra sweep a gust of fresh air into the stuffy legal environment, she was also a crackerjack secretary and quickly made herself indispensable. She was wholly professional, asked for no special favors, took no advantage. She could even spell, a rarity in California, where spelling had apparently been dropped from the state educational curriculum shortly after the death of Father Junipero Serra.

By applying to office politics the sort of diplomacy which gave McSweeney Lane its national reputation, Nan managed to keep Debra even after her own secretary returned. And when Nan left McSweeney Lane, Debra went with her.

Gradually Debra had opened up to Nan, and it became clear that the only resemblance to that long-ago little girl was a fearless sense of adventure. Part of her charm was her naive awe of Los Angeles. Hopelessly starstruck, she spent her days at her word processor and her nights in music clubs. She bought maps to the stars' homes. She lined up to watch the stars arrive for the Oscars and the Grammies. It was never entirely clear to Nan when Debra slept.

But what on earth was she up to now? Violet was right. This letter was most peculiar.

Nan looked up Debra's number and dialed. A machine picked up on the second ring with a familiar cheerful voice. "Hi, this is Debra. I'll be away over Labor Day weekend, but if you leave a message, I'll get back to you next week."

A little shiver ran down Nan's spine. It was now the third week in September. As Nan automatically left her name and number, her mind raced. Debra's attention to detail, even in the midst of personal tragedy, had never wavered. She simply wasn't the sort of person to leave a three-week-old message on her phone machine.

So where was she, then?

And why was her mother sending her mail at the State Bar?

* * *

James Weston Richfield was predictably contrite. He'd aced a course in office management and listed the condo purchased after his divorce. He'd turned in the leased 450 SL and bought a second-hand Corolla. Another solo practitioner had straightened out some of his messier files while Richfield was in rehab. He was hitting those AA and NA meetings every night, and he'd become a born-again Christian to boot. His haircut was fresh, his suit neatly pressed, his briefcase buffed. He was going to be the best little boy who'd ever put an "esquire" after his name.

If only there were some way to avoid that nasty suspension and to skip that icky old rule 955, which required suspended attorneys to notify clients and other interested parties of the State Bar discipline.

"My clients will never understand," he moaned. "I'll be ruined. I'll lose what little is left of my practice."

"It's up to the State Bar Court," Nan told him. "They may not suspend you at all, and even if they do, you might be able to skip rule nine-fifty-five."

She stared at him, at the puppy dog eyes, the earnest expression. This one, she was certain, would manage just fine, no matter what they did to him. The same arrogance which had gotten him into such a mess would see him through and out of it. The Mercedes leasing agent probably hadn't even moved his records to the inactive file.

At last he was gone, in a final flurry of apologies. Nan checked her watch and went in search of Danny Harrington. Attorneys and investigators weren't formally paired, but Nan and Danny worked together often and got along well. He was a former PI who'd gone to work as an investigator for the district attorney's office, then moved to a similar position at the State Bar when he began attending law school nights. He was happy to join Nan for lunch.

Nan showed Danny the letter, hoping that he'd tell her to stop being such a worrywart. But he didn't.

"The message said *Labor Day*?"

Nan nodded.

"And her mother thinks she's working with us again?"

"Apparently."

He shook his head. "I don't like it. Maybe one or the other—but both, that's way out of character." He mooshed some fries in catsup unhappily.

Danny had been immensely fond of Debra when she was a co-worker, his interest chaste and avuncular. He was twice her age, for one thing—in his early fifties with four kids, two grandchildren, and a wife he called the Contessa who ran a dog-grooming service out of their West Covina home. Danny Harrington was a capital *F* family man.

Of course, even if he'd tried to make a pass at Debra, she'd have shot him down cold. Danny wasn't Debra's type. Debra's tastes ran to handsome young studs— unemployed, unemployable, or both—who treated her shabbily and broke her heart, an oft-mended organ. Nan was convinced Debra had a lifetime registration with the Hollywood Losers Bureau.

"So what should we do?" Nan asked.

"Maybe she's sick," Danny suggested, "or had an accident. Tell you what. I've got a light afternoon. I'll call around, check with the hospitals and everything."

Everything, Nan realized suddenly, meant the morgue. She shivered again. "I'll see if I can't find Tony Fontaine. Her ex. He was working at a Honda dealership out in the Valley last I knew."

The Honda dealership said Tony wouldn't be in till Saturday, and it was only Thursday afternoon. The number at Tony and Debra's house in Canyon Country was disconnected, with a forwarding number in Reseda. That phone rang and rang and rang. No service, no machine, no Tony.

Danny stopped by Nan's office around four. "Good news and bad news," he said. "The good news is she's not in the morgue and there aren't any Jane Does even close. Ditto the hospitals. I checked under LaRoche and Fontaine. And there's no record of her being arrested anywhere."

"So then what's the bad news?"

"That *is* the bad news, Nan. I can't find her, and I'm not sure where to look next."

* * *

Debra's bungalow on a quiet street in the Hollywood flat-lands sat in a neighborhood that hadn't quite decided whether to move into heavy renovation or continue its slide into slumdom.

The houses were stucco, interchangeable one-bedroom boxes slapped up all in a row by a forties developer cashing in on the postwar housing crunch. Over the years, time and vegetation had softened the block as each cube took on its own character. Some, inhabited by original owners too stubborn or feeble to leave, were heavily fortified with wrought-iron bars on windows and doors. Others, overflowing with extended Latino families, had front doors wide open, diapered babies playing on front lawns, cars on blocks in driveways. A few had been refurbished, renovated, gentrified in anticipation of a migration of young professionals yet to materialize in any significant numbers.

Nan pulled into the empty driveway where Debra's blue Camaro should have been parked and looked around, putting up the top on her convertible. This was not a neighborhood where she wanted her 1966 Mustang any more exposed than absolutely necessary.

Debra's house was painted white, distinguishable by a stately Norfolk pine on the front lawn and bright turquoise trim. The turquoise window boxes had been filled with red geraniums when Debra moved in, giving the place an oddly patriotic appearance.

Now the geraniums were dry brown stalks in the relentless September heat. Yellowed throwaway newspapers dotted the scraggly little patch of burned-out front lawn; one rested in the lower branches of the Norfolk pine. Circulars for pizzerias and roofing contractors and realtors littered the front porch. Nan scooped them all up reflexively, then rang the doorbell and banged once or twice for good measure.

A plaintive *meow* came from inside as she rang the bell again. The windows were all tightly closed, miniblinds drawn. One slat of the gray blind in the window by the door was bent just above the dusty dead geraniums.

Through the bent slat, Nan could see letters strewn across the pastel dhurrie rug and hardwood floor just beyond the mail slot in the door. Quite a lot of letters. A gray striped cat approached and this time the *meow* was louder, desperate.

Nan didn't like this, any of it.

Using one of the circulars to fan herself, she walked around into the tiny backyard. Somewhere along the line, the garage had been converted into an illegal apartment. Debra had liked the idea of having a tenant, Nan recalled, said that it would help with the mortgage and make her feel safer at the same time. But Nan couldn't remember anything about the tenant. A musician, maybe, or an actor. Knowing Debra, it was probably somebody male, good-looking, and wildly irresponsible.

The back apartment looked every bit as deserted as the house in front. A side window was covered with plywood and the screen door hung at an odd angle. The windows were all closed up tightly; had anybody been home, Nan was sure, they'd be wide open with fans blasting. These buildings, like most older housing west of downtown and south of the Santa Monica Mountains, had no air-conditioning. For fifty weeks of the year, there was no need, and for the other two, folks generally just sweated and complained.

Debra's back door was locked, but unlike the front, had no visible deadbolt. Feeling a bit silly and very apprehensive, Nan dug a Visa card out of her purse and twisted it nervously in her fingers. She looked around furtively, expecting neighbors with binoculars, circling police helicopters, pigeons fluttering past with Polaroids.

This, of course, would be when the security service or some off-duty cop or maybe an entire SWAT team would show up and there she'd be, Nan Robinson, enforcer of truth and justice for the California State Bar. Breaking and entering. Debra wouldn't mind, of course, but Debra wasn't around to . . .

Oh, the hell with it.

She slipped the credit card between the door and jamb, alarmed at how easily the door opened. There should at least have been some kind of sliding bolt or chain. She'd have to tell Debra to change that lock, pronto.

She'd have to find Debra first.

As Nan stepped inside, the gray-striped cat streaked past her into the yard. Nan wrinkled her nose. The place was an oven and it reeked of cat. No wonder the animal wanted out, even if it *was* the perp.

"Debra?" she called out brightly. There was no answer, of course. She set her purse on the kitchen table, suddenly very afraid of what she might find further inside. "Debra, are you here?" Her voice echoed hollowly.

The kitchen had a built-in dinette with benches on either side. On the table's white surface, feline paw prints were visible in a film of dust. There was a small old gas stove and a three-quarter-size refrigerator, a massive microwave oven on a rolling cart. The counters were clean, dishes put away. A bag of Purina Cat Chow by the refrigerator had a plastic clip holding it closed on top, but had been gnawed or clawed open on the bottom. In the corner a cat box overflowed with turds.

Nan clamped her fingers over her nose, then took a deep breath as she walked to the front of the house. She had been here only once, shortly after Debra moved in, bringing a basket of dried flowers as a housewarming gift. There'd been almost no furniture then. Debra had left behind the things she bought with Tony when they moved to the Santa Clarita Valley suburbs.

There wasn't much more furniture now. The living room held a pale blue futon on a wooden rack and a white lacquer coffee table, with three pastel dhurries scattered over the hardwood floor. Nan's basket of dried flowers sat on a dusty mantel over a bricked-up fireplace. A TV and VCR were on a white lacquer table next to a stereo cabinet with glass doors. Waist-high speakers flanked the futon. Apart from the electronic equipment, the whole place had proba-

bly been furnished in a one half-hour swing through Pier
One.

There was nobody in this room and it felt like there
hadn't been anybody here for a long time.

With a growing feeling of dread, Nan called Debra's
name once again as she pushed open the bedroom door.
Nobody here either, just a giant waterbed on a platform
with a satin cover in hot pink. The walls were painted a vibrant purple, and the place seemed half den of hedonism,
half Easter egg. Inside a single large closet, Nan found a
small chest of drawers and a fair amount of hanging clothing. She recognized a few relatively conventional outfits
Debra wore to her office jobs.

The rest was fun, eclectic clothing: odds and ends from
thrift shops, up-to-the-minute trendy accessories, a fake
leopard jumpsuit purportedly owned by Cher that still had
a tag on it from A Star is Worn. Debra got a real kick out
of buying celebrities' cast-off clothing and was small
enough to fit into the minuscule items sent on consignment
to the shop. Famous people were all too happy to recycle
anything size six or under but not about to put their names
on the "fat" clothes they wore after childbirth or carbohy-
drate benders.

Only the bathroom remained. Nan took another deep
breath as she pushed the door open. It too was empty.
There were hot pink towels and a shower curtain covered
with flamingos.

Tidily arranged on the counter was Debra's exhaustive
collection of celebrity fragrances. She had dozens. She'd
stood in line when Linda Evans shilled Krystle at the
Broadway, rhapsodized when Priscilla Presley introduced
Moments, went without lunch on the days when Jaclyn
Smith and Joan Collins brought "their" scents to the eagerly waiting masses.

Nan exhaled slowly, admitting to herself for the first time
that she had half expected to find a suicide. Debra wasn't
the sort of person you'd picture taking her own life, but after the events of the last year, anything was possible.

She walked slowly back to the kitchen. So, if Debra wasn't hanging from a light fixture or lying in a tub full of pink water, where was she?

Nan opened the refrigerator: a bottle of simulated cheese goo to squeeze on nachos, sweet pickles, several jars of sundae toppings, two liters of flat orange pop, a plate with a little piece of something covered entirely in lush green mold. The freezer held four flavors of Häagen-Dazs ice cream, an empty ice cube tray, and a microwave burrito. Nutrition was not one of Debra's passions.

A beefcake calendar hung on the wall, muscled young men wearing smarmy smiles and not much else. There were a few cryptic notes on it, but nothing that immediately suggested a long-term absence. It was necessary to lean over the pungent and disgusting cat box to get to the calendar, however, which made Nan literally gag.

Grimacing, she picked up the cat box and carried it at arm's length out to the back porch. She opened the kitchen windows wide and sprayed liberally from a can of Lysol she found under the sink.

Now what?

She took a glass from one of the cupboards and ran the faucet till the water was reasonably cool and not quite so rusty. On the kitchen counter, the digital counter on Debra's phone message machine read "24." Listening to somebody's messages was like reading their mail, horribly wrong.

On the other hand, twenty messages seemed like a staggering number. She pushed the play button and sat at the kitchen table to listen.

"This is Madeleine calling from Steinberger and Glass for Ms. Debra LaRoche," an efficient voice not unlike Debra's own office tone announced. "Mr. Glass asked me to remind you that your appearance will be on Monday, September tenth, at two P.M., to discuss the property settlement. He'd like to meet with you beforehand, at one here in the office. This is Thursday the sixth at three-thirty. Please call me to confirm at 555-1050. Thank you."

Beep.

A male voice next, slightly slurred. "So you're not home, huh. Catch you later."

Beep.

"Tony, Debra." Nan recognized the voice of Debra's almost ex-husband. He spoke slowly, persuasively. "We need to talk, babe. I'm up in Seattle this week, but I don't want to walk into that courtroom without talking to you first. I miss you, babe, you know that, and I love you. I'm at 206 555-7475. Call me anytime, babe. Anytime."

Beep.

The next voice was female, young, self-assured. "This is April, Debra. I thought you told me you'd be in this morning. Give me a call up here at the PLI when you get in. It's Friday afternoon."

Beep.

The same deep male voice from the second message spoke again. "So where the fuck are you, anyway? Thought you said you'd meet me after the show."

Beep.

"Tony again, babe. Sunday morning, I'm back in town, and I thought maybe we could go to brunch and talk. Didn't get any messages from you in Seattle and I'm hoping that's cause the hotel screwed up. I'll be working this afternoon, but we could get together before or after. Call me, babe."

Nan pushed the stop button. This was beyond peculiar. It made her flesh crawl. She was invading Debra's privacy here, peering into arenas of the young woman's personal life which were certainly none of her business. She wiped her sweaty forehead and considered. Could she stop listening? Not a chance.

The next message was even worse.

"Debbie? Debbie, are you there? It's Mom. I was wondering why you didn't call this afternoon, that's all. I don't have any news or anything, but I just thought ... Well, there's no point wasting money talking to some silly machine, honey. Lots of love. Love, Mom."

Debra called her mother in South Bend every Sunday afternoon without fail, Nan knew. Her father had died several years earlier. Debra didn't feel particularly close to her mother. She didn't look forward to the weekly calls, didn't greatly enjoy the conversations or give them much thought once she'd hung up.

But she never, ever, missed a Sunday.

Not until September ninth, anyway.

Beep . . . beep . . . beep. Two hang-ups in a row.

"This is Madeleine calling again from Steinberger and Glass for Ms. Debra LaRoche." The secretary sounded perturbed. "It's nine-fifteen on Monday the tenth, and Mr. Glass is quite concerned that you haven't confirmed your meeting with him this afternoon at one before your court appearance. Please call me at 555-1050 immediately. Thank you."

Beep.

"This is Madeleine at Steinberger and Glass." Perturbed had given way to irritated. Borderline furious, actually. "Mr. Glass was able to obtain a continuance because you missed the hearing this afternoon, but he must hear from you immediately to learn your intentions, Ms. LaRoche, before he can go any further on this matter. You may reach me at 555-1050."

Beep.

"Debra, babe, it's Tony. I dunno what happened this afternoon, but I'm hoping it means you don't want to go through with this. Talk to me, babe. Talk to me. I know you're hurting, but I'm hurting too. We can work it out, I know it."

Beep.

"Hey, this is Marty." The connection was faint, scratchy long distance. Marty had a high voice, but sounded masculine. "We're hung up in Denver, Debra, held over if you can believe it, how 'bout that, huh? Listen, I won't get back till the seventeenth or eighteenth, so I'll just pay you then, okay?"

Beep.

"Debra, this is April again. When are you going to be in? Give me a call, please, as soon as possible."

Beep.

"Dr. Blake's office is calling for Debra LaRoche to remind you that your appointment tomorrow morning is at nine-thirty."

Beep . . . beep. Another hang-up, followed by a new male voice.

"Uh, this is Jack Thurston. I don't know if you remember, we met a couple of weeks ago at the Westwind show. I was, uh, wondering if you'd like to, uh, get together or something. Uh, call me at 555-2359."

Beep.

"Babe, it's Tony. I came by but you weren't home and that guy out back wasn't around either. Listen, I guess you probably just went away for a while or something, but call me when you get back so's I won't worry, all right? Love ya, babe."

Beep.

"Debbie, it's Mom again." The voice was thin, quavery, distant. "Maybe you . . . I just . . . I guess I take your calls for granted, honey, but I'm starting to get really worried about you and I want you to call me whenever you get in, even if it isn't Sunday. You can reverse the charges if you want. Lots of love, Debbie. I said this was Mom, didn't I?"

Beep.

Mrs. LaRoche wasn't the only one starting to get really worried. So far Debra, the original Miss Conscientious, had missed a court appearance and two phone calls to her mother, which brought matters, according to the beefcake calendar on the kitchen wall, up to Sunday the sixteenth. Mrs. LaRoche had probably mailed the letter to her daughter at the State Bar right after that unreturned phone call.

"Debra, this is April at the PLI. We have that big session starting on Wednesday, remember, and you promised you'd help with the registration. These are some potentially important clients, and I know we can count on you. You're too efficient to lose the number, but I'll save you even looking it up. 555-9836, or you can call my apartment at 555-9839. Bye."

Beep . . . beep.

"So when are you gonna be around the club again, hey, Debra?" It was yet another male voice, one that sounded older than the others. "This is Alex if you didn't figure it out yet, and I was thinking maybe we could go to the Franny Brownfield concert this weekend. She's gonna be at the Looky-Loo. I'll be lookin' for you, loo."

Beep.

"Tony, babe. I guess you're not back yet. Call me, babe. I still love ya, you know that."

Beep.

"Debra, this is Nan. Today is Thursday, September twentieth and it's ten-forty-three A.M. You can reach me at work for the rest of the day, or at home tonight."

Beep.

That was it.

Nan's original suspicion that something was wrong had moved from inchoate concern to visceral fear.

She jumped at a voice behind her, male and accusatory and familiar. It was, she realized suddenly, a voice she had heard minutes earlier.

"Just who the hell are you?!"

CHAPTER 2

He was long and lanky in cutoff jeans and flipflops, with a dark blond shoulder-length mane in urgent need of both a hairbrush and a shampoo. A sheen of sweat covered the deep tan on his bare chest and arms. He was probably all of twenty-three. He blocked the doorway as if expecting Nan to bolt.

"I'm Nan Robinson," she answered evenly, ordering her heart to stop racing so frantically. Her heart didn't listen. "I'm an old friend of Debra's and I was concerned because I couldn't get in touch with her." She paused and stared up at him from her bench in the dinette. She felt cornered. "Your turn."

"Huh?"

"I said your turn. Who are *you*?"

He was still suspicious. Rightly so, Nan realized, even though she was obviously respectable. Burglars didn't generally wear linen dresses with high heels and stockings in the middle of a blistering heat wave. Nor did they lounge around listening to their victims' phone machines.

"I live here," he said, after a moment.

"With Debra?"

It was likely enough, Nan supposed. This guy had all the tickets to be one of Debra's beaux: nice features, surly attitude, lots of sex appeal. If he and Debra were actually cohabiting, however, he had a bit of explaining to do.

"In back," he answered.

"Oh, you're her tenant." That made more sense. "Do you have a name?"

"Marty."

The one whose message she'd just heard. "You called her from Denver, saying you were 'held over.' " She tried to smile. "Are you a movie?"

The corners of his mouth turned up slightly. "A musician. We were playing in Colorado."

"When did you get back?"

The smile vanished as a blank mask slipped down over his face. "What are you, a cop?"

"Just a friend of Debra's. I'm a lawyer. I knew her when she was a little girl and the last few years we worked together. Have you seen her since you've been back from Colorado?"

He shook his head. "How'd you get in here?"

Nan hesitated. "The back door."

"It was locked."

"Well, yeah. But not very well."

He slammed his fist on the doorjamb. "Shit. This place been robbed?"

Nan stared at him, confused. "I don't know. I don't think so. Why?"

" 'Cause my place was ripped off while I was gone. Some asshole broke the side window, took my TV and a brand-new CD player and a really fine guitar. I was kind of pissed with Debra for not noticing, but . . ." He walked across the room slowly. The cutoffs were shredded a bit across the seat and he wasn't wearing underwear. Just as slowly he turned around and leaned on the sink. "You say you're looking for her?"

Nan nodded.

"Why? Is she in trouble?"

"I hope not. But I'm starting to get a little worried. It looks like nobody's been here for a long time. Is there some reason you don't want to tell me when you got back to LA?"

He shook his head again. He had what Nan's father had called bird's-nest hair back in the sixties, and he was impossibly skinny, with bony ribs and no stomach at all and a cute little musician's ass. Nan wasn't sure why young rock musicians always had such nice butts, or why they all seemed to weigh about ninety pounds. Maybe it had to do with the hours they kept and improper eating habits. Or maybe it was just the drugs.

Marty seemed straight enough now, however. "I got in Sunday night, late. Find my window smashed and my stuff gone—welcome home, hey? So I bang on Debra's door and there's no answer, but I figured that anyway cause her car was gone. She was maybe out or something. No big deal except I was so pissed about my stuff being ripped off. I had the rent money and it was a little bit late, but I knew she was cool about that."

"Did you report the burglary to the police?"

He looked at her as if she'd suggested he crawl on his knees from Vladivostok to Madrid. "What for?"

"Burglars do get apprehended occasionally. Stolen goods are recovered. At the very least, your insurance company will want—" She broke off as he began to snicker. "Don't you have renter's insurance?"

"Yeah, right. For a million bucks. I told you, I'm a guitar player. I make jackshit. I had a chance to go on the road, get paid, even—I get back and find out some junkie's ripped me off. That stuff's history. It got fenced for about twenty bucks ten minutes after the asshole left here. Hell, I'd've given him twenty-five not to take it."

"I'm surprised Debra's place wasn't burgled too," Nan reflected. "It certainly didn't look like anybody was home, with those papers all over the lawn."

"Probably a light on," Marty said. "She's got her lights on timers, don't like coming into a dark house."

"I haven't been here for a while," Nan said carefully. Too damn long. She was a lousy excuse for a friend. "Would you be able to tell if anything was missing?"

He shrugged. "I can look around." He disappeared into the front of the house and Nan poured herself another glass of water. She'd sweat off the first one listening to Debra's messages. The front of her dress, she noticed, resembled a pleated window shade.

Marty returned a few minutes later, holding a couple of letters. For the first time Nan noticed that he had an odor, not terribly offensive, just healthy male sweat with a slightly sweet cast. Maybe being able to smell Marty meant the odor of cat box was finally starting to clear. Maybe buffalo could fly.

"Looks okay to me," he said. "TV's still there, stereo. There could be something gone I don't know about."

Nan wondered what he did know about, whether he maybe worked off part of the rent under the hot pink satin cover on Debra's waterbed. But there was no point asking; he'd reflexively deny it. "Is that part of her mail?" she asked.

"It's for me," he answered defensively. "My mail's delivered to the house here."

"Oh." She wished she'd looked at the letters on the floor before he showed up, but she couldn't very well ask him to relinquish his own mail. "When did you leave for Colorado?"

"Middle of July."

"So your place could have been ripped off anytime in the last two months."

He shook his head. "Debra'd notice, like I said. And I talked to her every couple of weeks."

"When was the last time you talked to her?"

He thought about that for a minute. "After we went from Boulder to Denver. Denver started the twenty-fourth."

"Of August?"

"Yeah. It was a couple days after that. The Denver thing came up out of nowhere—we weren't expecting it. She thought I was gonna be back by the first of the month and I wanted to tell her."

Nan considered. She wasn't terribly fond of this guy, and had absolutely no reason to trust him. Still, he was Debra's closest neighbor and quite possibly more than that.

"Do you have any idea where Debra might go if she wanted to get away for a while?"

He shook his head slowly. "Not really. She's been kind of down, but she never said nothing about going nowhere."

"If she *did* decide to go away, where do you think she might go?"

"I dunno. Hawaii? . . . What did you say your name was?"

"Nan. Nan Robinson."

"She's been talking a lot about reincarnation, Nan. She's pretty hyped on it. She was working someplace out in Malibu doing something like that."

"Reincarnation? Debra?"

"Yeah. I didn't pay much attention, but she was all the time talking about karma. Karma this, karma that. Bad karma to smash a spider. Good karma to put out soda cans for the bums to pick up. Got kind of boring after a while."

Nan wondered fleetingly what subjects might hold Marty's attention. "You say she has a job related to reincarnation?"

He shrugged. "I think. It's no nine-to-fiver or nothing, though. She wears shorts when she goes and sometimes she's home all day."

"It's in Malibu?"

"I think. I dunno. Like I said, in one ear, out the other."

Nan thought a minute. "Marty, this really bothers me. Debra's very conscientious and according to her messages, she's been missing important appointments. And for two weeks in a row, she hasn't called her mother. She *always* calls her mother on Sunday afternoons."

Marty grinned. He needed dental work, badly. "I know," he said. "One time we were . . . well, never mind. But you're right. She calls her old lady no matter what." The smile left his face. "You say she missed two weeks? I don't like that."

"I don't either. Do you know the neighbors here?"

"Not really. I asked the guy next door if he seen her, but he said no. Place on the other side's empty. Some old lady was living there—they took her away in an ambulance couple months ago."

"I'm going to look around and see if I can find something that shows where Debra might be," Nan said. "In the meantime, here's my card. I'll put my home number on the back. If you hear from her or run into anybody who's seen her, call me right away, all right?"

He shrugged as he took the card. "Sure."

"I know she likes to hang out around music clubs. Do you go to some of the same places?"

"Sometimes."

"Could you ask around?"

"I suppose."

After Marty left, Nan went systematically through the tiny house. There were three fresh packs of birth control pills in the medicine chest and a dazzling assortment of condoms in the headboard of the waterbed.

An accordion file on the closet shelf held receipts for paid bills, income tax returns, car registration and insurance, old pay stubs, mortgage papers for the house, correspondence relating both to Debra's divorce and the insurance settlement for her son's death. The back pocket of the file held a rubberbanded packet of letters from Mrs. LaRoche back in South Bend, all on the same dime store stationery as the one which had arrived at the office.

A key in the top drawer of the dresser, under a chartreuse teddy, opened the front door. Nan put it in her purse.

There was no Rolodex. Nan remembered Debra carrying a purple address book in her purse, but she'd apparently taken the purse with her. Nan copied all the phone numbers written on the card by the kitchen wall phone and took down the beefcake calendar, still set to August. There was a blank tape in the kitchen drawer by Debra's answering machine. She switched tapes and took the used one with her.

Then she went through the accumulated mail. There was another letter from Debra's mother, postmarked August 31, and two long vellum envelopes from the law firm of Steinberger and Glass. A Mastercard bill. A renewal notice from the DMV. All sorts of junk mail. The new *Cosmo*.

Nan stacked the mail neatly on the mantel beside the basket of dusty dried flowers, keeping out the two letters from Mrs. LaRoche. She turned them over and over.

Was opening somebody's mail that much worse than listening to her phone messages? Or breaking into her house and checking out the condom selection?

Where *did* one draw the line on invasion of privacy?

Probably a few miles behind where Nan was situated already, she decided, slitting open the letters from Mrs. LaRoche. She read the one delivered to the office first, a single sheet that urged Debra to call home immediately and expressed concern that her mother hadn't heard from her.

Then Nan opened the earlier letter. As she read the cramped handwriting, a more wrinkly version of Debra's own neat script, she became more and more puzzled.

I'm so glad you're back at the State Bar, Mrs. LaRoche wrote. *Even if you don't really need the money, it's better to be working. Nan Robinson is such a lovely girl and those people all seemed so very nice and devoted to you.*

Nan frowned. Did lovely girls read other people's mail? And how could Mrs. LaRoche have possibly formed an opinion of Debra's former co-workers? She had been in Los Angeles only once, so far as Nan knew, after little Timmy's accident. Of course Nan and the others had attended the services for Timmy, a hideously wrenching experience. But any exchanges Nan overheard between Debra's mother and her co-workers were brief and stilted. Only Violet Thomas had spoken with Mrs. LaRoche at any length. Violet was innately empathetic, and one of the few with any frame of reference for what it might feel like to have a grandchild killed.

The letter went on to relate some gossip from South Bend, news that meant nothing to Nan and probably not much more to Debra, who had been back to the Midwest only once since leaving for LA. She hated South Bend.

The closing of the letter was so curious that Nan read it three times: *Beware of charlatans who want to separate you from your money by exploiting your pain,* Mrs. LaRoche wrote. *There is one Lord God and one true church. Father Boyle has offered a special novena for you, that you will put this heresy behind you and return to the faith of your childhood.*

What might that heresy be? Nan wondered. Could it have anything to do with Debra's mysterious Malibu job and reincarnation? Nan hadn't learned much from her visit to Debra's house, but she knew now that it was no shot in the dark that had prompted Mrs. LaRoche to send that letter to Debra at the State Bar. Debra had deliberately led her mother to believe she was again working there.

Why?

By now it was too late to make her regular Thursday meeting of Adult Children of Alcoholics, but Nan wasn't really in the mood anyway. Besides, she no longer needed ACA the way she once had.

Over time she had satisfactorily resolved—or at least identified—most of the major problems her father's alcoholism had caused her. A seasoned ACA veteran, she went to meetings as a somewhat voyeuristic habit, taking slightly guilty comfort in the reminder that many people had problems considerably worse than her own.

Still, she felt antsy and out of sorts. On impulse, she picked up Debra's phone and called Tom Hannah. He was about to go to dinner, he told her. Did she want to come up to his house or meet him somewhere?

Nan opted for the house, and ten minutes later she was walking down the steep driveway behind a huge stone house in the Hollywood Hills. When she turned the corner at the foot of the drive, she found Tom lying on a chaise longue on the patio with his eyes closed. He held a nearly empty bottle of Grenzquell in one hand and wore a Walkman. Opera blasted out of the windows above. Tom rented the ground floor apartment from a stone-deaf old lady who'd automatically be labeled the town crazy anywhere but Hollywood. Here she was simply one of the gang.

Tom smiled and stood when Nan walked in front of him and blocked the sun pouring onto his face. He pulled off the Walkman and kissed her cheek. "You look hot," he told her.

"I was hoping I could talk you out of a beer and a shower," Nan answered.

"Sure," he answered easily, holding the door for her to go inside. The apartment was built right into the side of the hill and was almost cool. But not quite. A casual observer might have suspected tornado damage. Tom's housekeeping was pretty loose. "I've got Augsburger. Also a kind of interesting brew from Liberia. You can practically taste the blood of oppressed natives."

Nan laughed and twisted the cap off the Augsburger longneck. "Some other time. I need familiarity today."

Tom loved beer and was incapable of leaving Trader Joe's without at least one sixpack of unfamiliar brew. A few years earlier, he had systematically collected one bottle from each variety he tried. Before a 5.6 tremor knocked over his display shelf into a glittering mountain of green and brown shards, he had saved over a hundred different bottles.

"Something kind of weird is going on," she told him, after a healthy swig of Augsburger. It was a personal favorite, a Wisconsin German beer she'd introduced to Tom. "I want to tell you about it and see what you think. But first, I *really* need a shower."

"No problem," he told her. "Want your back washed?"

She laughed. "No thanks, but I'd sure like to borrow something else to wear." Nan and Tom had been lovers briefly many years earlier, the only period of their relationship she hadn't thoroughly enjoyed. Backing off into a simple and solid friendship was tricky at first, but far more satisfying in the long run.

She felt much better once she was clean, dressed in a pair of Tom's running shorts, and a TEACHERS DO IT BY THE BOOK T-shirt Tom had been given one Christmas by a smitten student. Tom taught English at Beverly Hills High, where teenage girls wrote him embarrassing love poems and drove cars worth several years of his pay. He was adept at deflecting teenage crushes. His hair was salt and pepper—heavy on the salt—but his face was youthful and he looked much younger than thirty-eight.

When Nan came back outside, Mrs. Finkelstein had turned off the opera. Jungly vegetation ran rampant down the hill below Tom's apartment, all but covering a little shack at the bottom inhabited sporadically by various citizens of the Homeless Nation. It was a rather serene and lovely yard, even in neglect, even with squatters at its base. A massive stand of birds-of-paradise bloomed just beside the patio.

"So," he said, "you hungry?" It was a safe bet that Tom himself would be. He had some sort of metabolic imbalance that forced him to eat at least three thousand calories a day.

"Sort of," Nan answered. "I guess I could eat a salad or something."

"How about gyros? A nice little Greek place opened just down the hill last month."

The Greek place looked authentic enough, and the spiced lamb sliced off the huge cylinder of meat smelled delicious. Seating, however, was limited to one small counter and a pair of tiny tables, all occupied. Nan and Tom huddled, then placed their order to go.

Back on Tom's patio, Nan picked at the feta cheese in her salad and told him about visiting Debra's house.

"She just ran off somewhere," Tom said. "You know, she met some dude on his way to Vegas and tagged along."

"The last time she did that, she came back married," Nan reminded him. "Besides, that doesn't explain away three weeks." A police helicopter came thup-thup-thupping overhead and she waited till it was gone before she spoke again. "So, what should I do about Debra?" she asked Tom.

"Forget about her," he advised. "She's off partying somewhere, Nan, and I guarantee she's not worrying about you."

By the time Nan got home to Playa del Rey, she'd sweated through Tom's shorts and T-shirt. She stripped them off and didn't bother putting on anything else. Her air-conditioning was a joke, the equivalent of setting a couple of ice cubes on the table. The serviceman she called during last year's heat wave didn't show till after the temperature finally broke. Then he wanted eight hundred bucks, and Nan told him to forget it.

She was sorry now she'd been so cheap.

While the air-conditioner puffed an occasional desultory snatch of cool air through the vents, she tried to promote ocean breezes through an open patio door that faced west toward the Pacific. Theoretically this should have worked, but the ocean was two miles away, blocked by a solid network of three-story condos. Nan lived on the second floor.

Finally she slipped into a swimsuit and went down to the pool. She was able to get wet, but that was it. Laps were hopeless. It was dark now, but the pool was still jampacked with frazzled mothers and their whining offspring, splashing young salesmen with deep tans, and nymphets in string bikinis with no apparent concerns beyond their next nail sculptures.

She went back upstairs, pulled off the wet swimsuit and sat naked in front of the air-conditioning vent, drinking an iced Molsen Golden and worrying.

Where was Debra LaRoche?

Debra was twenty-eight now, old enough to take care of herself. Never mind her waiflike quality, the fact that she looked like a strong Santa Ana could blow her clear to Baja. Tom could easily be right, that she'd met some guy and gone off on an impulsive vacation. She had the means, the settlement for Timmy's death. She had nobody to answer to. Maybe she was tired of being responsible.

But to not call her mother two weeks in a row? The missed court appearance was troubling, too. And surely she would have made some kind of arrangement for the cat.

After a while Nan showered and went to bed wet, lying on top of the sheets and hoping evaporation would cool her enough so she could get to sleep. She had just settled herself when the ceiling creaked above her. Dammit!

The condo immediately above Nan's was occupied by a pair of flight attendants who weren't airborne nearly often enough. One was a willowy brunette, the other a bubbly little redhead. And whoever had the bedroom directly above Nan's own was a creature of voracious sexual appetites. It wasn't simply a matter of creaking bedsprings, either. She was a screamer. Crash landings were frequent.

Circumstantial evidence suggested that the offender was the redhead. She'd been down at the pool earlier with a hearty, musclebound fellow with sun-bleached hair and a bronzed body. The kind of jock who spends every non-working hour in gym shorts and owns athletic shoes for a dozen different sports.

After a while, Nan got up and went to the living room. She put Debra's message tape in her own phone machine and listened again, taking notes on a legal pad, making lists. Nan liked making lists. It might not actually accomplish anything, but it provided the illusion of busyness.

By the time she was finished, so was the flight attendant.

In the morning Nan called Steinberger and Glass and asked for Joe Glass, the former UCLA law classmate and family law specialist to whom she'd sent Debra. Joe had handled Nan's own divorce. Neatly.

He came on the line almost immediately. "You sent poor Madeleine's blood pressure right into the stratosphere. We don't get a lot of calls from the State Bar here."

"I should hope not," Nan answered. "I didn't mean to upset her. And I did say it was personal."

"That scared her even more."

"Hey, I figured out a long time ago you get less run-arounds from support staff when you say you're with State Bar investigations."

"So this isn't an official call?" he asked carefully.

"If it were, I wouldn't be the one making it."

"Then what's up?" Joe asked, sounding considerably relieved.

He was a cheerful fellow of great patience and compassion, prerequisites for a successful family law practice. Family law was one of the meanest and messiest of all legal specialties, there being nothing quite like a divorce for bringing out the absolute worst in everybody. Family law was like an endlessly looped country-western song, full of heartache and broken dreams, anguish and recriminations, soured hopes and plain old vitriol. Amazingly, Joe never let it bother him. A former football player whose body had begun to turn on him, Joe had already been through arthroscopic surgery on both knees and was contemplating work on his right rotator cuff.

"I'm trying to find Debra LaRoche," Nan said.

"Aren't we all?" Joe chuckled. "You didn't tell me she was a flake."

"She isn't, Joe. That's just the point." Nan explained what had happened.

Joe listened carefully. "I don't know what to tell you, Nan. She's certainly not the first client I've had who took a powder when it came time to actually split up the property and say bye-bye. That's one of the givens in this field. Folks are emotional, unpredictable. I guess I'm lucky nobody's shot me. Judge Horton is pretty easygoing. He just gave us a continuance till November. Of course Tony Fontaine doesn't want to get divorced at all, so he wasn't making any kind of fuss. He did seem concerned about where Debra was, though."

Nan rang off with promises to have lunch the next time Joe was in court downtown. She tried Tony Fontaine's numbers and again got no response.

She didn't feel quite like trying to track down the guys who had called Debra's machine and wasn't sure where to start anyway. Somebody named Alex hoped to go to a Franny Brownfield concert and mentioned a club without further elaboration. Another guy called twice without leaving any ID at all.

Jack Thurston, however, was kind enough to leave both a last name and number. He was out, a groggy male voice told Nan, at work. Work was a Three-Day Miniblind store in West LA. Thurston seemed reluctant to discuss Debra, but did say that she hadn't returned his call and he hadn't seen her for a month.

That left April from the PLI, whatever that might be. April had left three separate messages for Debra, spaced over two weeks, and two numbers. Nan dialed the first and a cheerful young female voice answered.

"Past Lives Institute. Good morning, this is Marsha."

My, my, my. Nan asked to speak to April.

"Ms. Henley's in a meeting right now," Marsha said. "May I take a message?"

"This is Nan Robinson with the California State Bar. I'm a friend of Debra LaRoche's and I'm trying to get in touch with her. I believe Debra was doing some work for you?"

A moment's silence. "Could you hold please?"

It was almost three minutes before the well-modulated, self-assured voice from Debra's machine came on the line. "April Henley speaking. May I help you?"

"I certainly hope so," Nan told her, identifying herself again. "I'm looking for Debra LaRoche. Is she working for you now?"

"She has been." April Henley sounded cautious, tentative. "She hasn't been in recently, though."

"Not at all?"

"Not at all. What's this about, anyway?"

Nan sighed. "I'm not really sure. She had some mail sent to the State Bar and she hasn't worked here for quite a while. I've been trying to reach her, but it seems nobody's heard from her since late August."

"She was here over Labor Day weekend," April said.

"She was? When did she leave?"

"Monday night. We had a weekend seminar and Debra was assisting. Actually, I expected her back before now. Do you suppose . . . something's wrong?" The woman sounded perplexed.

"I don't know what to suppose," Nan said. "I've known Debra for a long time, and it's not like her to go off like this. I'm starting to get really worried." As she spoke, Nan realized that she was well beyond *starting* to get worried.

"Have you tried her ex-husband?"

"I haven't been able to reach him," Nan said, "but I'm still trying. Listen, let me give you my numbers. If you hear anything from Debra, would you call me?"

"Of course," April Henley agreed. "If you'll promise to do the same if you hear from her first."

There only seemed to be one thing left to do. After work, Nan drove to the Hollywood division of the Los Angeles Police Department to file a missing persons report.

Her expectations weren't high. She expected the runaround, with an admonition that nothing could be done for twenty-four hours. She was half right.

LAPD no longer maintained a minimum waiting period on missing persons, the desk officer explained. He was hatchet faced, a bit paunchy, maybe fifty—a guy who should probably have taken retirement five years ago. He punched Debra's name into the computer and determined that she wasn't in jail or the victim of an accident or crime. This fit Danny Harrington's research, but it wasn't much comfort.

"I'll make out a report," he said, asking routine questions with the enthusiasm he might have put into getting the specs on a stolen tricycle. Missing young women didn't seem to be a high priority in Hollywood.

Still, Nan tried to express her concern as clearly and concisely as she could. She was overdressed for the neighborhood, she knew, and hoped that being an attorney would give her at least a little leverage.

Fat chance.

"Look," the bored old cop said finally, "this information will go down to our Missing Persons Bureau at Parker Center, and they'll be in touch."

"How soon?"

"Couple days."

"A couple *days*? Do you mean to say if I came in here and said my eight-year-old didn't get home from school, somebody would call me in a couple *days*?"

"A missing eight-year-old, ma'am, we'd get that on the streets right off." He stifled a yawn. "But you're telling me about an adult with no responsibilities, somebody you haven't even talked to in three months. You say you looked at her place and there's no evidence of a struggle or a robbery. She's probably in Vegas. Maybe she went off to find herself." The last two words carried a decided sneer.

"Surely you can do something here, now," Nan said, trying to be beguiling and authoritative at the same time.

"Take a look around here," the officer said. For the first time he met Nan's gaze. His own eyes were the palest possible shade of blue and frighteningly empty; she didn't want to think about what they'd witnessed over the years. "We've got rapes, robberies, murders, junkies, kids who'll off each other for two hours worth of crack. Your friend's on file. She'll show up."

"And that's it?" Nan asked, equally irritated and incredulous.

"What do you want us to do?" His smile was sardonic. "Call out the National Guard?"

Nan swallowed the half dozen smart remarks that sprang to the tip of her tongue, smiled sweetly, and left. It was almost dark outside. She reached her car neck and neck with a pair of young Latino gentlemen in hairnets, who seemed truly disappointed by her arrival.

Hurray for Hollywood.

❋

The killer hurtled down the arrow-straight desert highway, elated. The September night was clear and crisp, full of stars and promise. There was such a wonderful sense of freedom now, with the Debra problem so neatly resolved.

Freedom.

That was what this was all about, ultimately. Freedom, choices, the ability to follow through on a plan and make things happen as they were supposed to. When all this ended, when all this was done, that freedom would still be there, like an endless caress.

As for Debra, well, that was just too bad. One of these days Debra would turn up again, and they'd all get the surprise of their lives.

Just as Debra had.

CHAPTER 3

On Saturday morning, Nan finally reached Tony Fontaine at the Honda dealership where he was a salesman. He shared Nan's dismay at Debra's disappearance. He'd be on the floor all day, he told her, but if she could possibly come out and meet him for a break, he'd really like to talk to her.

It was another scorcher. The condo pool was full of screaming kids when Nan left, and the weekend tanners were well basted, chairs facing east. The odor of coconut oil was overpowering. The redheaded flight attendant and her friend weren't down yet; their morning wake-up call was still in progress when Nan left her condo at nine-thirty.

The temperature rose steadily as Nan's car climbed the Sepulveda pass on 405. When she crossed the summit at Mulholland, the Valley below shimmered with hazy heat in layered shades of grungy gray. By the time she hit the Valley floor, it was easily over a hundred degrees. She had the top up and the windows open, and worried that she might have to turn on the car heater to keep the engine from overheating.

Tony was seated at a corner desk with a young couple when she arrived. He waved a cheery hello and held up a finger to signify he'd be with her in a minute. As she waited, she wandered around the showroom. It had a comfortable, homey feeling to her; she had grown up around her father's Ford dealership back in Illinois. There was something terribly exciting about a showroom: gleaming vehicles with lots of zeros on the odometers, that great new-car interior smell, eager salesmen ready to put you into the car of your dreams.

Tony's prospects left, and he crossed to where Nan waited in the luxurious front seat of an Accord.

"Nice, eh?" Tony said. He smiled crookedly at her. "We can make you a honey of a deal."

"Not today, thanks." Nan's domestic auto bias ran strong, even years after her father's death, and she loved her Mustang convertible. "But on a day like this, with no air, I do fantasize a little."

He smiled. Tony Fontaine was a handsome man, around thirty, with jet black hair, dark brown eyes, and a warm Mediterranean complexion he kept tanned year-round. He was only about five-nine and weighed maybe one forty-five, but he carried himself with great assurance and gave the initial impression of being a much larger man. He was also a snappy dresser, always looking fashionable without being overtly trendy. Today he wore crisply creased white slacks and a mint-green shirt, a white tie, and beige jacket.

The first time Nan ever saw him, she understood immediately why Debra had fallen in love. He was energetic, cheerful, and obviously determined to make a good impression on Debra's boss. Nan couldn't help liking him. At the same time, he winked so frequently that she wondered if he had a tic.

She'd been certain, of course, that he was somehow grievously flawed; that was a given with Debra's boyfriends. Regrettably she was right. Tony had a temper.

"Let's go across the street," he suggested now, catching the eye of another salesman across the room. He tapped his watch and flexed his fingers in the air twice to show he'd be gone twenty minutes.

They hurried through the smothering heat to a donut shop in the nearby pod mall. Nan ordered iced tea and Tony had a Coke with a couple of gooey concoctions that made Nan cringe. She could only imagine what kind of meals he and Debra had shared in their married life;

Debra's notion of a balanced breakfast was one Ding Dong for every Ho-Ho.

Tony listened as Nan told of her visit to Debra's house and the reception she'd gotten from the Hollywood police.

"I realized then," Nan said, "that if I want to find Debra, I'll have to do it myself. But I don't know if I'm being silly and overreacting, or if I ought to be really worried."

"For whatever it's worth, *I'm* really worried," Tony said. There were no gratuitous winks this morning. "Dammit, I should've broken in myself. I went down there and the place looked deserted. But I figured Debra'd be pissed and she was just looking for some kind of excuse to go harder on me. I've been on my best behavior, Nan, I don't mind telling you. I want that girl back. Letting her go is the biggest mistake I ever made."

Tony hadn't exactly let Debra go, Nan knew. Debra had walked out on him, and she'd done it with bruises on her body.

"I'd crawl through broken glass if I could get her back," Tony went on. "I told her I'd go anywhere, do anything, go back to that counselor if she thought it would help." Debra and Tony had both seen a therapist after Timmy's death, though Tony checked out after a session or two. "I worship the ground she walks on."

"Is that why you hit her?"

Nan hadn't intended to say anything, but here, face-to-face with Tony for the first time since she'd learned of his physical abuse of Debra, she just couldn't help herself. She was horrified when Debra admitted that Tony knocked her around and that the beating before she left was not an isolated incident. Even more horrifying was Debra's suggestion that she was partly to blame. Nan hadn't asked why Debra felt that way. Spousal brutality was not an issue in which Nan recognized shades of gray; it was flat-out wrong and there was no such thing as an extenuating circumstance.

Tony closed his eyes for a moment and looked genuinely pained. "If I could undo that . . . Christ, you think I haven't told myself a million times what a fool I was? I had the greatest girl in the world and I was such an asshole I hurt her."

"Where do you think she's gone?" Nan asked. There was no point in pursuing the subject further. She wanted Tony as an ally right now, and if she thought about what he'd done she'd only work herself into an unproductive lather.

"I can't imagine," he answered, looking grateful to have the subject changed. "I don't think she'd go back home to see her mom."

"Her mom hasn't heard from her."

"I guess . . . maybe some other guy?" He sounded pained at the suggestion. Nan presumed Debra had been faithful to Tony while whey were together, but it was possible she hadn't, particularly after Timmy's death. Maybe that was why Debra thought she deserved being beaten. "She kind of missed the club scene way out there in the boonies. She didn't talk about it much, but I could tell. I could never quite figure it, I get her a beautiful three-bedroom house, brand-new, in a nice safe neighborhood and then she splits and goes back to Hollywood, for Chrissakes. *Hollyweird*. And then she's never home nights when I call."

"Maybe it was just too painful being in the house where she lived with Timmy," Nan suggested.

"You think I don't understand that? You think it wasn't hard for me, too, expecting him to come running around a corner, looking at the closed door to his room? I hear a kid say, 'Daddy,' it's a knife in my heart. You know, she never could bring herself to do anything about his room. It was all still there for months, the crib, the little trucks, the whole bit. She'd go in there and close the door and cry. For hours. My ma came out from Jersey to visit—she packed it all up, said it was sick leaving it like that. Debra came home and found out, she threw a real shitfit."

Rightly so, Nan thought. "The house is for sale now, isn't it?"

"Yeah, but the market's kind of soft. Realtor says it's easier to sell a house looks like somebody's living there, so

I left all the stuff there. Got a furnished apartment near work. I keep hoping when Debra gets all this whatever it is out of her system, she'll want to come back and it'll all be waiting for her." He looked at Nan as a co-conspirator. "Got the house priced kind of high, too. Don't want somebody buying it before Debra changes her mind."

"Did Debra ever say anything to you about working at a place called the Past Lives Institute?"

Tony's laugh was bitter. "Did she ever! What a crock! I took Debra out to dinner, oh, about two months ago. Made it real special, her favorite restaurant, brought her flowers to that dump she's living in, two pounds of those rum truffles she loves. So what does she talk about all night? This mumbo-jumbo bullshit about how she and I used to be together in some past life and what happened to Timmy was our karma 'cause we were supposed to be taking care of some kid and we let the kid get sick and die. I mean, is that bullshit or what?"

"It sounds pretty strange," Nan agreed readily. "Is that something she got from the Past Lives Institute?"

"Yeah. She's telling me she's had all these regressions and gone back to past lives and it just isn't our karma to be together anymore. Karma, shmarma, I tell her. I mean, I think all this reincarnation stuff is hooey. I was raised Catholic and so was she. We didn't get married in the church and neither one of us was going anymore, but you grow up believing in heaven and hell, you don't just one day say, oh, hey, I bet I'll come back as a butterfly and have me a nice new life."

Nan couldn't help but laugh. Tony was obviously overwrought, but his own views weren't too far from her own. Not only did she not believe in reincarnation, she wasn't sure she believed in any kind of afterlife at all.

"So you weren't too receptive when she talked about it."

He was instantly defensive. "You think I shoulda been? Listen, I'm willing to do a lot for that girl, but I can't handle chanting and incense burning and the rest of that New Age crap."

"Did she say much about the PLI?"

He shook his head. "She got furious with me. She started out all excited, wanted to tell me everything, and I just couldn't handle it. I mean, if it makes her feel better thinking she's gonna run into Timmy in some life down the line, that's her business I guess. Maybe no screwier than thinking he's waiting for her in heaven. But leave me out of it, I told her."

"Do you have any idea how long she's been going there?"

He cocked his head. "She moved out in April. I kinda got the idea she's been going there almost since then. Maybe before, who knows? She wasn't working, hadn't worked since she quit before Timmy was born. I'm gone long hours—she coulda been anywhere, but she never said diddly to me."

"I'd like to check that place out," Nan told him.

"Hang onto your wallet," he advised her with a brief, bitter laugh. "I got curious and drove up there. It's this big redwood-and-glass place spread out on top of a hill over Malibu. I just turned around and left, didn't want to make more waves with Debra, but I hate to think what she's paying those people."

"I thought she was working for them," Nan said.

"I can't tell you. She got so damn mad at me for not wanting to talk about our life together in ancient Egypt or wherever the hell it was I never brought it up again."

After Tony went back to work, Nan flipped through the *Thomas Guide* in her car and found where he had told her the Past Lives Institute was located. The Topanga exit came up quickly on the uncrowded Ventura Freeway.

She passed through the subdivisions of Woodland Hills and climbed into Topanga Canyon. There seemed to be fire warning signs every hundred yards. It was years since there'd been a respectable rainy season in Southern California, and to worsen matters, bark beetles and some rare funky fungus were attacking the already parched and brittle vegetation. It was only a matter of time before flames swept through the acres of bone-dry chaparral in one or more of the LA canyons.

At times like this, Nan was quite content to live where she did. True, her Playa del Rey condo was built on landfill. In a serious earthquake, liquefaction might turn the soil beneath it into Jell-O. A tsunami might sweep it out toward Honolulu. But there were natural disasters everywhere. Somebody who wanted guaranteed environmental protection would probably have to move into a North Dakota missile silo. And wouldn't *that* be fun?

Even dry and dusty, Topanga was a wonderful, almost magical place. A young woman in a long flowing paisley skirt carried a baby in a sling across her front as she walked barefoot along the side of the road, her waist-length hair swinging behind her. She looked like a color plate from a book of sixties photographs. Topanga had a definite timelessness to it, a sense that life had stopped somewhere around 1968 and there was still a chance to stop the war and save the world.

That was one of the things Nan loved about LA. All over town people lived in their own little time warp fantasy worlds. Interior designers had recreated complete Art Deco households from the twenties, trendoids grouped fifties Danish modern chairs around kidney-shaped Formica coffee tables. There were probably even people dressing up in white suits and dancing to disco somewhere. If you found a period of history you particularly liked, you could just step off the linear time line and live there.

The descent to the Pacific Coast Highway brought Nan squarely back to the present. Nothing anachronistic about *this* stretch of land. The folks who could afford this beachfront property were so up-to-the minute their chronometers told time in fifteen world capitals. In microseconds.

She followed Tony's directions and wound up into the hills on a two-lane paved road, passing the occasional security gate, following discreet redwood arrows toward the

Past Lives Institute. The road narrowed as she neared the summit, became more winding and treacherous as it hugged the side of the hill.

At last she rounded a final curve and saw it spread before her: a complex of half a dozen low buildings, all positioned for maximal views of the Pacific Ocean far below. It was a breathtaking location and Tony Fontaine was right: it stank of money.

She parked in a small lot and stepped out into blast-furnace heat. The lot held a dozen cars, mostly exotic and all expensive. Except for the Duesenberg, not one was over a year old. How in the hell had a Duesenberg negotiated that road? Airlift?

She went through tall glass double doors into a small and blessedly chilled reception area. Soft low chairs and couches in beige glove leather were grouped around heavy glass tables holding understated arrangements of unfamiliar tropical flowers. A small sign on a marble table near an interior door read: WELCOME TO THE PAST LIVES INSTITUTE. PLEASE RING FOR ASSISTANCE.

Nan pushed the button, which made no sound in the room, then took a seat by the window. Far out on the ocean, the white triangles of sailboats bobbed.

A few moments later, the interior door opened and a slender brunette in her mid thirties came out. She wore iridescent aqua spandex shorts and an artfully knotted gauze overshirt.

"May I help you?" she asked, puzzled. Evidently the PLI didn't get a lot of drop-in trade.

Nan recognized the voice she had spoken with the previous day. "Are you April Henley?"

The woman nodded. As Nan introduced herself, April stepped forward to shake her hand. Her grip was cool and firm.

"I wasn't expecting you," she said, mildly accusatory. "I've just been working out."

"I'm sorry to interrupt. I was driving this way and I thought I'd just drop by to meet you. It was an impulse; I should have called." Actually Nan had arrived unannounced intentionally.

"No problem," April Henley said warmly. "Do come in."

She led Nan through the door and down a corridor past several closed doors. The corridor forked, ending to the right in padded double doors labeled AUDITORIUM. April Henley continued to the left almost to the end of the hall, finally turning into an office with a panoramic view of the ocean through floor-to-ceiling windows.

Seated across from April's desk, a sleek affair in some undoubtedly endangered tropical wood, Nan told her story again. By now it was practically a rote recitation.

"You're getting me really upset," April said finally. "I've been wondering if I shouldn't do something or call somebody, but I wasn't really sure what or who."

"You told me last night that Debra was here over Labor Day weekend. Was she working?"

April smiled. Her thick, dark brown hair was shoulder length and layered, with a fringe of bangs across the forehead. She seemed vibrant and energetic, almost pretty but not quite. Too many of her features were just a bit off. Her hazel eyes were set a little too close to her nose, and the nose itself turned up just a smidgen too much. Her lips were a little thin, her mouth a trifle wide. Still, the overall impression was of a very attractive woman, one who clearly worked at her looks. Though she claimed to have been working out, her hair and skin were untouched by sweat, her makeup unsmudged.

"She was helping with a weekend seminar," April said. "What has Debra told you about the PLI?"

"Actually," Nan admitted, "not a thing. I haven't been in close touch with her recently. I didn't know that she was working here or even, I have to admit, that you *were* here."

April Henley leaned back in her chair, seeming to relax a bit more. "Perhaps it would help if I gave you a little background on the Past Lives Institute, then. We've been here four years. My brother and I began the PLI because we believed that many of the problems in people's lives are the result of situations they weren't even aware of that had occurred during previous existences. Do you believe in reincarnation?"

"As much as Santa Claus or the Easter Bunny," Nan answered politely.

April's smile this time was gentle. "Many people don't," she said, "but you might be surprised to learn that a quarter of the American public believe that they have lived before and will live again. Have you ever had the feeling that some aspects of your life don't quite make sense?"

Nan laughed. "Who hasn't?"

"If you take the position that the life you're leading right now is only one step on a continuum, you'd be likely to find that aspects of life which are puzzling, even inexplicable, become perfectly logical. Take, for instance, someone who suffers greatly in this life. Debra LaRoche came to us initially because she was devastated by the death of her son. She couldn't understand what she had done to deserve such a terrible experience, why little Timmy had been taken away from her before he had a chance to experience more than a tiny part of life. Through her studies and therapy, through an examination of her past lives, Debra's reached a greater understanding of those questions."

"That may well be," Nan said, "but I'm a lot more concerned about where she is now than where she was in some other life. If she even *had* some other life."

"I won't try to convince you if you don't want to consider these issues, Nan. I'm just trying to give you a little overview."

"What exactly do you do up here, anyway?"

"We offer a wide variety of programs to meet a wide variety of needs." April sounded rather like a late-night TV huckster. "Much of our work is done through hypnotic regression. You're an attorney. You may know that sometimes witnesses to a crime recall critical information when they're hypnotized and taken back in time to the event in question."

"I also know that the California Supreme Court has ruled that hypnotized witnesses can't testify in court."

"That's unfortunate. Hypnosis is also used in conventional psychotherapy, to take a person back to the root causes of a phobia or to alter a type of behavior the patient wishes to modify. In fact, the first business my brother and I had in the field was directly related to behavior modification. We used hypnosis to help people who wanted to eliminate addictive behavior, with great success."

April got up and walked toward her window. "I can tell you're still very resistant, and that's all right, Nan. But there are millions of people who've stopped smoking or lost cravings for drugs or food as a direct result of hypnosis. You probably know some of them."

She scored on that one. Danny Harrington tried a dozen different times to quit smoking, went through program after program before he finally learned some kind of self-hypnotic technique and licked cigarettes. On the other hand, Danny now chewed a box of toothpicks a day, leaving behind him a trail of weirdly twisted little wooden twigs.

April perched on the edge of her desk. "Debra came to us as a client and began seeing one of our therapists as part of her program. From the very beginning we all liked her, a lot. It was also clear that even though she anticipated receiving a substantial settlement for her son's death, she wasn't in an economic position to fully avail herself of the counseling she needed and wanted. Her counselor made a rather unorthodox suggestion, that Debra be allowed to perform secretarial services for the PLI in exchange for her continued personal participation."

"What, like a scholarship? A reincarnation work-study program?" It sounded utterly loony.

"I know you're being facetious, but actually that's just about exactly the arrangement we made. I don't have to tell you how special Debra is. I know you've known her a long time. She speaks of you very fondly."

Oh really? Just what was Debra telling this lady with the rain forest desk and shiny spandex shorts? It was unsettling to realize that April Henley had apparently known all along just who Nan was. "I'm flattered."

"You know," April said, "when Carleen first suggested the arrangement to me, I was doubtful. Of course I love Debra. She's a delightful girl. But I was dubious about bringing her in as an employee at the same time she was a client. I couldn't have been more wrong. I have to tell you, Nan, I don't know how we ever got along without that girl. We were just starting to computerize some of our operations at the time, and I was the only one who had the slightest interest in doing it at all, much less doing it properly. Of course that's part of my job."

"If you don't mind my asking," Nan said carefully, "just what exactly *is* your job?"

"I'm the head of operations. I oversee the business affairs of the PLI, supervise the regional offices, handle our mail-order enterprises, coordinate the tour program. I work with the advertising people, the lawyers, the accountants. I schedule the seminars. I do all the nitty-gritty sorts of things that are necessary for the operation of a successful business."

Nan nodded. It was easy to picture this woman handling all those different aspects of the business, once you got her out of the exercise clothes. She was intelligent, enthusiastic, dedicated. Put her in a power suit and she'd fit right into boardrooms from coast to coast.

"What I needed was an assistant who not only believed in the principles behind the PLI, but could handle a word processor at the same time. I've had secretaries and assistants, lots of them, but the problem is that most of them were really deficient in basic office skills. And the really good ones aren't content to stay in the job. They want ... they want to be in jobs that aren't perceived as subordinate. The last secretary I had was going to night school in marketing. She left to enter a management training program. Debra, on the other hand, seems to genuinely enjoy secretarial work. And I don't have to tell you, of all people, just how good she is at it."

Nan laughed. "She's the best secretary I've ever had. By miles. One of my father's friends was a bank president. He had a secretary who was with him forever. Miss Perkins, her name was, only everybody called her Miss Perfect because there was no record that she'd ever once made any kind of mistake. She was from the old school, and Debra's just about as modern as you can get. But I always thought of Debra as my own Miss Perfect."

"I like that," April said. "You're right, of course. I offered to put her on staff full-time, as a matter of fact, but she didn't want that. Debra's going through a really difficult period in her life and she doesn't seem ready yet for a commitment to a regular job. The irony is that she ends up putting in more time than she probably would have as a straight employee."

"And you didn't wonder when she just stopped showing up?"

April frowned. "Of course I did. But much of the work that I initially had for her to do was finished. If she wants more time to herself, more space to reconstruct her own life, I thought it only fair that she take it." She smiled again. "I guess I have to admit I was afraid if I pressured her too much, she'd leave. And then where would I be?"

Still sitting on top of what was evidently a multimillion-dollar enterprise, Nan thought. But maybe the PLI wasn't as flush as it appeared to be. April seemed to know all about Debra's insurance settlement. Did the Past Lives Institute have plans for Debra's money, as well as plans for Debra?

As she smiled politely, wondering just how to broach that subject, the door swung open abruptly.

CHAPTER 4

A handsome male head popped in through the open doorway. "April, are you about—" He broke off, seeing Nan.
"Excuse me, I didn't realize you were with somebody."

"That's all right, Jonathan," April answered. "Come on in."

He walked into the room. Actually, he *strode* into the
room. This was a guy with presence. He moved with the
serene self-confidence of a just-nominated presidential candidate or a movie star accepting an Academy Award.

"Jonathan, this is Nan Robinson," April said. "Debra
used to work for her and Nan's worried because she can't
find her. Nan, I'd like you to meet my brother, Jonathan."

He was at Nan's side before she could get out of her chair,
offering a firm handshake and the sort of intense eye contact
that would have made a lesser woman swoon. Maybe, Nan
decided as she sank back in her chair, *any* woman.

Was Jonathan Henley the draw for Debra here at the PLI?

He was certainly handsome enough. The family resemblance to April was strong. They had the same cheekbones,
the same angle of jaw, the same thick wavy hair. In Jonathan's case, however, there was nothing off. All the pieces
came together perfectly.

He was probably forty, but his hair was untouched by
gray, with no hint of the male baldness pattern now plag-
uing so many of Nan's contemporaries. His hazel eyes were
flecked with shards of amber around the irises, his skin
golden with a tawny underlay of fresh sunburn. He wore
white tennis shorts and carried a racket. His body was a lit-

49

tle chunky for a tennis player, but it was solid, conspicuously lacking in paunch.

He pulled a chair up beside Nan's. "You're looking for Debra?"

Nan nodded. "Nobody seems to have seen or heard from her in weeks, since she left here after your Labor Day whatever it was."

"The introductory weekend," he said absentmindedly. "We had a dozen new clients for an intensive workshop. You say *nobody's* seen her?"

"Not as far as I can tell. She missed a court appearance, she hasn't called her mother, which is a weekly ritual, her tenant doesn't know where she is."

He shook his head. Worry lines furrowed his brow as he turned to his sister. "When did she leave here, April?"

"Monday night late, I think. You know, we had the final session from two to four, and then after the clients left Debra stuck around and helped get things straightened out. She stayed for dinner, remember? Later I saw her drive out. Maybe she stayed for a while with Bartholomew."

"Who's that?" Nan asked.

"Brother Bartholomew is associated with the PLI," April explained. "He's studied meditation in the Far East and is responsible for most of our more spiritual programs, meditation, *chakras* and so on."

"You seem to have a lot of different things going on up here," Nan said carefully, wondering what April was talking about. *Chakras* sounded like a breakfast cereal, the kind laced with chunks of orange marshmallow. "Is there some kind of guide to your programs? Where do you find the people who come here?"

"Most of them find us," Jonathan answered. "We have an international reputation with clients from across the country and around the world. We do a little advertising, but we rely heavily on word of mouth to bring us new clients."

"Was that how Debra came here?"

Jonathan frowned. "You know, I'm not really sure. She

came to one of our introductory sessions and after that, she was just here. Do you remember who referred her, April?"

April shook her head. "Nope. You might ask Bartholomew. Perhaps one of her friends?"

"Maybe," Nan said doubtfully. Debra had lots of acquaintances and club scene compadres, but not all that many actual friends. And nobody Nan had spoken to seemed terribly spiritual. "Where would I find this Brother Bartholomew?"

Jonathan looked at his watch. "He's in session right now with a meditation workshop, but he should be available in about half an hour." He grinned at April. "Think we could hold off on the tennis game a little while, Sis? Maybe I can show Nan around till Bartholomew's finished. Who knows, by then the heat may break. I'd be awfully embarrassed if I had to be carted away for heat prostration."

"Sure," April answered, without much enthusiasm. "I've got some stuff to catch up on. Find me when you're ready."

"You bet," he told her, holding out a hand to Nan.

Nan let him help her from the chair, feeling rather odd. This was a really fine piece of manflesh here, not the type she normally was attracted to, but quite nice nonetheless. She was embarrassed by some of the wild thoughts running through her brain. *Debra.* That was why she was here. First things first.

He led her down the hallway.

"Our administrative offices and therapy rooms are mostly back here," he explained, opening a door. Inside was a small sitting room with two couches and a couple of chairs in soft pastels. Japanese prints hung on the walls and vertical blinds opened on a rose garden in dazzling bloom. "This is a typical therapy room. We try to stay away from the more formal traditional type of doctor's office."

"Exactly what sort of therapy are we talking about?"

"It varies. We have three licensed psychologists on staff. One of them's on maternity leave right now. They work with people using hypnotic regression to explore the relationship between past life situations and relationships and their contemporary lives and problems."

Oh. "Which means?"

He smiled at her. "Say, for instance, you've always had an extreme fear of heights, and you can't figure any reason for it. No childhood falls or anything like that, never trapped at the top of a Ferris wheel. But it's starting to interfere with your life, or maybe you're just sick of not being able to work above the second floor. You might discover in a regression that in a past life you fell to your death from a great height."

"Uh huh," Nan murmured noncommittally.

"A skeptic, eh?" He crinkled his face into nicely worn smile lines. "Or try this one. You meet somebody and you're really attracted to him, you feel like you've known him forever even though you just met five minutes ago."

Nan cocked her head. Was this a New Age come-on?

"It may be," he went on, "that the two of you had a relationship in a past life. Maybe you were friends or lovers or relatives. Or, the other side of the same coin, maybe you meet some people and you take a strong and instant dislike to them. Nothing rational, not even anything specific like you don't like the way they comb their hair. You just know that you don't trust them or whatever. That might go back to a past life relationship as well. Maybe that person betrayed you or hurt you in some past life."

"If," Nan felt compelled to interject, "you actually had a past life."

"I can see you're going to be hard to convince," he said. "So I'll lay off. But do come along and see the rest of the place. You say you're a friend of Debra's?"

Nan explained the relationship as Jonathan Henley took her around the Past Lives Institute. The physical plant was rambling and extensive, its various components connected by shaded trellises and redwood latticing. Drought-tolerant sea lavender and coreopsis bloomed around the buildings.

In addition to the administrative building where they began the tour, Jonathan showed her a residential complex with a solar-paneled central house, servants' quarters, and a cluster of several smaller buildings. A gym full of fancy exercise equipment opened onto a tennis court and swimming pool. Half a dozen tiny cottages, currently unoccupied, served as a sort of residential hotel to accommodate special clients in town for prolonged periods of time. Two slightly larger cottages stood behind them.

"Bartholomew lives in that one," Jonathan said, indicating a building nestled into a eucalyptus grove. A bed of gray and green succulents outside its door bore striking red blossoms on tall stalks. "And the other is April's. She prefers it to living in the main house with me, likes having her own space."

"Did you build this all?" Nan asked. The idea was staggering.

"We were prepared to build," he told her, "but then we got lucky. We bought this place from a movie producer who went bust. He'd been running his business out of here. Into the ground, as it turned out. We were fortunate in not having to make a lot of changes in the physical plant. Our auditorium was his screening room, the offices were offices already, he had the guest houses for—" He broke off. "You know, I don't have any idea what he used them for. But anyway, it was set up and ready to go."

"It's all very impressive," Nan told him, as they returned to the main building through a kitchen entrance. He opened a hotel-sized refrigerator stocked with all manner of mineral waters, juices, and soft drinks. There were also a dozen varieties of imported beer; after a moment's hesitation, Nan helped herself to a Grolsch and turned down the offer of a glass. Jonathan took an Evian and clinked bottles with her.

"How did you ever get into this in the first place?" she asked him. Jonathan Henley didn't seem like a religious zealot, or even your standard LA flake.

He grinned at her. "You probably won't believe this, but for the first twenty, twenty-five years of her life, my sister April had a real weight problem. She'd diet, lose some weight, put it back on, diet some more. She used to joke she'd lost ten tons, but it really bothered her. Then she went to a hypnotist. He taught her self-hypnosis and biofeedback, and for the first time ever, she was able to get her weight down and keep it there. She was living in Denver and I was out here. I saw her at Christmas and I just couldn't believe how terrific she looked. It didn't even bother her not eating cookies and stuff, and I knew how she'd always had a thing for holiday food. Well, I was a smoker back then and I wanted to quit but not really. You know?"

Nan nodded.

"I figured if this guy could get April skinny, maybe he could get me off cigarettes. So I tried it for that, and damned if it didn't work. We were two for two, the Henleys. I talked April into coming to LA, and we started a small business teaching self-hypnosis for behavior mod. Dieters and smokers. We started with our own testimonials and built on that. To make a long story short, we were a big success. The Henley Health Institute was bought out for big bucks after a few years by Slim 'n' Trim."

Nan whistled softly. Slim 'n' Trim was a major weight control business with franchises in all the overfed nations of the world and storefronts in a thousand American mini-malls. "I had no idea," she said.

"We weren't allowed to talk about it," he explained. "It was part of the contract we signed. We also had to agree to stay out of the business of weight and addiction control for five years. I was looking into some new ideas and selling commercial real estate while I tried to figure out what to do next. Then one day, during my self-hypnosis, I accidentally regressed myself to a previous life."

Nan raised an eyebrow politely. Flying saucer time.

"I can see I'm losing you," he chuckled, looking at his watch. "The meditation session should be finishing up now. If you'll wait here a minute, I'll see if I can find Bartholomew."

Nan perched on a barstool at a butcher block island and sipped her beer. The inside of the building was pleasantly cool. Even outside she hadn't been as aware of the heat as earlier down in the Valley. Maybe it was because of the covered porticos between the buildings, or some special design arrangement that maximized ocean breezes. Or maybe it was simply the chilling effect of so much money.

This would seem an intriguing place to Debra LaRoche, Nan realized. There were probably celebrities passing through here, for one thing, and after nine years Debra still hadn't quite lost her fascination with the stars.

More important, however, the Past Lives Institute had come into Debra's life at a time when she was both relatively affluent and emotionally needy, always a dicey combination. The death of a child, which everyone seemed to agree was the greatest devastation any parent could endure, came to Debra out of nowhere. One morning in her new house in the new subdivision two mountain ranges north of LA, she got up and poured Timmy some apple juice and a bowl of Cheerios. Then she dressed her son in his Oshkosh overalls and red-and-blue striped T-shirt, pulled on his little socks, and fastened his Velcroed tennies, all routine motions, maintenance functions inherent in the mommy job.

Before noon, it was all over. Timmy was on life-support systems in a helicopter racing to Children's Hospital in LA, where all the king's horses and all the king's men shook their heads and ran CAT scans and MRIs, spoke softly to Debra and Tony as they delivered the terrible final truth.

Whatever these people at the Past Lives Institute had told Debra now, she was more than eager to hear. In times of senseless tragedy, the question *Why?* has a particularly insistent, hollow echo to it. Debra needed answers to the *Why?* and *Why me?* questions and the PLI had given her some. It was a pity that Tony hadn't paid closer attention to what Debra wanted to share with him.

Nan didn't hear the door open, but sensed a presence in the room. When she looked up, Jonathan was back.

Beside him stood a tall ascetic in a flowing homespun robe and rope sandals. A braided leather thong was tied around his waist. Prematurely white hair reached his shoulders. His beard hung long and untrimmed. He was probably around fifty, pale complected with opaque turquoise eyes

that resembled glacial lakes. The hand that shook Nan's
was soft and gentle, the fingers long and smooth.

In a way, he reminded Nan of the pictures of Jesus at the
garden gate which had hung in the Sunday school of the
First Methodist Church back in Spring Hill. Age that picture twenty years, turn the brown hair white and the brown
eyes blue, and you'd have Brother Bartholomew.

With one significant difference. The Jesus of those pictures was a benign, asexual man. Brother Bartholomew, despite the aggressive simplicity of his appearance, moved in
a cloud of pheromones. He exuded an almost feral sensual-
ity. If he wore any underwear at all beneath that monastic
robe, it was probably scarlet minibriefs.

Here, Nan was certain, was the PLI's ultimate draw for
Debra LaRoche. Forget Jonathan Henley and his boy-next-
door charm. The more time Nan spent with Jonathan, the
less she thought he'd appeal to Debra. He was too straight,
too wholesome, too earnest.

Brother Bartholomew, on the other hand, was exotic and
sexy and undoubtedly versed in all manner of interesting Eastern techniques of sensual massage. If he was simultaneously
trying to nourish Debra's soul, the girl would be a goner.

"I've been dreadfully worried about Debra," he told Nan
now. His voice was deep and he spoke slowly and deliberately. "I wish there were some way I could help you."

But there wasn't, really. Brother Bartholomew had last
seen Debra at dinner on Labor Day, and claimed to have
nothing to add to what Nan had already been told by the
Henleys. Nan was certain he could have told her more,
would have been willing to stake her law license that Debra
was sleeping with this aging guru.

Was Brother Bartholomew the kind of guy who routinely
boffed the help? Was sleeping with clients a normal service
provided by the Past Lives Institute? Or had he made an
exception for Debra LaRoche, the apparent PLI mascot?

After Bartholomew excused himself for his afternoon
meditation, Jonathan surprised Nan with an invitation to
join him for dinner that night. It seemed pointless to pre-

tend she had a previous engagement, she decided quickly. It was months since she'd had anything approximating a real date and even longer since she'd met any man she found genuinely interesting. This guy was pleasant and good-looking and also her best lead so far to finding Debra.

So she agreed to meet him at eight at Shells 'n' Fins on the beach.

Shells 'n' Fins occupied an oceanfront building which had housed a succession of seafood restaurants over the years. This one had been in operation just over a year and was still considered very chic in the fickle world of LA foodies. On any Saturday night it was invariably packed. But on this second Saturday night of a blistering heat wave, folks were packed in like sardines. Mesquite grilled, of course.

Jonathan was already waiting in the bar when Nan arrived, and he made it clear from the outset that his interest in Nan was purely incidental to the whereabouts of any missing young women.

Which was nice, Nan realized by her second beer. She was getting a little tired of the Debra problem, and it didn't take much internal urging to convince herself that the whole thing was probably just a false alarm. Any time now, Debra would waltz into town from some spur-of-the-moment junket she'd made with a guy she picked up at a rock concert. She'd be apologetic about everybody's concern, and probably a bit baffled too. What did it matter where she went or with whom?

What did it matter indeed?

By the time they were finally seated, Nan had practically forgotten how she met Jonathan in the first place. He was a splendid conversationalist, initially keeping far afield from the Past Lives Institute and his work.

He had grown up in a small Wyoming town where his family owned and operated a Texaco station.

"It's odd," he said, leaning across the table. The racket in the restaurant was deafening, but Jonathan seemed oblivious, focused entirely on Nan and their conversation. "I

watched Rocky Glen go from dirt-scrabble poor to giddy
rich and back to poor again in the space of about three
years, all based on a tiny little titanium discovery. We were
perfectly positioned to watch it all. Before the boom,
folks'd be driving these beat-up old junker pickups, nursing
them along. They'd come in and buy three bucks worth of
gas, try to barter for a new fan belt. My dad would give
anybody credit, but Mom and April were both real firm
about getting paid up front."

"And where did you stand on the issue?"

Jonathan chuckled. "Depended on who I was talking to.
It was a real family operation, with us living in a little place
out back of the station, so it wasn't like Daddy could keep
any big secrets about who was in or what they wanted. We
all knew everything. I could see Daddy lost money giving
credit to folks who couldn't pay without selling their kids,
and I could see how that upset Mom and April when they
were buying sale sheets out of the Sears catalog and cutting
them up to make new dresses. Still, we always had food
and we knew folks would always need gas."

It wasn't easy for Nan to picture Jonathan as a teenager
in a dusty little western town. But it was virtually impossible
to place sleek April Henley in a feedsack apron, scrubbing
pots in a chipped porcelain sink. Even if she *had* been fat.

"And then came the boom."

He nodded. "Then came the boom. All of a sudden
Rocky Glen was just awash in money, and the first thing
most folks did was buy the biggest, fanciest pickup trucks
Detroit had to offer. Bought a lot of other stuff, too. Tony
Lama ostrich-skin boots and sheepskin jackets. Shotguns
and rifles with handcarved walnut stocks. Fishing reels and
tackle that could've landed Moby Dick. Top-of-the-line ra-
dial saws and for the little lady, a mink coat and the grand
deluxe kitchen from Sears."

It was a difficult syndrome for Nan to imagine. Her own
Illinois home town had always been modestly prosperous,
never obviously affected economically beyond her father's
occasional mildly racist grousing about Arabs and the price

of crude oil. He had taken the need to produce gas-economical automobiles as a personal affront.

"For a while there," Jonathan went on, "my daddy was one of the all-time big spenders of Rocky Glen, and that was a crowd to beat. I don't think it ever really occurred to him that he was just a service industry. Those new trucks needed less work than the old clunkers and they didn't use any more gas. About the only way he profited was selling everybody snow tires and junk to hang off the rearview mirror. Did a brisk business in gunracks, too, for a while."

"Did he get hurt when it ended?"

Jonathan cocked his head and considered. "Not as bad as a lot of folks. Most people were in debt up the wazoo, lucky to end up where they started. Daddy still had the station and his family helping run the place for free, so he was ahead of the game."

"Some people must have come out ahead, though."

"Oh sure. Uncle Bob, for one. I had an uncle," he explained, "who was dubious about the titanium from the very beginning. But he had mineral rights to sell just like everybody else, and he sold them. Used the proceeds to buy land. Not a lot, but enough. He picked up a couple of lots with rundown houses on them, places the owners moved out of to get into nicer places. Let the old owners keep the mineral rights, even. Then Uncle Bob fixed them up as rent houses for the mineral company employees who came to town. Used the money he made from rent to buy another one, fixed that up and sold it to one of the company executives."

"A shrewd man, your Uncle Bob."

Jonathan smiled. "You could say that. When the titanium played out and the mineral company executives went back to Cheyenne or Denver or wherever it was they'd come from, Uncle Bob picked up more property cheap, at bank auction. Folks were overextended and some of them lost it all. It was kind of like the grasshopper and the ant. Of course a lot of folks were pissed with Uncle Bob for taking advantage. But they didn't call it taking advantage until the boom was over and the finance company was coming to repo everything."

"What did you sell during the boom?" Nan asked. She realized, as she heard her question, that there was no question in her mind but that Jonathan Henley had profited somehow.

"What do you think?"

Nan considered. "I don't see you as either the grasshopper or the ant, actually. I kind of picture you as the guy selling the refrigerator with the fancy icemaker and raking in the commissions."

He laughed. "I was a little young for that. But in a way you're right. As a kid I sold door-to-door, mostly. Greeting cards and wrapping paper. My mom's homemade candy and fruitcakes at Christmas. Magazine subscriptions. Vegetable seeds. Folks had cash around and they knew me, so they'd buy."

They'd have bought even if he were a stranger, Nan knew. He had that sort of charm. As a thirteen-year-old with a cowlick, he must have been irresistible. Even now, a quarter century later, it was hard to imagine saying no to him.

But no she did say, much later, when they finished coffee and dessert, when the crowd was finally starting to thin a bit, when the noise level had abated to a surflike roar.

No, she didn't think she'd come back out to the PLI with him just now, and no, she was really too tired for him to follow her home to Playa del Rey. Maybe some other time.

The persistent salesman, his fangs in the ankle of a prospect, nailed her down before he let her go.

Thursday evening there was an introductory lecture at the Past Lives Institute. Nan let herself be talked into attending, on the house, skepticism checked at the door. After that, it took no effort at all to agree to dinner again the following Saturday night. She wasn't entirely certain what Jonathan Henley was trying to sell her, but she was pretty sure she hadn't bought any yet.

When she got home just after midnight, there were three hang-ups on her answering machine and the flight attendants were having some kind of a party.

It took a long time to get to sleep.

CHAPTER 5

No mere heat wave could stop the Venice Boardwalk; a nuclear explosion would probably be necessary. Venice Beach was jumping on Sunday morning and, as always, it was easy to forget there was an ocean just a few hundred feet to the west.

Nan threaded her way through crowds of Rollerbladers, jugglers, spaced-out neon-bikinied teenagers, whining children, cops in Bermuda shorts, bodybuilders with grotesquely overdeveloped muscles and teeny little swimsuits. GI Joes crawled on their bellies near a toy vendor, stopping periodically to fire a few rounds. A pathetically untalented guitarist sang old James Taylor songs beside a nearly empty straw hat. A black evangelist loudly extolled the role Jesus played in his life and handed out pamphlets.

Nearby another black man swallowed fire. Given the weather, the act seemed redundant.

Nan walked on, passing a bum in a heavy gray wool overcoat and stained deerstalker hat. He pushed a battered Vons shopping cart with a crudely lettered placard on its front: MY OTHER CART IS A RALPHS.

Chuckling, she turned in at the Wave Café. It wasn't quite eleven, but Shannon Revell was already seated and drinking a papaya spritzer on the patio. Shannon waved a cheerful hello as Nan picked her way among the tiny outdoor tables. Most of the brunch crowd had opted to stay indoors on this beastly Sunday morning, but Shannon was a certified sun freak. She'd managed to find a table that provided an umbrella to protect Nan even while she nursed her own mahogany tan.

"So!" Shannon said when Nan sat down. "How's your life?"

Nan wrinkled her nose. "Kind of crazy," she replied.

"I sold the Lattimore place yesterday," Shannon announced. "So we're celebrating."

"Does that mean brunch is on you?"

Shannon laughed, a wonderful tinkling sound reminiscent of sleigh bells. "Of course. I was beginning to worry that I'd never see another commission."

The Los Angeles real estate market, notorious for its absurd overpricing and frenetic binges, was currently in a bit of a slump. Not a stall, Shannon swore, because that would never happen, and neither would, God forbid, a serious reversal. Maybe she was right; there always seemed to be some group of affluent foreigners eager to pump their funds into Southern California real estate. Now that the Iranians were all settled in, the Japanese were buying property as investments. Million-dollar fixer bungalows were considered bargains by a nation accustoming itself to the hundred-year multigenerational mortgage.

"I'm glad," Nan told her.

Shannon's triumphs were always fun to share, her life usually interesting, if tumultuous. Shannon had spent six childhood years as the cherubic imp on *Our Family*, one of those early TV dramas where the weekly plotline centered on a misplaced plate of church bazaar cookies and was invariably resolved by the final credits. It seemed fitting, somehow, that Nan had met Shannon through Adult Children of Alcoholics.

"Are the lawyers behaving this week?" Shannon asked.

"About as much as they ever do. But the legal secretaries, now, that's a different matter."

A waiter appeared, introduced himself as Randy and recited the brunch specials with great passion and a subtle dance step. Someday Nan hoped to be served in an LA restaurant by somebody whose secret ambition wasn't a multipicture deal with Paramount and the cover of *People*. She ordered a mimosa and a fruit salad. It was too hot to even think about heavier food.

Then she told Shannon about Debra's disappearance. Shannon didn't really know Debra, but she knew about Timmy and had been horrified at the time of the boy's death. Shannon had kids of her own, a teenage daughter from her second marriage who lived with her and two boys from her third marriage who lived with their father in Arizona.

"She'll turn up," Shannon said confidently when Nan finished. "I'll bet you anything she's up in the mountains somewhere, meditating."

"Debra isn't the meditative type. And anyway, if she just wanted to meditate, why didn't she stay here and do it with Brother Bartholomew, the old lech?"

"Now, Nan, you don't know that he's a lech. He may be just exactly what he says he is."

Nan shook her head. "I don't believe it. The more I think about him, the phonier he seems."

"Based on what?"

"Based on I don't know. Just a feeling I have. I deal with shysters and con men a lot, you know. Just 'cause this one's wearing tatty robes instead of a Ralph Lauren suit doesn't make him a real man of God."

"You'd be more comfortable if he were wearing a clerical collar?"

"I'd be more comfortable if Debra'd never hooked up with those people in the first place."

"Wait a minute," Shannon said, as Randy the soft-shoe waiter brought their food. The fruit plates looked wonderful, succulent rainbow-colored melon balls dotted with grapes and blueberries. Fresh chopped mint was sprinkled on top. "It sounds to me like the Past Lives Institute is the perfect place for her to be. Once she figures out the karma involved in losing her little boy, she'll be able to get on better with her own life."

"You mean to say you believe in this crap?"

"Of course. Don't you?"

Nan shook her head. "Nope. I don't believe in aliens in our midst, either, with the possible exception of that waiter."

"What about life after death in general?"

"I go back and forth on that one," Nan admitted. "For the most part, I think that this is it. Here we are, and when it's over, it's over. I suppose I'd like to believe in heaven, the way I was raised to, but then I'd have to believe in hell, too. When I was a kid I used to lie awake at night worrying about unbaptized babies and the people in Africa who never heard about Jesus. Of course maybe Bruce Jay Friedman is right and God's a Puerto Rican janitor."

Shannon speared a honeydew ball. "Well, let me ask you this. Do you think there's any kind of pattern to life, any kind of big picture? Or is it all random and crazy?"

"You're asking an Angeleno? Random and crazy, of course."

"But *why*?"

"Wait a minute," Nan said. "That's *my* question. Are you saying you believe there really is an order to the universe?"

"Sure."

Nan sipped her drink and ate some more fruit. It wasn't really surprising that Shannon believed in reincarnation. After all, the woman was a native Californian. Still . . .

"Why do you think so?"

"I guess," Shannon answered slowly, "because if you believe in reincarnation, a lot of things that otherwise wouldn't make any sense fall into place."

"Such as?"

"Such as why some people who seem totally undeserving have such incredibly good luck. Or why some people who are decent and wonderful have such horrible things happen to them. Like the woman who spent ten years working with Mothers Against Drunk Drivers *before* her own kid was killed by one. Or, bringing the matter closer to home for both of us, why some kids have the experience of living with an alcoholic parent."

"Are you saying that that was our fault?" Nan frowned. The entire tenet of ACA was the precise opposite.

"Not our fault so much as our karma."

"And precisely how are we defining karma?"

"What goes down goes around is the glib answer. Karma is really just the accumulation of all the good and bad things you've done in all your lives. From the karmic viewpoint, you and I were probably both alcoholic parents in some past lives. Because of that, we had to experience in our current lives what effect that has on a child."

"So you're just supposed to accept whatever happens to you, whether it seems right or fair or anything? That everything is just your karma and you can't do anything about it?"

Shannon smiled. "Not necessarily. You can interpret karma actively or passively. In passive karma, you'd say, 'This is my lot in life, my destiny. I must endure.' In a more active interpretation, you might say, 'Well, obviously I have some bad karma to work off in the area of such and such, so I'll really put myself into it.' Do you think you'll ever be an alcoholic parent?"

"No. But I'll probably never be a parent at all, as my mother keeps reminding me."

Shannon laughed again. She had the kind of laugh that made people nearby turn their heads and smile in contagion. "Well, Counselor Cautious, let me put it in personal terms. I *did* turn out to be an alcoholic parent. But I caught on to what was happening and I went to AA and I stopped drinking. Now that's an example of active karma. If I'd caught on a little quicker, maybe my drinking wouldn't have gotten out of hand, or I'd have stopped sooner. If I hadn't caught on at all, I'd be facedown in a gutter somewhere and my kids would be even more screwed up than they already are."

"Your kids aren't screwed up."

"How would you know?" A sudden edge tinged Shannon's voice.

Nan winced. "I'm sorry. I guess I don't know. But Becky

seems like a fine kid to me." Becky was a high school senior, a pretty, quiet girl with a professed interest in anthropology and a part-time job at a frozen yogurt shop.

"Becky, who's decided she wants to be called Rebecca, has a new boyfriend," Shannon said in clipped, precise tones. "She claims he's only nineteen, but he looks a lot older to me. He drives a Harley-Davidson the size of Rhode Island and he has tattoos."

"Oh, no!"

"Oh, yes. He probably has a record, too, but I'm not sure how to find that out."

"I could check if you'd like."

Shannon closed her eyes. "I'm afraid to find out," she said after a moment, "but I think I'm more afraid not to know. His name if Rick Oleander, spelled just like the poisonous plant, and he lives in Santa Monica. Do it."

Nan ate some cantaloupe. "Consider it done. Now. Is karma always so literal?"

"The Hindu version is, particularly in terms of retribution. Others are looser. But for Debra, my guess is she was responsible for the death of someone else's child in a past life, so she had to experience what it felt like to lose one of your own this time out."

Which sounded like what Tony Fontaine had said yesterday. Debra was claiming ... what was it? That she and Tony had neglected a child together.

"They use hypnotic regressions at that place," Nan said. "Do you know anything about that?"

"Do I know anything about it? Girl, I've *done* it."

"At the Past Lives Institute?"

Shannon shook her head. "No. It was in Tucson, when I was married to Dave. There was this psychic hypnotist I used to go see. I was trying to figure out why Dave and I were so miserable together, why I felt compelled to keep sneaking around and seeing other men. That was during my country-western period—I think I've told you about it. When I was hanging out in honky-tonks. Anyway, she regressed me to a past life in sixteenth or seventeenth century

Ireland—I was never sure which—where he and I had been together before, only that time he was the one cheating on me. With my sister, as a matter of fact."

This was getting a bit never-never land. "Wait a minute. You're saying that some woman told you that Dave had an affair with your sister in Ireland four hundred years ago, so that's why you were fucking cowboys in Arizona now?"

Shannon winced. "Do you need to be so blunt about it?"

"I can't help myself. It sounds ridiculous."

"Maybe to you. Besides, she didn't tell me. I was the one who told her, who saw the whole thing when I was hypnotized. It really helped me, Nan. Once I realized what I was doing, I was able to stop it and leave the marriage. In my heart of hearts, I knew marrying Dave was a big mistake, but then we had the boys and I just couldn't face the fact that I'd struck out for the third time."

"I'm not sure I find all this a terribly compelling argument for reincarnation," Nan said after a moment.

"Oh, there was more to it. I'd also had these weird headaches, right above my left ear, for years and years. I discovered I'd been killed once being shot in the head."

Nan shook her head. "Somehow, Shannon, I don't think I'm being convinced."

"Would you believe it if you read it in a book?"

"Not necessarily. There are books that say there was never a Holocaust. Books that say women should subordinate themselves to men. There's probably a book that says eating Cracker Jacks cures cancer."

Shannon laughed as she signaled for the check. "Good lord, you're a hard sell. Listen, come on back to my place and I'll give you some stuff to read. I want to show you something anyway."

What Shannon wanted to show Nan was a house across from her own, three doors down on a Venice walk street.

"Shannon, I'm not looking to move."

"This place would be perfect for you."

"I'm happy in my condo." Come again? The flight attendants, the screaming kids at the pool, the numbing anonymity of the endless warrens stretching along Manitoba Street?

"It's been on the market for six months and they're antsy to sell. I think we can get a contingency on selling your condo—"

"Which would be absolutely impossible to do."

"—and then price the condo just a little below market to a first-time buyer. But don't worry about the details yet. Just promise me you'll keep an open mind." Shannon unlocked the door of the freshly painted pink stucco house at 924 Glorioso Way and stepped back. "Voilà!"

The house was tiny, a dollhouse in realtorspeak. It sat far back on the walk street lot, separated only by a white picket fence and sidewalk from the opposite houses. There was a little porch in front, a massive magenta bougainvillea shading a side patio, and an alley almost directly behind it.

Inside, the place was empty. Everything had been painted Navajo white, the floors carpeted in white Berber. A freestanding fireplace stood in a corner of the living room. Nan prowled through the house. It didn't take long.

"It's nice enough, what there is of it," she said finally. "But it probably isn't even half as big as my condo."

"Which has more space than you use, face it. Here you've got the same number of rooms, just a little cozier."

"I'd have to step outside to change my mind."

Shannon laughed again. "If you're changing it to say you'll buy the house, let me just open the door for you. The absolute best feature," she went on, "is right across the walkway. Nine-seventeen."

Which was Shannon's own house, where she and Becky had lived for four or five years now. Nan liked Shannon's place, always enjoyed visiting her here. These walk streets seemed a world unto themselves. It would, Nan realized suddenly, be really nice to live across the street from a friend, to be able to visit without making complicated advance plans and driving half an hour on the freeway.

They crossed to Shannon's house and Nan listened while her friend outlined strategy. The house on Glorioso Way was outrageously expensive, but the amount Shannon thought the condo would bring was equally preposterous. In general, LA real estate prices made Nan break into a cold sweat. As far as she was concerned, the down on the bungalow was what the whole thing should have cost.

"Look," Nan finally told Shannon, "don't get your heart set on this. I'm really not looking to move and if I were, this would be a bassackward way to go about it anyhow. The best I can promise is I'll think about it." She took an armload of books about reincarnation and headed home.

As she drove through the gate into the condo complex, a jumbo jet on an LAX flight path roared past, rattling windows in the three-storied buildings looming on every side of her. It even blocked out the juvenile shrieks from the pool. She envisioned the flight attendant waiting for the sound of Nan's stereo to begin her afternoon sexual aerobics workout . . . and suddenly the idea of owning a little house on a quiet street seemed a lot more appealing.

There were two more hang-ups on her machine when she got home, as well as a message from Carleen McIlheney, who said she was Debra's therapist at the PLI. Nan dialed her number, a West LA exchange, and a little boy answered the phone.

"Hello? Hello?" he asked over and over again. Nan asked to speak to Carleen, which brought more hellos. Then she suggested he find his mother, no more successfully. She was ready to pound the phone into the wall by the time a breathless adult female voice picked up and said that yes, she was Carleen McIlheney. Nan identified herself.

"Oh, I'm so *glad* you called," Carleen said. She sounded fairly young. "I was out in the garage with the dryer banging away full of tennis shoes and I didn't hear the phone. April told me you were out at the PLI yesterday."

Nan began her looking-for-Debra speech, but Carleen cut her off.

"Oh, I know who you are," she said. "Debra's spoken of you. I can't talk about that, of course—confidentiality and all—but I'm just so *relieved* that somebody's finally paying attention to her being missing."

"Then you don't think she's gone off to meditate?" Nan asked dryly.

"I don't know what to think," the woman admitted, "and I was starting to think I ought to do something myself, only I couldn't imagine what. I don't have your expertise at that sort of thing."

Just exactly what had Debra told these people about her, anyway? Nan wasn't terribly impressed with Carleen McIlheney's take on confidentiality, either.

"Finding missing people is pretty far removed from what I do," she explained.

"But I thought you were an investigator."

"I am. But the people we investigate aren't generally missing, Dr. McIlheney. We know right where to find them." Cowering under their desks, most often.

"Oh, please. I don't have a doctorate. Call me Carleen."

Nan had not, till that very moment, given any thought to the credentials possessed by PLI therapists. It might be interesting to look into the subject.

"Carleen, do you have any idea where Debra might go if she went off for a while to, I don't know, get herself together or something?"

There was a moment of silence. "I don't guess there's any problem if I tell you no."

"I take that to mean you don't know where she is. Do you have any ideas where she *might* be, even if you don't think you can share them with me?"

Again hesitation. "Not really. Look, this is all rather . . ." Her voice trailed off uncertainly. In the background, Nan could hear a small voice whining, "Mommy."

"I won't keep you then," Nan said. "If you think of anything, could you give me a call? I don't want to intrude on Debra's privacy, but I do want to be sure she's all right."

"Of course," the therapist agreed.

After getting off the phone with Carleen McIlheney, Nan showered and called her mother in Spring Hill, Illinois.

Was Debra LaRoche calling her own mother from somewhere today? Nan fervently hoped so. Tomorrow she herself would have to call Mrs. LaRoche, she'd decided. Up until now there had seemed no reason to further worry the woman, but if three Sundays went by with no word from her daughter, Nan wanted to know about it.

June Robinson picked up the phone on the first ring, full of cheerful chatter about a community picnic she'd just attended. Nan half listened; for the most part, her mother referred to people she hadn't seen in years and never thought about.

Nan carefully avoided any mention of Debra LaRoche, not wanting the Midwestern old girls' network involved unless it became truly essential. The mere possibility that a native daughter was missing in lotusland would sweep terrified mothers into a tizzy across three states within an hour.

She did, however, tell her mother about looking at the house on Glorioso Way, and was surprised by the enthusiastic response.

"Why, Nan, I think it would be wonderful for you to get out of that apartment," her mother said. June Robinson recognized little distinction between apartments and condominiums and considered the detached single-family dwelling to be the only truly proper abode.

"I can't afford it, I don't think," Nan said. "The prices are just too ridiculous. If I were at some hotsy-totsy law firm working eighty hours a week it wouldn't be a problem, but I'm a civil servant, remember."

"Perhaps I could help you out," her mother suggested.

Nan was stunned into silence. She had never asked her mother for money, nor had any been offered in the past.

"I couldn't do that, Mom."

"I don't see why not," June Robinson answered. "I was just talking to Binky Hart at the bank this week and I really have quite a lot of money, more than I even realized. Your father left me very well provided for." It was Mr. Hart who had the original Miss Perfect, Nan realized with a stab.

"But, Mom—"

"You'll get it when I die anyway, you and Julie. Would you rather have me dead?"

"Mom! I can't believe you'd say such a thing!"

"Well, just because you're a fancy lawyer doesn't mean I can't want to help you out. If you're not going to get married and have a family, you might at least move into a respectable house."

Nan was somehow doubtful that her mother would consider the place on Glorioso Way a respectable house; *shack* or *shanty* were terms that would probably come more trippingly to Mom's tongue. She explained that there was no rush, but that Shannon claimed a set of initially greedy Eastern heirs were now getting antsy and ready to haggle.

"Is there something wrong with the place that you haven't mentioned?" Mom asked suspiciously.

"It's a little cozy." Even acquiring a gerbil might render it overcrowded, though there was little danger of Nan taking on a pet. At the moment she wasn't responsible for a single living thing, and she liked it that way.

"Well, you think about it, dear. And now I'll let you go, before you run your phone bill up."

Nan hung up, chuckling. To avoid squandering an additional fifty cents, her mother had cut short a conversation about whether or not to spend the equivalent of some developing country's gross national product on a cottage that would barely fit Hansel and Gretel.

After they'd been made into cookies.

CHAPTER 6

Late at night the killer paced and pondered.

Things had dragged on far too long. Why hadn't Debra's body been discovered yet? It was so *obvious*. Didn't anybody pay attention to anything?

Not that it really mattered, probably. Delayed discovery would just confuse the time of death. The *cause* of death would still be apparent. Would *seem* apparent.

If they didn't find Debra soon, maybe it would be time to direct a little attention. Make a suggestion.

There was a lot to be said for the anonymous phone tip.

Right now, though, the big question mark was Nan Robinson. Her intrusion was amusing, but it had potential for trouble. Debra had spoken about the Robinson woman with respect and even reverence. Nan was like a pit bull when she got her teeth into a problem, Debra had said. She wouldn't let go until she was absolutely satisfied. That shouldn't be a problem, but still . . .

Everything had been set up so painstakingly. All the plans had been made so carefully, been carried out so well. There was room in the general scheme of things for an interested old friend, of course. It might even be helpful in the short run.

The danger lay in letting the Robinson woman dig around, in having her stir things up unnecessarily. She claimed not to have spoken with Debra recently, and it seemed fairly obvious that Debra hadn't told her anything critical. Still, there was no way to be absolutely certain. She could be more sly than she seemed, might give away less than she appeared to.

But right now there was no way she could actually *know* anything. Was there?

Caution. That was the byword. Caution and maybe a little distraction. It couldn't hurt to rattle Nan Robinson a little.

Nothing too obvious. Nothing traceable. There was a fine line between muddying the waters and stirring up needless suspicion.

Still, it couldn't hurt to continue the hang-ups. Single women living alone always found that unnerving. Maybe a breather call or two, ones that couldn't be traced. Mail was risky: fingerprints, handwriting, typefaces.

But maybe . . . There were unpleasant things that could happen to anybody in Los Angeles, whether or not they were poking around where their attentions were unwanted.

Nobody could say it wasn't a coincidence if something disagreeable happened to that buttinsky attorney.

Could they?

☀

On Monday morning, Nan woke early and restless, the events of the past four days swirling through her brain. Her room was hot, her bedding tangled around her naked body. She dimly recalled dreams of Debra fleeing in terror from something large and formless.

For the first time since her initial suicide fears, she permitted herself to think seriously about the possibility that Debra was dead. California abounded in crazed murderers, after all. Serial killers, too. With over two thousand homicides annually in Los Angeles alone, it often took five or six deaths before anybody even noticed a pattern. The Hillside Strangler, the Zodiac Killer, the Trailside Slayer, the Night Stalker, the Sunset Slayer, the Skid Row Slasher, the Trash Bag Killer—all had killed repeatedly and many had been apprehended only by accident. Kenneth Bianchi had been questioned and released, more than once, because in the context of his Hollywood neighborhood he seemed so normal.

Unless Debra had changed dramatically in the past six months—and her recent phone messages suggested otherwise—she'd be all too likely to go home with some nice-looking sociopath who spouted a good line and showed a little interest. Like Bianchi or Ted Bundy.

Nan got out of bed shivering. This was the perfect antidote to a miserable heat wave: suspect a friend has fallen victim to a yet-unnamed serial killer.

Clearly she wouldn't be able to get back to sleep. She showered, dressed, and headed for the office with a breakfast bag of grapes in her lap. Early rush hour traffic on the Santa Monica Freeway swept in a tidal wave toward downtown LA. A woman in a Mazda drove alongside Nan for several miles, expertly applying mascara at sixty-three miles an hour. Nan wondered, as she did every morning, where all these bleary-eyed folks navigating by rote were going. And why.

At the office, she plowed through paperwork on a half dozen cases, dictating letters and reports, forcing Debra to the back of her mind.

It bothered her that so much of what she did now seemed so routine. Nan had come to the State Bar full of enthusiasm and rectitude, anxious to root out the dishonest and duplicitous, disillusioned with large firm practice. It seemed an eternity now since she'd experienced the euphoria of getting a job offer from McSweeney Lane.

McSweeney Lane had proven a fine place to be at first, a Los Angeles firm with a prestigious national reputation, respectable clients, and a partnership track which had even been known to reward the female gender. Nan didn't notice until later that the place was also riddled with hypertension, bleeding ulcers, premature coronaries, and skittering, consumptive anxiety.

The associates who labored endlessly, billed impossibly, and abandoned any semblance of personal lives told each other—in rare, unguarded moments of social interaction—

that things would be different once they made partner, when they'd no longer be working eighty hours a week. Theirs was the chilling myopia of the classic Type A. With the exception of certain rainmakers most often found at the Jonathan Club or on first class junkets to Washington, D.C., and San Francisco, the partners worked equally appalling hours. One litigation partner was rumored to require name tags for his nine children during those few weekend hours he spent at the family homestead enjoying quality time and begetting more offspring.

Finally Nan realized that it didn't matter how much money she was making or that attorneys in New York and Chicago and Houston were familiar with their firm. It didn't even matter that she had an excellent chance of making partner. She was over thirty, divorced, and in dire need of a personal life, even if it only consisted of sleeping till ten on an occasional Saturday morning. She was ready for a radical change and the job with the State Bar offered it.

From the very beginning, she had liked her work here. Today, however, she found it almost impossible to concentrate.

By the time Danny Harrington breezed in at eight-thirty with a bag of donuts, she had organized her lists for Operation Debra. Danny listened with growing alarm as Nan reported on what she had learned over the weekend. He munched his breakfast while Nan talked.

"Let's check in with her tenant first," he said, "and if he hasn't heard anything, you've got to call her mother."

"And tell her what?"

Danny frowned. "The truth."

"Danny, Debra's spent the last nine years keeping the details of her personal life from her mother."

"While calling her every Sunday." He shook his head. Nan had never seen Danny look quite so worried. His open Irish face looked gaunt and naked without the smiles it usually wore, vibrant laugh lines reduced to simple wrinkles. "Listen, Nan, I'm sure my kids have kept plenty from me over the years, too. But if one of them turned up missing, I'd want to know about it."

"Because you're an investigator."

"Because I'm a *father*, you nitwit!"

"Danny, if we tell her, we'll just worry her more."

"If she hasn't heard from Debra in three weeks, she's already frantic. Besides, maybe she'll say she got a call yesterday. Now come on, be a good girl. Call that guy in Debra's back house."

"He won't be up."

"So?" Danny took out the first toothpick of the day and began chewing.

Nan dutifully dialed Marty and listened through nineteen rings. She hung up, pushed her chair back, and started to stand.

Danny shook his head, tossed his greasy white donut bag in the trash, and pointed to the phone. "Her mother."

Nan inhaled deeply, then followed instructions before she had time to think about it. It was nearly eleven A.M. in South Bend, Indiana. Maybe Mrs. LaRoche would be at the grocery store or checking on white sales at the mall or kaffeeklatsching at a neighbor's. Maybe she'd be at work.

But Marie LaRoche answered on the second ring, her voice tentative and low, familiar from the messages on Debra's machine. Nan took a deep breath and spoke. "Mrs. LaRoche, this is Nan Robinson, calling from Los Angeles. Debra's friend."

"Something's happened to Debbie!" No preliminaries, no how-have-you-beens, no nothing. Which meant that Debra hadn't called yesterday. Damn!

Nan ignored the chill that swept over her and swallowed deeply. "I don't know," she answered quickly. "But I *am* concerned. Mrs. LaRoche, I don't want to alarm you, but I've been trying to get in touch with Debra and I haven't been able to reach her. I was wondering if perhaps you've heard from her recently?"

That was at least mildly ambivalent.

"You mean she hasn't been to work?" A note of near-hysteria raised Marie LaRoche's voice. Nan could picture her standing beside the phone. No, probably she'd be sitting, would have collapsed into a chair expecting horrific news when Nan identified herself. Mrs. LaRoche was a small woman, tiny like Debra, with fluttery mannerisms and an unconscious habit of running her fingers through her hair when she was upset.

"Well, no," Nan answered, after a moment's hesitation. "She, uh, wanted to take some time off." Nan was not a fluent liar, had never been able to easily make even small social fibs. The Big Lie was virtually impossible. It helped to be doing this on the phone, but not much.

Nan went on to explain, ever so carefully, that she had already visited Missing Persons. In response, Marie LaRoche made a strangled noise somewhere between a moan and a wail.

"I always knew something like this would happen," Debra's mother whimpered. "She should never have left here. I begged her not to go." That Debra had left nine years earlier seemed an insignificant detail. "I warned her something horrible would happen, that it was dangerous, that . . ." Her voice trailed off miserably.

"Now, now, Mrs. LaRoche," Nan said, in her most soothing tones. She was terrible at this sort of thing, no better at false assurances than white lies. "I'm sure Debra's just fine, that she simply forgot to let us know where she was going."

Danny smiled encouragement as Nan fumbled on. By the time she hung up five minutes later, she was shaking. She had established that Debra's last call to her mother came on the Sunday of Labor Day weekend and that Marie LaRoche believed her daughter had been working at the State Bar for the past four months. Nan thought she had convinced Mrs. LaRoche that there was no reason for her to drop everything and come to California, and had promised to call the instant she heard anything.

Now she would have to call her own mother and repeat the entire story. As soon as Marie LaRoche made her first phone call, the story would spread like a Midwestern prairie fire. June Robinson would never forgive her daughter if she first learned of Debra's disappearance from somebody else.

"I feel sick to my stomach," she told Danny.

"You were great," he reassured her. "Now let's split up the leads we have, starting with the boyfriends."

"Most of them should be split with a meat ax," Nan said bitterly. "I think about those jokers and it's hard for me to believe there's ever been a women's movement. But I honestly don't think we can find very many of them. I never knew that much detail about her—" she paused, looking for a polite way to say *one night stands*—"her more casual relationships. She just told me about the guys who stuck around for a while. Danny, she's been here nine years and it's been one loser after another."

"So we concentrate on the most recent ones. They have anything in common?"

Nan grimaced. "They're all good-looking and great in bed. Or so Debra always says. But, Danny, these aren't exactly meaningful relationships. One of them she actually took to small claims court because he trashed her apartment."

Danny looked truly baffled. "I don't get it. She's such a sweet little thing. Why would she . . ." He let his voice trail off. He had always, Nan realized suddenly, thought of Debra in the same category as his daughters and nieces, girls he knew and cherished and wanted to see happily ensconced in their own little American dreams.

"What can I say, Danny? You want the pop psych answers? Insecurity, low self-esteem, a poor self-image? She's mixed up, that's all. And she's got a healthy libido."

"Healthy?"

"Active, anyway."

"But there are so many nice, respectable fellows."

Nan smiled despite herself. "You obviously haven't been in the dating arena lately, Danny. Nice respectable fellows aren't nearly as easy to find as you seem to think. Besides which, she always says professional men are boring. I think she's spent too much time in law offices."

Danny left finally, promising to follow up in any spare time on the boyfriends from hell. Nan dialed her mother and was both relieved and concerned to find the line busy.

She closed her eyes as she considered the love life of Debra LaRoche.

Most of Debra's long-term beaux had been so appalling that Nan did her best to ignore their existence while they were around, then promptly repressed them once they left the scene. She thought of them not by name, but rather by classification: the one who beat Debra, the one who stole her Mastercard, the one who trashed her apartment, the one with the coke habit, the alcoholic, the one who gave her genital warts, the one who wrecked her car, the several with other women on the side. A few categories overlapped. Nan had seen pictures of some, but Tony was the first she ever met. In this company, Tony was a real prince.

She tried her mother again. Still busy.

Before she began on her own part of the boyfriend list, she decided to try Debra's hairdresser, Alistair. Debra's calendar showed a hair appointment on the Thursday before Labor Day.

Nan had copied two numbers for Alistair from the wall by Debra's kitchen phone. The first rang three times. Then a machine played a few bars from "Cabaret" before a male voice coyly said, "You know what to do, darlings." At the beep, Nan left her name and number and what she hoped was a logical, coherent message. She wasn't sure if Alistair would remember her personally, so she repeated Debra's name three times.

The second number was answered by a man who was either in a drug-induced stupor or startled out of delta sleep by the ringing phone. He had only a vague idea who Alistair was but was sure he wasn't there. Somebody named Jay might know. He groaned when Nan begged for Jay's number and was gone for so long she began to suspect he'd slipped into a coma. Finally he returned with a phone number that yielded yet another message machine. This one just said, "On your mark, get set, GO!"

After she hung up, Nan decided that these were probably a fairly representative sample of Alistair's friends. Alistair was a grand champion, world-class flake. It was years since Nan had last seen him, but just thinking about Alistair brought a smile to her lips. He was more than a flake, really. He was warm, caring, and the quintessential LA character.

Alistair used no last name and refused to talk about his past. He claimed to have emerged some fifteen years earlier in San Francisco, an exotic moth unfolding his wings from the construction of a fast-discarded cocoon.

Like all true eccentrics, he genuinely believed himself perfectly normal. At the same time, no goofy trend went past that Alistair didn't embrace headlong. No fashion escaped him, no wacked-out fad eluded him, no quirk of social mores avoided his attention.

Nan had no idea where Debra had first found Alistair, but by the time Debra began actually working for Nan, he was already doing her hair. Over nine years he'd done everything to Debra's head but shave it. She'd been hennaed, permed, spiked, colored, moussed, streaked, cropped, and bobbed.

She had once appeared at McSweeney Lane with a skunk streak the precise shade of the turquoise buttons on her very proper little secretarial dress, precipitating an office uproar and the threat of a dress code for all support staff. The female attorneys, of course, adhered to their own rigid self-inflicted code, identical peas in the law firm pod, each in her own grim, sexless power suit with the teeniest speck of color at the throat.

The remarkable thing was that no matter what atrocities Alistair performed on her hair, Debra never looked bad. Somehow, even when she had little orange corkscrews framing her face, she never lost her look of innocent charm.

At Debra's suggestion-turned-nagging-turned-dare, Nan had even gone to Alistair herself for a few years, after extracting his solemn promise that he would do nothing—*nothing!*—inappropriate to her hair. To her vast relief, he never did. He also gave her some of the best haircuts of her life, and for a while she relished the experience of being one of his clients.

The problem was that Alistair was self-employed in the most literal sense. He answered to no one, not even the IRS. A gypsy always half a step ahead of miscellaneous creditors, Alistair had no bank accounts and never worked in a shop. He moved frequently and cut hair out of the kitchen wherever he happened to be living. After Nan kept an appointment in what appeared to be a bondage brothel in one of Hollywood's seamier neighborhoods, she vowed never to go back.

It was a promise she had little trouble keeping, since Alistair did a bunk shortly thereafter and was gone for six months. He was forever disappearing on short notice, showing up months later with a tale of adventuring in the Amazonian jungle, cavorting with New Mexican sheepdogs, or serving as personal hairdresser to a U.S. cabinet member. His tales were as impossible to verify as they were titillating, and most of his clientele eagerly canceled their appointments at more mundane salons at the first breath of Alistair's return.

Wherever he was now, Nan hoped he was at least checking his messages.

"This is a ridiculous idea," Tom Hannah said, for the nineteenth time.

"Then I'll go by myself," Nan shot back. "I'll drop you off and come back alone."

"That's even more ridiculous. Nan, nobody's going to talk to us. They probably won't even let us in. We look like narks."

Nan felt relieved that Tom hadn't agreed to go home. This was not an excursion she particularly wanted to make herself, or at all. They were headed down Sunset Boulevard from Tom's house to Papillon, a music club popular with, as Tom kept pointing out, people who thought life was pretty much over by the age of twenty-five. Debra's tenant,

Marty, had identified it as one of her favorite hangouts, promising to meet Nan there at eleven.

"Tom, I have to do something. This thing is turning me into a total wreck."

It was only Tuesday night but it felt as if weeks had passed, long unproductive weeks full of phone calls to losers who'd shared the life of someone Nan was starting to realize she had never really known at all.

Plus, there were the hang-ups on her home message machine, coming in at the rate of two or three a day. Ordinarily she would have viewed them simply as an irritation, but now they worried her. Was somebody trying to get in touch with her, unwilling to leave a message? Did somebody know something they were reluctant to share with a machine?

Probably not. Most likely it was just some kook with a redial feature on his phone.

"Up ahead on the right," Tom said, pointing. "Youth in action for a better tomorrow."

A dozen or so young people milled about on the sidewalk outside a storefront whose windows were painted an unrelieved black. White Art Deco lettering on the window read PAPILLON. Did anybody in that crowd have a clue what the word even meant? What Art Deco was? Nan turned a corner and parked a block away.

Tom was still grousing. "I'll probably run into some of my students, and what in God's name will I tell them?"

"That they're underage and ought to get their butts back home," Nan suggested. "Tom, we're adults. We have the right to go anywhere we want to."

"They probably won't even let us in. They'll leave us out on the sidewalk looking like jerks. Middle-aged jerks."

"Speak for yourself," Nan told him, getting out of the car. She had dressed as casually and unobtrusively as she was able, in jeans and a black tank top, but Tom was right. They could never blend into this crowd.

The kids on the sidewalk looked like children to her. Debra must have been the oldest one by at least six years.

Not that she looked her age. And she wouldn't have been
dressing to melt into the woodwork, either. She'd have
been decked out like that girl leaning on the wall over
there. The slightly chubby blonde wore a full-length zebra-
striped bodysuit under the briefest of black miniskirts, with
a ratty red feather boa wrapped around her neck.

The doorman looked like he'd been letting people into
LA music clubs since the days of Buffalo Springfield. He
raised an eyebrow at Nan and Tom but let them in without
comment after making a big production out of checking
their IDs.

Inside, loud rock music that Nan didn't recognize poured
out of speakers beside a small empty stage. Papillon was
not a classy place. The floor was sticky and even in very
dim light it was clear that everything was filthy. The little
Formica table where Nan waited while Tom visited the bar
was bisected by an irregular brown stain.

The room was half full of people, all of whom pointedly
ignored Nan and Tom. Though it was fantastically late by
Nan's standards, quarter to eleven on a weeknight, she had
a strong sense that the evening was only beginning for most
of these folks, and not necessarily because they'd just gotten off the swing shift.

"Now what?" Tom asked, setting down two bottles of
Corona.

"I don't know," she admitted. "I don't recognize a soul.
Marty said he'd be here, but I don't see him."

They waited and waited, Tom stifling yawns and Nan
growing increasingly miserable. A few people danced, including the blonde in the zebra-striped bodysuit, but mostly
folks lounged around tables, looking bored and drinking.
There didn't seem to be a lot of heavy conversations going
on, even when the loud music stopped briefly. There was
no live entertainment on weeknights.

Nan couldn't bring herself to start accosting people at
random, waving Debra's picture. In fact, it took her nearly
twenty minutes to get up nerve enough to speak to the bartender. This sort of thing was so easy in detective novels.

The gumshoe would slip a twenty to a guy named Mack behind the bar, surreptitiously flash a photograph, and learn that the subject had left twenty minutes earlier in the company of a sinister man with a scar under his right eye.

Here, the bartender ignored Nan for five minutes, then said he'd only been working at Papillon a week. He barely glanced at the picture of Debra. Somehow Nan was sure no amount of money would refresh his memory, though a bit of cocaine might have prompted a few lies in gratitude.

It was nearly midnight and Marty had promised to be there at eleven. Why on earth had she believed him? Tom, who normally rose at 5 A.M. to run three miles, was all but slapping himself on the cheeks to stay awake.

Finally, when Nan was ready to give up, Marty sauntered in with two other guys cut from the same musician's cloth: skinny, sallow, mildly dazed, unfashionably lengthy hair. One of them had an earring through his eyebrow. As they crossed the room, Nan moved to intercept Marty. He seemed startled to see her.

"Didn't think you'd come," he mumbled. "Was gonna call but I lost your number."

"Well, I'm here," she answered. "Can I talk to you a minute?"

Marty shrugged. His friends moved on and sat at a large table with a mixed group who hadn't changed positions in half an hour. They looked like mannequins in a Melrose Avenue boutique.

"Yeah?"

"I was wondering if you could point out anybody Debra knows or hangs out with," Nan said. "Maybe introduce me."

Marty shuffled. "Yeah, well, uh . . ."

Nan smiled ingratiatingly and fought a rising wave of anger. "Marty, somebody must know something! You've got to help me."

He looked around the room slowly, hesitating for a moment and narrowing his eyes when he saw Tom Hannah.

"He's with me," Nan said shortly.

Marty chuckled. "A cop?"

"A teacher, if it matters."

"Same difference." Marty fixed his gaze on a table in the corner. The blonde in the bodysuit was half-sprawled against the wall. Fifteen minutes ago, she'd been dancing provocatively by herself on the small dance floor, swinging around the ratty red feather boa. Now she sat beside a chunky guy with tawny skin and broad flat Indio features locked into a permanent scowl. "Over there. That chick in the corner. Linny."

"She's a friend of Debra's?"

"They hang together sometimes."

"Anybody else?"

Marty shrugged, his most common gesture. His friends at the group table were now watching him and Nan with unabashed curiosity. "She's maybe gone home with some of the guys here, but I don't know nothing about that. Try Linny."

"Could you introduce me?"

Marty smiled for the first time. "I could, but her old man might throw me into a speaker. Me 'n' him don't get along."

"Thanks," Nan told him. "And here's another one of my cards, so you can call me if you need to. Hell, take two." He took the cards and turned away. From the corner of her eye, she saw the small white rectangles drift to the floor before Marty reached his friends at the group table.

Before she gave herself time to think about it too much, Nan crossed the room and pulled an empty chair up beside Linny and her hulky Latino friend.

"Linny?" she asked.

"Who wants to know?" the hulk growled. He'd seen too many tough-guy movies.

"I'm Nan Robinson, and I'm trying to find a friend of mine. I believe you know her, Debra LaRoche?"

Linny leaned forward on an elbow and tried to focus. "Who?"

Nan brought out the picture. "Debra LaRoche."

Linny took the Polaroid and tried to focus again. She seemed very drunk. Then she smiled slowly. "Oh, yeah. Debra. Don't know her last name."

"LaRoche. Have you seen her recently?"

Linny closed her eyes a minute. Nan wasn't sure if the girl was thinking or passing out. Slowly Linny shook her head.

"When was the last time you saw her?"

Linny opened her bleary eyes and held one hand palm upward. "Long time ago. Long time."

"A week? A month?"

Linny shook her head. "Long time." Her chin dipped down onto her chest and she slowly tipped forward onto the table, snoring softly.

Nan sighed. The hulk sat there, still glaring. "Do you know Debra?" she asked, showing him the picture.

He shook his head. "Seen her around, maybe."

Nan took out two more cards. She slipped one into the pocket of Linny's miniskirt and set the other in front of the hulk. "If you think of anything, or if Linny does," she said, "call me anytime. There's a reward."

Nan's own reward, when she got home at nearly one in the morning, was two more hang-ups on her machine. She had just pushed the rewind button when the phone rang, loud and startling in the quiet night.

"Hello?" The line sounded hollow and empty. Nobody said anything. "Hello? Hello? Is somebody there, dammit?"

Nan heard what sounded like a very faint, deep, distant chuckle, followed by a sharp *click* as the connection was broken.

❋

At a booth in Westwood, the killer cradled the telephone, smiling in anticipation. That had been fun, hearing the note of fear and hysteria in Nan Robinson's voice.

Tomorrow would be even better.

CHAPTER 7

The next morning, Nan was edgy and exhausted, haunted by the image of Linny passing out onto the grimy Formica table at Papillon. It was painful to think of Linny as representative of Debra's crowd.

Midmorning, finally wakened by half a dozen cups of coffee, she achieved a minor victory, managing to reach one of Debra's old boyfriends. Walker Hess was an actor, a fellow who'd met some minor success on a TV sitcom since the days when he shared his venereal diseases with Debra. Nan had seen his picture once in a group shot on the cover of *TV Guide*. She got hold of him through his agent, insinuating that the alternative to calling Nan would be an on-set visit from the LAPD.

"I haven't seen her in four years," Walker Hess told Nan over the phone, in a bored, indifferent tone. "She was a neat chick, but that was like five or six lifetimes ago." Which was, alas, far too easy to believe.

Now what? She was saved from plotting an immediate next move by a call from Detective Wainwright of Missing Persons. He seemed surprised to hear that Debra was still missing.

"As far as I can tell," Nan told him, "she's been gone for weeks. Why would she reappear just because I filed a report?"

"I'm sorry," he said. He sounded young, earnest, relatively obliging. "But about eighty-five percent of the reports we get are on people who turn up just fine." He went over the information Nan had given the desk officer in Hollywood. There wasn't much she could add to it.

"I know you're worried," he said finally, "and I promise that a detective will be assigned to her case today. If you think of anything else that can help, give me a call."

Danny Harrington didn't seem heartened at lunch to learn that Debra was now an assigned case.

"They've got what, eight detectives? For four thousand missing persons a year?"

"Most of whom are apparently already back home safe and sound by the time LAPD makes the follow-up call," Nan reminded him.

"True. But the others could be pretty tricky." Danny spoke with an investigator's weariness. "Consider the guy who *wants* to get lost. He's got ex-wives after him for child support, or some drug dealer out to make an overdue collection. Maybe he just hates his life. Had a neighbor did that once, a guy with four kids and a mortgage and a bitch of a wife. Went down to Seven-Eleven for milk one night and never came back."

"How did you find him?" Nan asked.

"I didn't. Nobody asked me. But his oldest boy tracked him down a couple years later. The guy always had this big thing about going down to see the grunion run. His kid showed up at the place they used to go with the old man and there he was. Complete with new wife and baby."

Swell. "So if we can't count on LAPD, Danny, what have you got? I hope your half of the boyfriend list has been more productive than mine."

But it hadn't. One of the two old flames Danny found claimed to not even remember Debra and the other, the fellow she'd taken to small-claims court, had been living in Houston for years.

Nan concentrated on work to take her mind off Debra. Most of the cases she was currently handling were routine, with a depressing similarity to them. An attorney might spend years, even decades in uneventful practice. Then along came the divorce, the affair, the substance abuse, the family illness. Personal problems became all-consuming, spilling over into professional time, the lines blurring between the various sectors of a lawyer's life.

Nan found herself contrasting the messed-up lives of these attorneys to that of Debra LaRoche. Whatever chaos existed in Debra's life, and certainly there was plenty of it, took place strictly on her own time. While she was at work, Debra was invariably calm, efficient, and productive. She simply turned a mental switch when she walked through her office door, setting aside anything that might distract from the job at hand. Perhaps she viewed her job as a respite from her personal life, an oasis of certainty where she could rest for eight hours a day before returning to madness and confusion.

This made her, of course, a fantastic employee. But over the years, Nan had found herself increasingly frustrated by Debra's dispassionate approach to work. She always performed her tasks correctly and conscientiously. She never did a half-assed job.

But she had no apparent ambition beyond being a legal secretary.

Nan reminded herself that there was nothing ignoble about secretarial work, that it hadn't been devalued in the workplace until women took it over. Nan's own grandmother, a woman of considerable talents, had spoken with enormous pride of being the first woman ever promoted to work in the correspondence department at Sears Roebuck in Chicago before World War I.

"I work to support my life," Debra would say, when Nan suggested that maybe she strike out, do more, find some kind of challenging career. "Maybe you like your job, Nan, but you don't understand. Most of us just do it 'cause we have to."

"But what if you found something you really loved to do?"

"I've already found it, silly. I love to party!" Debra's infectious grin always ended the conversation, and she'd go back to her word processor.

But Nan remembered the little girl who climbed all the neighborhood trees, the pixie who swung by her knees from the highest bars on the jungle gym at the park. She wondered.

Debra had seemed to find something else she wanted to do with the birth of her son. Nan remembered the beatific expression on Debra's face as she watched Timmy crawl across the carpet in the family room of the house out in Canyon Country. Timmy could do no wrong. Timmy was bright, beautiful, mischievous. Timmy was, Nan thought for a while, perhaps what Debra needed all along.

Then came the accident.

Afterward, Debra seemed lost, adrift, barely alive herself. Nan could only imagine the enormity of Debra and Tony's pain, felt helpless and totally out of her element. There was nothing you could say to somebody in their horrible situation, nothing you could do that could possibly make a difference. Nan knew enough not to tell them they'd have other children, that they were still young, that it was part of God's plan. Nan didn't much believe in God anyway, and she wanted no part of a deity who would kill children.

She was ashamed now to realize that one way she'd reacted was to withdraw. Yep, she was a dandy friend. But on the few occasions when Nan did see Debra, she seemed less vital, more subdued, perpetually somnolent. It came as no surprise when Debra announced she was leaving Tony. Tony had seemed right for Debra only in that Debra believed he was right for her.

She had claimed, with marriage and childbirth, to have found what she was looking for. Now she had neither husband nor child. It was the kind of situation that made people dump it all and go off to Alaska or Tahiti, join the Peace Corps, take a swan dive off the Golden Gate Bridge.

Where had it led Debra?

* * *

Wednesday evening, when Nan left the office, she figured she had just enough time to get home, shower, and make it to Moira Callahan's for dinner. She plunged into the outside heat, a sensation akin to diving into boiling molasses, and walked briskly to the lot where she normally left her car. The Mustang was parked, as always, in the rear, in a location where so far it had escaped any noticeable nicks or dents.

She unlocked the driver's side and was almost knocked over by a blast of pungent insecticide. Startled, she opened the door wide and stepped back, noticing for the first time a slit in the canvas convertible top. On the backseat of the car sat a huge can of Zodiac flea killer.

What the hell?

The smell of insecticide was overpowering. First things first. She circled the car and opened the other door wide, rolled down all the windows. Then she held her breath long enough to put the top down.

Coughing, she stepped out of the car and reached into the backseat for the can of flea killer. It was the type you'd use to bomb a house or apartment, setting it off as you walked out the door. The label said it would cover ten thousand cubic feet, an area roughly four hundred times the size of the Mustang's interior.

Was it safe to drive the car, even safe to get inside? Nan read the directions on the can, growing angrier and angrier. Open doors and windows after two hours, the directions read, then leave again for at least thirty minutes.

Terrific. It had been a hundred and three downtown earlier in the day and wasn't much cooler now. There was nobody else in the lot that she recognized and she certainly couldn't go off and leave the car wide open with the top down. No enterprising car thief would be stopped by a little insecticide odor or have the foresight to worry about getting cancer in five or six years.

She left the car open and walked up to the booth near the front. Manuel, the afternoon attendant, sat listening to salsa music on a boom box. He wore a wrinkled blue Guayabera shirt and baggy khaki pants. His wide brown face remained impassive and his dark eyes blank as Nan asked, in her halting extension-course Spanish, if he'd seen anybody near her car.

He hadn't seen a thing, he told her, and only when she insisted did he even bother to come look at the Mustang. *"No sé,"* he muttered several times, circling the car, looking at the can of flea bomb. It wasn't until he'd turned it over several times that Nan even thought about the fingerprints he might be obliterating.

She laughed out loud at the idea. Fingerprints indeed. Some screwed-up kid played a prank on her and she was going to check fingerprints? She was lucky it was only a flea bomb and not something truly explosive. She could just imagine what LAPD would say if she called indignantly to announce that her car had been subjected to an unauthorized fumigation. She'd end up on their crackpot list forever.

She found a pay phone, called Moira, and told her to have dinner without her. Then she sat down cross-legged in the shadiest spot she could find with a view of the Mustang and waited a full hour. It was just her luck that something like this would happen in the middle of one of the worst heat waves she could remember.

The weather had been ghastly for weeks now. A high-pressure system sat stationary over the Four Corners of Colorado, New Mexico, Utah, and Arizona. Heat continued to blast the Los Angeles basin. It was 119° in Palm Springs, 110° in Pasadena, 106° in Long Beach. Increasingly, people abandoned overheated cars on the sides of the freeway, and tempers grew short as surface streets neared gridlock.

The only people who seemed pleased were the TV weather clowns, ecstatic at a chance to actually discuss a meteorological phenomenon. LA weather for the most part was reliable, predictable. But this . . . this was *news*. They lectured on high-pressure systems and used maps with swirling computer-generated graphics. One had likened the weather situation to placing a sheet of aluminum foil over a turkey in order to better roast it. The turkey being the entire southwestern United States.

When the hour ended, Nan got a paper towel from Manuel and wiped off the seats, then braced herself and started the car. With the top down, most of the residual odor would blow out as she drove. It would probably be the freshest part of the charming chemical stew that hovered permanently over the freeway.

She was still furious when she got home, and she had a splitting headache as well. No surprise, really. The poison was guaranteed strong enough to kill fleas and their descendants for weeks to come. At least she wouldn't have to worry about getting any bug bites while driving.

She showered and shampooed, tied the clothing she'd been wearing into a heavy-duty trash bag for the dry cleaner and drank a fast beer. She called Moira, promised to be at her place by eight, then decided she simply had to swim first. Down at the pool it took a dozen or so laps before she felt she'd washed the smell out of her nostrils, or at least replaced it with chlorine. Life in Southern California was just one big chemical cocktail.

Moira Callahan was waiting anxiously when Nan arrived at her Culver City bungalow. Moira was fifty-seven and warmly maternal, with softly curled gray hair and dark blue eyes barely visible behind thick glasses.

"You poor girl," Moira murmured, pouring two glasses from a pitcher of lemonade as Nan began what was intended to be a breezy recital of the flea bomb incident. Suddenly, without warning, Nan burst into tears.

Moira was shocked, but only for a moment. Nan had never cried in front of her before, never appeared less than totally competent and composed. She found herself now sitting on Moira's overstuffed couch, pouring out her anger about the flea bomb, her worries about Debra, her certainty that something was terribly wrong, and her fury at being unable to do anything about any of it.

Moira listened sympathetically.

"What an awful thing for you to have to go through," she said finally. "No wonder you're so upset."

The most upsetting part, Nan realized, was that she hadn't noticed just how strung out she was. It shamed her to make that discovery in front of Moira, who had sufficient problems of her own. Shortly after their youngest child left home, her husband of thirty-four years had dumped her for a younger woman. Roy Callahan was a carpet layer, his new wife a waitress at the coffee shop where he stopped each morning before heading out into the field. He had left behind a house full of luxurious wall-to-wall carpeting and four shelves of bowling trophies, now boxed in Moira's garage.

His departure left Moira in the same leaky boat as millions of other women, except that Moira's craft was missing a paddle. Due to a combination of extremely poor eyesight and a father who considered female education frivolous, Moira had never really learned how to read.

Moira's priest referred her to the California Literacy Project, who in turn referred her to Nan. Moira was the fourth adult Nan had tutored and in many ways was her favorite. After seven months of intensive sessions, Moira was reading at a ninth grade level and planning to enroll in a high school equivalency course.

"We could just skip our session tonight, dear," Moira offered.

"Don't be silly!" Nan told her. "This is the high spot of my day. But before we start, there's one thing I'd really like."

"If I've got it, it's yours."

"Tell me some good news about something."

Moira beamed. "That I can do for you, dear, that I can do. Elise's husband just got a wonderful promotion, and little Jeremy's soccer team is undefeated."

For ten minutes, Moira shared her daughter's reflected glory, and Nan leaned back and soaked it all in. Moira visited her grandchildren out in Lancaster every weekend and spoke at length with her daughter every night. It was a relationship which Nan vaguely envied, even as she realized she wouldn't want it for herself.

After that, the session went smoothly. There was a real comfort to being with Moira, sharing her triumphs and looking toward a future vastly different from what it might have been.

Nan had left the top down on her car while it was parked in Moira's driveway, but the residual odor of insecticide was still strong and she had another roaring headache by the time she got home. She took two Tylenols and fell asleep quickly.

Wakened by the ringing phone, she fumbled to answer it and read 3:17 on the digital clock by her bedstand. Calls in the middle of the night frightened her. There was no way they would ever be good news.

At first she thought there was nobody there, that she had a breather on the line. Then a deep guttural voice said, "Bug off!" and broke the connection.

Bug off.

By now thoroughly awake and damn scared, she turned on the light. The first thing she saw was the flea bomb sitting on her dresser. Shaking, she crossed the room and picked up the empty canister.

Bug off.

Was some angry attorney harassing her, exacting a pound or two of Nan's nervous system in exchange for the humiliation and inconvenience of suspension or disbarment?

She paced into the kitchen and poured herself a glass of water. Think, dammit.

Her phone number was unlisted, and certainly never made available to any attorney under investigation. True, an unscrupulous lawyer with a buddy at the phone company could probably find it out in about three minutes.

But why bother? Why go for such a petty revenge? Besides, Nan was only one of a dozen people involved in any individual lawyer's disciplinary proceedings.

Debra.

She realized, with a little tremor, that for the past week she'd been handing out business cards like confetti, carefully writing her home phone number on the back of each and every one of them. She'd left her number on countless message machines, with all sorts of unknown friends of friends who promised to have so-and-so get back to her. What's more, it was hardly a secret where she worked, and she drove a conspicuous car.

She remembered the little white cards fluttering to the floor at Papillon, where she had parked just around the corner and departed at what was, for the club, an early hour. Somebody might easily have followed her when she left, and the denizens of Papillon probably had plenty of free time during normal working hours.

So somebody wanted her to bug off, did they?

The possibility that Debra was alive and well, off somewhere being irresponsible, suddenly seemed less likely than ever.

CHAPTER 8

A couple years earlier, Nan had thrown herself a Third-of-a-Century party. She was emerging from a time of great stress and major change. Her divorce was final, she had bought the condo, she had come to terms with her father's death through therapy and ACA, she was happy with her job.

This is my life, she realized, looking around the room at the collective friends of thirty-three and a third years: hiking companions, co-workers from the State Bar, old buddies from McSweeney Lane, workout compadres, ACA fellow travelers, college and law school classmates. It was an odd lot, people who for the most part had nothing in common but their varied links to Nan Robinson. Danny Harrington and his wonderful no-nonsense wife, the Contessa, came all the way from West Covina. Shannon Revell was with husband number four. Tom Hannah was with wife number three. Debra and Tony were there, newlyweds.

That night, when everyone was finally gone and Nan moved through her home gathering stray plates and glasses, she felt none of the letdown she normally associated with the end of a party. Her life wasn't perfect, but she was comfortable with it. There were no white picket fences, but there wasn't a lot of barbed wire, either.

Her unstated assumption then had been that with her life so fabulously in order, she would have no trouble finding an appropriate companion to share it.

It hadn't happened yet.

Now, as she wound up the twisting road to the Past Lives

Institute on Thursday evening, her radio set to a soft rock station, she thought about Jonathan Henley. She had found him popping into her mind often over the course of the week. Which was odd, given everything that had happened since she last saw him. She had felt no powerful frisson on meeting him, no overwhelming sense that he was Mr. Right. Still, there'd been no indication that he was Mr. Totally Wrong, either, and she'd grown expert at picking out those guys at thirty paces. Perhaps the strongest clue that she was interested in Jonathan was the simple fact that she was attending tonight's introductory seminar on past lives therapy at all.

Even though she'd rationalized that it was important to understand the state of Debra's mind, the better to find the missing girl.

She parked between a Lexus and an Infiniti in the nearly full lot at the Past Lives Institute. Inside, an earnest young woman whose name tag identified her as Marsha was handing out registration materials in the reception area, impressive packets of pamphlets, brochures, and photocopied articles. This place was so different from Papillon, from that other side of Debra's life. Nan wondered which one was the real Debra, if Debra herself even knew.

She was flipping through the folder when Jonathan appeared at her elbow. His touch on her arm felt mildly electric.

"You look wonderful," he told her softly, and she was glad to have taken the extra time on her hair and makeup, to have tried three outfits before settling on the simple emerald sundress that played up the green in her eyes. Vanity grew correspondingly more time-consuming as the years passed by. It took a lot of time, effort, and cosmetic assistance to get that fresh, dewy, no-makeup look.

"So do I fall into a trance right now, or is that scheduled for later?" She kept her tone light. He looked mighty good himself.

"Ever the cynic, eh?"

Nan was aware of Marsha's curious gaze as Jonathan led

her out of the reception area. The auditorium doors were open, exposing plush red velvet seats that were almost armchairs. The first seminar participants were self-consciously settling themselves in the auditorium. Nan started to follow, but Jonathan stopped her.

"I want to talk to you a minute first," he said, leading her around the corner into a small therapy room. This one was done in lacquered rattan with puffy apricot pillows. The early evening light glowed on the blooms in the rose garden outside. "Have you had any news about Debra?"

She shook her head. "I've talked to a lot of people, been some places. I stopped by her place again on my way home today, but there's no sign she's been back."

There had been one more message on the machine, another unfamiliar male who left only a first name and no number. The new mail was mostly junk, except for a Visa bill that showed no charges after August 27. The cat was living with Marty, who'd been stoned out of his mind, eating Cheetos and listening to hard rock on a new stereo. That rent money must have been eating a hole in his pocket. Marty was not surprised to find that Nan had learned nothing from Debra's friend Linny. And he had no new ideas.

"I just don't know what to think," Jonathan told her, sounding genuinely worried.

At his insistence, Nan described her latest fruitless attempts to locate Debra. She left out the flea bomb, but reported the haunting conversation with Marie LaRoche.

He winced. "Poor lady. Nan, is there any way I can help?"

"I don't think so," she answered slowly. "Unless you know of people she's friendly with through whatever she does here."

He shook his head slowly. "You've met April and Carleen told me she spoke with you on the phone. She's here tonight, by the way, asked if you could stop by and see her before you leave."

Nan was frankly curious about Debra's therapist. This

morning Danny Harrington had stopped by her office to report something disturbing he'd learned about the woman. Nan considered mentioning it to Jonathan, then decided to wait.

"I was thinking more of people she'd met through . . . I don't know. Does Debra take your workshops or just work in the office or what?"

"A little bit of everything. I know she's been a huge help to April setting up computer files or whatever. I'm lousy at that kind of thing myself. Every computer I've ever met has been user hostile. But April says Debra's really great at it."

Nan smiled. "She sure is. Before she went on maternity leave, we had a complicated fraud case at the State Bar. It wasn't really part of Debra's job, but she was fascinated by the whole thing. The information we needed was buried in a lot of computer gobbledygook, but she figured out a way to get at it. I was pretty impressed."

Jonathan glanced at a malachite clock sitting on a rattan table. "We should go on in. I do the introductory remarks and it's time to get started."

"Tell me what happens. I hate surprises."

He grinned. "It's all on the program in your folder, but basically this is our broad overview for people who're interested in the PLI but not sure which avenues they want to pursue. Some of them will end up in meditation programs, others in group or individual therapy. Most everybody will undergo hypnosis. Tonight I'll speak first, then Brother Bartholomew will explain his meditation programs. After that we'll have a fairly short group hypnosis."

"Does Brother Bartholomew do the group hypnosis?" The idea was mildly alarming, for reasons Nan couldn't articulate.

"No. He doesn't do any hypnosis. As a matter of fact, I'll be doing the group induction tonight."

"You make it sound so military!"

He laughed. "You're the first person who's ever said that. Come on, now. My public's waiting."

* * *

Nan took a seat midway down an outside aisle, where she could see most of the other people in the room without obvious rubbernecking. They were a mixed lot, twenty-five altogether. About two-thirds were female and only a handful were over sixty. Nearly all were white, with the exception of a young Japanese woman, two middle-aged ladies who looked Indian or Pakistani, and a very nervous Latino couple in their late forties. The common denominator, so far as Nan could tell, was an air of easy affluence. A few middle-aged matrons wore sufficient jewelry to finance a Third World revolution.

Jonathan spoke first, soothing gentle talk that rippled through the room and caused people to shed tension almost perceptibly, like snake skins. Nan paid less attention to his actual words than to their effect as he welcomed everyone and introduced himself. He was a salesman, she reminded herself. He might be selling spiritual awakening, but a reading of the list of PLI programs and services in her information packet made it clear that spiritual awakening could be mighty pricey.

"Many of you are here today because you believe in reincarnation. Others"—here he smiled directly at Nan, who was startled by the intensity of his gaze—"are less certain. What all of us have in common is a seeking for truth, a hope for a better and more perfect present life. I believe in reincarnation, and often I meet people who say, well, where's your proof? Can I prove that I've lived before, that you've lived before? Not in terms the scientists will accept. But there's a reason that a Gallup poll showed a quarter of the people in America believe in reincarnation, and I don't think it's because we're all crackpots. You might be surprised to hear some of the famous people who believe, and I don't just mean Shirley MacLaine."

He paused during the appreciative chuckle. This was an LA audience, Nan thought, and some of them probably expected to meet Shirley tonight. Some of them probably thought they'd *already* met her, as actors working together on Aeschylus's new play in Athens.

"No," he went on, "I'm talking about people like Henry Ford and Julius Caesar and Ralph Waldo Emerson and Henry David Thoreau and David Lloyd George. Wagner and Mahler and Yeats and Gauguin and Michelangelo and James Joyce. Not exactly crackpots. But we aren't here tonight to talk about what other people believe. We're here to talk about how learning about your own past lives can help you better understand the life you're living right now, to do your work in this life in a positive and productive way."

Nan looked around the room as he continued. Most of his audience seemed truly spellbound. Of course they'd already paid plenty for the pleasure of hearing him and were getting ready to shell out a bundle more. Or maybe, and this was a chilling notion, he was already subtly hypnotizing them.

"I've seen," he told them, "hundreds and thousands of cases that demonstrate the effects that previous existences and relationships have on people's current lives. But never mind the statistics. Let me give you an example from my own life. I was married for seven years to a woman I loved passionately, a woman I adored. I thought our life together was perfect. Then she came to me one day and said, 'Jonathan, I'm leaving you for somebody else.' Well, I was such a fool I hadn't even realized there *was* somebody else. I was devastated. For years I carried around a lot of pain and bitterness from that experience."

Nan took her eyes off Jonathan just long enough to see that the audience was rapt, voyeuristic. Was this a significant component of the PLI program as well, this sort of sharing through group hypnosis and group therapy? She knew from her experiences with Adult Children of Alcoholics that there was a powerful purgative effect in sharing accumulated pain and anxiety with people whose experiences were similar. With a start, she realized that her own ACA group was in session right now back in town.

Jonathan went on, "It was only when I began doing my own past life regressions that I began to understand what had happened. My ex-wife and I were together in Florence during the Renaissance. In that former life, I was the one who treated her badly, who had other women. I never left her, but I shamed her. We came together again in this life to balance the bad energy from the past experience. We had chosen to be together again to work out that relationship. Perhaps we'll be with each other again in a future life, or maybe all we needed to do was clear our slate."

Nan was relieved when he ended the personal anecdote and went on to explain the programs available through the PLI. They were many and varied: individual and group hypnotic regressions; individual and group therapies; meditation techniques, classes and consultations; video and audio cassettes; directed research programs aimed at verifying or pinning down specifics of individual past lives.

Her favorite, she decided when Jonathan finished, was the past lives travel program. Special group tours were assembled for people who wished to visit the sites of past lives they had uncovered. She stifled a chuckle at the image of bevies of Cleopatra's former handmaidens cruising blissfully down the Nile.

Brother Bartholomew came out next, in his sandals and homespun robes, blue eyes vibrant, white hair flowing around his shoulders. His simple, understated appearance made a stunning contrast to the red velvet opulence of the auditorium. The size of the group, however, did nothing to diminish his rampant sexuality. Nan sensed panties moistening all around her.

Bartholomew spoke of the similarities and differences between Eastern and Western religions. He emphasized that one needn't abandon previous spiritual beliefs before exploring new ones, a focus clearly aimed at staunch followers of the Judeo-Christian tradition who wished to cautiously dip their toes in Eastern mysticism before taking any headlong plunges. Then he demonstrated a few simple breathing techniques and Nan watched as the audience members dutifully inhaled and exhaled on cue.

When Brother Bartholomew had finished, the lights were dimmed for a twenty-minute film. It was a slick effort, with high production values and lots of magnificent shots of mountain ranges and sunsets. The audio portion, however, seemed almost totally unrelated to the breathtaking visuals.

Nan made a serious effort to understand the film, which included a hodgepodge of personal testimonials, philosophical statements, and promises that greater self-awareness was the only guarantee of a truly fulfilled life. By the time the lights came up again and Jonathan stood at the front of the room, she was hopelessly confused. The cynic in her felt certain that was the film's intention.

Jonathan now instructed the men and women in the room to find comfortable positions for a group hypnosis session. Papers were shuffled and set on the floor, handbags stuffed beside chairs. Several people stood and stretched before settling in their seats, and a young man in his twenties assumed the lotus position in an aisle.

"Those of you who aren't comfortable with the idea of being hypnotized," he said, again smiling at Nan, "can simply follow along what the rest of us are doing. Don't be afraid to relax as you listen, and if at some point you feel you wish to join us, simply close your eyes and let yourself come along."

Nan was not about to be hypnotized in a group of twenty-five strangers, even though she was fairly certain that there wouldn't be any embarrassing parlor tricks where people clucked like chickens or publicly confessed their most humiliating sexual experiences. This was far too slick an operation for such tactics, and the whole point was to enthuse people into signing on for the long haul.

She watched as the others closed their eyes and followed Jonathan's instructions on breathing. His voice was dreamy, soothing and—well, hypnotic was probably the best word for it. Nan didn't believe that it was possible for a subject to be hypnotized against her will. Even so, she made a particular effort not to listen too closely to the lulling cadence of his voice, lest she be shanghaied into a state of altered consciousness and find herself ... What? Where? It was scary to think of the power a hypnotist wielded. How could these people so blithely trust a virtual stranger?

When Jonathan seemed satisfied that the others in the room were properly entranced, he instructed his subjects to move backward in time to a moment when they were totally happy, filled with overwhelming joy and love. Smiles crossed their faces as he began moving among them, lightly touching shoulders and asking them to share their memories. This part was fascinating: tales of lakefront picnics and Hawaiian fern trails and childbirth and experiences both grand and humble shared with loved ones. There were also a few bizarre notes, like the woman who described attending the presentation of the fall fashion lines in Paris and the nondescript man who spoke of making love with his wife in a stone grotto at the Madonna Inn on their twenty-fifth anniversary.

When Jonathan had finished the recitation of joyous moments, he instructed his subjects that they would remember these moments fully and completely when they returned to consciousness, and that over the course of the next few weeks, whenever they felt upset or depressed, these images—and their attendant feelings of happiness—would come to them.

Then he asked each of them to focus on a problem area in their current lives they wished to resolve. Working from cards filled out in advance by the participants, he began moving around the room, looking at name tags and murmuring what were presumably encouraging thoughts.

Nan decided this was as good a time as any to bail out. She quietly gathered her things and slipped up the side aisle and out the auditorium doors. As she left, she gave a discreet smile and wave to Jonathan, who was bent over the young Japanese woman, speaking softly. He smiled and waved back.

The lighted hallway was jarring after the dimly lit, womblike velvet auditorium. She took a moment to adjust to the environmental change, then started down the hall of administrative offices.

Marsha, the young woman who'd handed out registration materials, hurried out of an open office door as Nan passed. "The ladies' room is down the other hall on the right," she said helpfully.

"Thanks, but what I'm really looking for is Carleen McIlheney," Nan told her. "Do you know where I could find her?"

The girl frowned. "I'm not sure if Carleen's still here. If you'd like to wait . . ." She pointed at a chair inside the cubicle she'd just left and waited till Nan was seated before leaving. The PLI didn't encourage casual roaming about.

About two minutes later, a mildly plump woman with a wild cloud of frizzy red hair appeared in the doorway. Her glasses had trendy designer frames and her turquoise and purple Hawaiian shirt hung loose over white pants.

"Nan!" she effused, with the warmth of one greeting a beloved relative returning from war. She offered a soft, squishy, and as far as Nan was concerned, entirely gratuitous hug. "I'm so glad to meet you. I'm Carleen. Come along to my office. Would you like something to drink? Mineral water, juice, decaf?"

"How about a Diet Coke?"

"Caffeine-free?"

Nan laughed. "Not if there's a choice. I've got a long drive ahead of me and I'm pretty beat."

Carleen McIlheney smiled. "Marsha, could you bring us a couple regular Diet Cokes? And maybe some of those chocolate macaroons, too? Thanks."

As Marsha set off toward the kitchen, Carleen took Nan down the hall into her office, where the furniture was lush blond wood and the walls a deep royal blue. Primitive children's drawings hung everywhere in expensive frames.

"My kids' work," Carleen explained when she saw Nan's curious stares at the pictures. One of them seemed to be a dragon eating a red-haired lady. "Jonathan says you haven't heard anything more about Debra."

"Not a peep. And I'm running out of leads, unless you've thought of something that might help me."

Marsha brought in a tray with iced drinks in cut-crystal glasses. There was also a generous platter of macaroons that the American Heart Association would probably have wanted to imprint with a skull and crossbones.

After Marsha left, Carleen sighed and sat in an armchair by the low coffee table. She picked up a cookie and munched absentmindedly. "It's just so disturbing," she said after a moment. "Of course people sometimes drop out of therapy, but usually not so abruptly. And Debra's situation is such an interesting one. Her regression tapes are some of the most fascinating I've ever listened to."

"Tapes?"

Carleen nodded. "The way it works, the client is hypnotized and regressed and the whole thing is recorded on tape. Some hypnosis programs would leave it at that, just use posthypnotic suggestions. But we carry it one step farther. After the hypnosis session, the client and therapist listen to the tapes and go through the information together, using it to piece together what's happening both in past lives and the present."

"You believe there's a correlation, then?"

Carleen stared at Nan as if she'd suggested joining the Flat Earth Society. "Of course there's a correlation! In Debra's case, it was striking. But we've hardly finished all the work she wanted to do. In some cases, we've barely scratched the surface. There are entire tapes we've only listened to once, intending to go back and review later. But each time she's hypnotized, she comes up with more wonderful stuff. Debra's a terrific hypnotic subject."

"Do you hypnotize her yourself?"

"Uh-huh. It's much more efficient that way, because of course the therapist knows a client so well. Except like now when Yvonne's having her baby, I'm doing some of her people. When I was on vacation earlier, April did a couple of Debra's regressions because she didn't want to wait till I got back." Carleen smiled. "Debra's not a very patient woman."

Nan smiled back. "She used to call herself the Instant

Gratification Kid. But you know, it bothers me that you say she's still got a lot of tapes to go over. Don't you think that makes it unlikely that she'd leave without telling anybody she wasn't coming back?"

Carleen nodded, shaking her thick red hair. A clump of it fell forward over her eyes and she brushed it back. "Absolutely. But of course if you've been to Debra's house, you've probably seen her past lives journal."

"Her what?"

"Oh. Oh my goodness." Carleen waved her hands, mildly flustered. "You mean you *didn't* find her journal?"

Nan shook her head. "Not only did I not find it, I don't have any idea what you're talking about."

"Hmmm. Well, we encourage our clients to keep past lives journals as they proceed with their therapy. It's strictly for their own benefit; we don't even look at them unless the client requests it. Debra never did. But I know she had one and that it was fairly extensive because she talked about how she wrote in it almost every day. I know she'd sometimes go out in the Serenity Garden after she finished a session and write for a while." Carleen brightened. "She probably took it with her."

"Took it where?"

The therapist shrugged. "Wherever she went. But I still don't think she'd just up and leave. Completely apart from continuing her therapy, Debra has other responsibilities here and she takes them very seriously. We've really been in a bit of a tizzy since she's been gone. April's had a couple of temps in, but they only seem to make things worse."

"I can understand how you'd be missing Debra," Nan said. "It was a nightmare for me when she went on maternity leave. In my heart of hearts, I was always hoping she'd come back after Timmy was in school, but . . ."

"Such a senseless tragedy," Carleen agreed, picking up another cookie.

Nan looked at the therapist. Her initial impression that the woman was far too loose-lipped hadn't been helped by the information Danny Harrington had brought this morning. And she'd been prattling on without a thought for Debra's privacy just now. Maybe it would be better to wait for some other time to bring up what Danny had found out. But Nan was tired and worried and niceties didn't seem terribly important.

"You must have had some personal conflicts when you learned where Debra used to work," Nan said.

Carleen looked up. Initial bafflement turned to a sort of guilty flush as she glanced away. "I can't imagine what you mean."

"I would think the concept of professional disciplinary agencies would be a rather painful one for you."

The therapist's jaw set. "I'm not following you."

"I think you're following me all too closely," Nan told her. "I found out some interesting things today about Eugene Rochman."

Carleen set down her cookie abruptly and stood. The chair was too low to make it a fluid movement and she was too angry to move gracefully anyway.

"That's totally irrelevant."

"Is it?"

"Absolutely."

"I don't think Eugene's parents thought what happened was irrelevant," Nan said.

"It's all over, long past."

"I'm told that the death of a child is something that never passes," Nan said. She was goading the woman now, and it felt oddly good. Carleen McIlheney was a little too touchy-feely sweet. "Surely that's something you went over with Debra in the course of therapy. Maybe the coincidence even struck you: here was somebody who lost a male child, somebody who worked for a place that lifted licenses from professionals who screwed up."

Carleen turned and glared at Nan. "I was twenty-five years old, just out of school. I made a mistake in judgment and I paid for it."

"I'd say it was Eugene Rochman who paid for your mistake. He blew his brains out because he couldn't stand the rejection when his therapist broke off the affair she was having with him."

"Oh, for God's sake," Carleen muttered. She came back to the table, took another chocolate macaroon, and began pacing. "What possible business of yours is any of this?"

Nan shrugged. "Maybe none."

"Then let's just drop it, all right?"

"We could," Nan agreed slowly. "But quite frankly, I'm fascinated by how reluctant you are to discuss all this."

"It's nobody's business but my own," the therapist said defiantly.

"That argument would be more convincing if there weren't somebody missing whom you might have good reason to resent."

Carleen McIlheney stared in shock. "Are you suggesting that I have something to do with Debra being missing?"

"Do you?"

"Of course not! My God, what do you think I am? And why on earth would I resent Debra?"

Nan sighed. "I don't have any idea what you are, and I already told you why I think you might resent her. She used to work for a place that lifted professional licenses. The way yours got lifted."

"That's absolutely ridiculous! I love Debra."

Nan said nothing.

"Well, I do," Carleen went on defiantly after a moment. "I think she's a dear sweet girl and she's had an absolutely horrible time and I told you how worried I am about her."

"You weren't worried enough to do anything."

"What could I do?"

Nan sighed again. Carleen's indignation seemed entirely authentic. "I don't know. All I know is that there's a very unsavory episode in your past, one that might possibly have something to do with Debra's disappearance."

"Well, it doesn't. It has absolutely nothing to do with Debra and I certainly wouldn't ever discuss it with a patient anyway." Carleen's anger raised bright red circles on her cheeks. "But since you seem to think you know what happened, maybe you'd be interested in *my* side of the story."

"By all means. I'd like very much to hear your side." Nan sat back and took a macaroon herself. It was shockingly rich. No wonder Carleen had such rounded contours.

"Eugene was all messed up," Carleen began, indignation still strong in her voice. "His parents had programmed him that he had to be a lawyer like his father was, go into his father's firm. What he wanted to be was an actor, and his parents belittled that, told him they'd never support him, he'd be a failure, they'd disown him if he didn't get with the program. When he dropped out of UCLA, they were outraged. They sent him into therapy hoping to find somebody who'd tell him what they wanted. I told him to do what he wanted to do, to be himself, that he was the one who was going to live his life, not his parents."

She sat down again. "He was really a wonderful boy. He was only twenty, but he seemed older and wiser. I think he was a talented actor, too. When he . . . started coming on to me, I put him off, just the way you're supposed to. It went on for months like that. He was teasing me, I think. And he was very . . . appealing. I was young, single, a little overweight." She picked up another macaroon with no apparent sense of irony. "Then one day when he was leaving, he put his arms around me and . . . oh, hell, I was an idiot. Being young isn't an excuse."

"It can be a mitigating circumstance," Nan said gently. Despite herself, she was beginning to feel a certain measure of sympathy.

"The affair didn't last long. After I stopped it, that was all he wanted to talk about. I told him he'd have to find another therapist. He talked me into one more session, and I told him that was absolutely the last time I'd see him. Then he went home and killed himself. I still can't figure out why. He didn't love me. I think he was trying to punish all of us, me, his parents, the casting directors who wouldn't hire him."

Carleen McIlheney sighed deeply. "You know what happened. I lost my license and I was lucky to ever get it back. I can damn sure tell you I'll never sleep with a patient again. There isn't a day that goes by when I don't think about Eugene. But it's over." She stood up, looking pale and drained. "And now, I need to get home. I waited to see you, so I missed getting to put my kids to bed." She smiled grimly. "Better I should have just left."

Nan rose and started for the door. "I'm sorry to have kept you," she said, "and I'm sure it wasn't easy for you talking about all this. But there's one thing I need to know. Are you absolutely certain Debra doesn't know about Eugene?"

"Of course she doesn't," Carleen answered, genuinely shocked. "I would never—" She brushed her hair back from her face again. "I need a haircut," she muttered.

A thought skittered across Nan's brain. "But your hairdresser's out of town?" she asked.

"How did you—" Carleen's eyes widened in confusion.

"Does Alistair cut your hair?"

"Why, yeah, but . . . Oh, of course. Debra."

"Did Debra tell you about Alistair?" This strange coincidence didn't fit into anything Nan had already learned.

"Oh, no," Carleen told her. "It was the other way around. Alistair's been coming up here for years. He brings his bag and cuts everybody's hair, mine, April's, a bunch of other people. It was Alistair who first brought Debra here, after Timmy died."

As Nan drove home, she wondered why April and Jonathan had both claimed not to know who first recommended that Debra visit the Past Lives Institute.

CHAPTER 9

When the receptionist buzzed at eleven on Friday morning to tell her two LAPD detectives were waiting to see her, Nan's stomach clenched into granite. Missing Persons wouldn't drop by; they'd already picked her brain and seemed mostly to work by phone anyway. Nor would LAPD pop in to chat about an ambulance chaser or some public defender caught scoring a half-pound of coke. She practiced deep breathing. To no avail.

"I'm Detective C. J. Bennett," the young man told her, when they were back in Nan's office. He was in his early thirties, five-ten and wiry, with a pale crewcut so short he could have passed for a skinhead in low light. He wore a sale-rack polyester suit in mud brown with a yellow shirt and an ugly orange-and-yellow tie. The bulge below his left armpit was enormous, suggesting weaponry capable of downing fighter jets. "And this is my partner, Detective Rosalie O'Brien."

She had a good fifteen years on him in age and at first glance could probably dance circles around him in the class department. Her hair was steel gray, thick, and styled short, framing a face that managed to look both kind and severe at the same time. She knew how to wear makeup and took good care of her slim, fit body. She looked understated and professional in an oversized white jacket, peach silk T-shirt, and straight gray skirt. She shook Nan's hand, then took a chair slightly behind her partner and let him do the talking.

C. J. Bennett was matter-of-fact. "Debra LaRoche's body was found this morning," he announced.

Nan felt suddenly weak and dizzy. It was one thing to imagine the worst, even to know with virtual certainty that her visitors were bringing bad news. But to hear it stated so baldly . . .

"Where?" she asked, trying to be businesslike, trying not to think of Debra dead. "What happened?"

"She was in the trunk of her car," Bennett said, "in one of the remote lots out at LAX."

Nan closed her eyes. "Poor Debra."

"You filed a missing persons report on her," Bennett went on. "Why'd you do that?"

"Because I couldn't find her and I was worried," Nan answered. She told them of the letter from Debra's mother that arrived at the State Bar, Danny's preliminary calls to hospitals, jails, and morgue. When she got to her first visit to Debra's house, she hesitated only a moment over the issue of how she got in.

"I had a key," she lied, "that Debra gave me when she first moved in." There seemed no point in implicating herself for breaking and entering. "It was obvious once I got inside that nobody'd been in the place for weeks." She told them about the cat box, the accumulated mail, the phone messages. As she went through her story, she could see C. J. Bennett growing more and more irritated.

"You really messed things up, didn't you?" he said finally. "Any evidence that might have been in her place, you've got your fingerprints all over it, stuff rearranged, things taken away."

"I wasn't thinking she was dead," Nan pointed out irritably. "I was just concerned because I couldn't find her. I didn't start to get really worried until after I'd been in her place. And when I took my concerns to the police, they weren't particularly interested."

Rosalie O'Brien spoke up. "You can go with me to her house," she said, "and show me precisely what you did and touched. That will help our forensics people."

"Do you think she was killed in her house?" Nan asked. "How *was* she killed?"

The detectives exchanged glances and C. J. Bennett shook his head slightly. "We'll have to wait for the coroner on that one."

Nan frowned. "Does that mean there weren't any obvious marks on her body?"

"It means we'll have to wait for the coroner's report," he repeated. "Why do you ask about 'marks' on the body?"

"I'm just trying to figure out why you won't tell me, if it's because you don't know or because there was something unusual about what . . . killed her." Nan wondered if time and repetition would make it easier to speak about Debra being dead. The words kept sticking in her throat.

"There was indication of trauma," Detective O'Brien said. "The preliminary report suggests she was hit on the head."

Tony.

Rosalie O'Brien stared intently at Nan. "That seems to suggest something to you," she said quietly. "What?"

Tony, whose temper didn't flare up "very often," Debra had said in his defense. Tony who had hit her.

"Her ex-husband," Nan said. There was no reason to protect Tony, every reason to bring him to the attention of the police. Still, she felt vaguely disloyal. Debra hadn't wanted to admit she was physically abused, chose not to make an issue of the matter in her divorce proceedings.

But Debra was dead now, and violence was clearly an issue. Nan told them about Tony, and that she'd spoken with him the previous Saturday.

This time C. J. Bennett really looked mad. "Nothing like a damned amateur blundering around to screw up a murder investigation. Anybody you *didn't* talk to?"

Nan was annoyed herself. "Nobody I could think of who might have been able to help find her," she snapped back. "All the people I talked to about Debra were concerned, but they didn't have any idea what to do about it. Of course I talked to everybody I could think of. I work as an investigator; it's my nature to look for answers. The police seemed mighty indifferent. Maybe you're here to see me now because I filed that missing persons report, but I'd bet both your pensions that Debra wasn't found because somebody was following up on it."

There was a moment's silence before Rosalie O'Brien smiled. "No," she admitted, "she wasn't."

"How *was* she found?" Nan didn't like to think too much about the answer to that one. The heat had been so awful for so long. "Did somebody notice, uh, a smell?"

Detective O'Brien shook her head. "An anonymous phone call."

"Can't you trace it?"

"It didn't come in on nine-one-one."

"Oh." Nan thought a moment. "How long had the car been there—does anybody know?"

"We're not clear on that. Probably a while."

"Do you mean to tell me that her body's been sitting in a car trunk at the airport for three weeks and nobody ever noticed it?" The idea was outrageous, unsettling. People walking past day after day, nobody aware of the horror only inches away.

"We don't know yet," Detective O'Brien said. "What I'd like to do now is have you come with me to her house, while Detective Bennett takes care of some other matters."

Like Tony Fontaine, Nan was quite sure.

Now that Nan knew Debra would never be coming back to her little house in the Hollywood flatlands, the neighborhood looked even more decrepit and seedy. She was conscious of eyes on her as she stepped out of Detective O'Brien's unmarked car. A black-and-white was waiting out front; the detective spoke briefly with the two uniformed officers inside, and they began canvasing the nearby houses. The forensics people arrived just as they were walking up the front path past the parched lawn.

Inside was even more depressing. The tentative beginnings of Debra's new life alone seemed pathetic and forlorn. She wouldn't sit on the futon watching MTV, wouldn't listen to the collection of CDs of groups Nan had never heard of, wouldn't set out cat food or make herself a megacaloric ice cream sundae.

Nan and Rosalie O'Brien moved through the house with the fingerprint man, a businesslike young fellow who nodded and said little as Nan pointed out the things she had touched, the places she had looked. Her searching for clues to Debra's whereabouts had seemed forgivable at the time, but now it all felt intrusive. She was embarrassed to explain she'd been through Debra's drawers, had looked through the accordion file of personal papers.

But when they got to the bathroom and the collection of dusty perfume bottles, she was struck with an overwhelming sense of sadness and loss. She felt silent tears pour down her face as she remembered Debra talking about training at the Indianapolis secretarial school.

"You're never completely dressed until you've applied your scent," Debra had said, mimicking the voice of an elderly spinster, Miss Whozit who ran the school. And indeed Debra always smelled nice, always wafted a pleasant odor as she entered and left Nan's office. Her delight in those stupid overpriced celebrity perfumes had seemed funny at the time, just another little quirk to be enjoyed not so much at Debra's expense but with her tacit approval. Debra didn't mind being considered idiosyncratic; indeed, in the often stultifying legal environments where she and Nan spent most of their time together, she found it essential.

When it became clear that she wasn't going to be able to stop crying, Nan went outside and sat on the back stoop and just let the tears flow. Debra couldn't be dead. She was too young, too vital. There were too many new rock groups she hadn't heard yet, too many nights to stay out dancing, too many handsome young men to meet.

She thought about the guys at Papillon, wondered about other clubs where Debra hung out. Could someone she met in one of those places have lulled her into a false sense of security, a belief that because the environment was well-known, its inhabitants were safe?

Had Debra made one error in judgment too many?

* * *

After a while, Rosalie O'Brien came out of the house and suggested that they get some lunch. Marty's apartment out back was closed up tightly and he hadn't answered several insistent knocks. An unpaid bill slipped through the mail slot was addressed to Marty Mitchum, but it was anyone's guess where he was now.

They went to a nearby coffee shop, not one of the self-consciously funky ones that served designer meatloaf, but a basic place where the waitresses all looked like they had sore feet and everything was drenched in thirty-weight. Nan was sure she couldn't eat, and the salad they brought clinched it: brown-edged iceberg lettuce topped with a pink tomato wedge and a glop of gelatinous Italian dressing.

"I thought of something I didn't mention earlier," Nan said, pushing the chunks of lettuce around her bowl. "Somebody put a flea bomb in my car two days ago."

Rosalie O'Brien stared. "A flea bomb?"

"Uh-huh. The kind you'd use to fumigate your house." She told the detective what had happened, could see the beginnings of a smile twisting at the edges of her mouth.

"I suppose it *is* kind of funny when you look back on it," Nan admitted. "But it was a damned inconvenience when it happened, not to mention breathing in all that poison on my way home. Even so, if it hadn't been for the phone call, I probably wouldn't have connected it with Debra."

"And it may not be connected."

"Maybe not, but it's an awfully big coincidence if it isn't. I still have the flea bomb canister, if you want it."

"We'll check on it," Detective O'Brien promised. "But don't expect too much. If you and the parking attendant both handled it, there probably aren't any prints. The best we could do is track down where it was purchased and even that's iffy. Now, tell me what happened to Debra's baby. That seems to be the single most significant thing that ever happened to her."

"Until somebody killed her," Nan reminded.

"Of course," the detective agreed. Her chef's salad was

a larger version of Nan's, with a couple strips of Spam and Velveeta. Wisely, she ate it dry.

"It happened about a year and a half ago," Nan began, "out in Canyon Country. Debra and Tony lived on a curve in a brand-new subdivision. They were out in the front yard with little Timmy. He was seventeen months old and really a pistol—into everything, racing around all the time. Debra was doing some kind of yard work and Tony was washing his car. Timmy was playing with a ball and he chased it into the street just as a car came around the curve."

Rosalie O'Brien flinched and gave a small moan.

"I don't think the car was going very fast, and I don't think there was any way the driver could have stopped, either. It was just one of those horrible, senseless accidents that happen."

"Who was supposed to be watching Timmy?"

"Ah, yes," Nan said. "Cutting to the heart of the matter. They each thought the other one was. So they both felt equally guilty, which of course made it all worse. You know, the kind of—'You were supposed to . . .' 'No, *you* were . . .' 'But I thought'—the kind of situation that just feeds on itself. They put a lot of energy into trying to assign blame, I think. When they should have been hanging on to each other." Nan shrugged. "Monday morning psychoanalysis. I guess it's easy enough for me to have an opinion. It wasn't my baby and it wasn't my guilt."

"You have children?" Rosalie O'Brien asked.

Somehow the question startled Nan. She thought her childlessness was obvious to even the most casual observer, like the color of her eyes or her height. "No," she answered. "You?"

The detective nodded and her voice softened. "Three. And two granddaughters."

"Then you'd know what it was like for them, losing Timmy."

The detective's brown eyes were sad and serious. "You don't know," she said, "until it happens to you. You can imagine, and of course I have, being a cop. But you never know. The worst part of my job is when I have to deal with parents of young people who get killed. It never gets easier. Was Timmy killed instantly?"

"Oh no. He hung on for a week and it was just awful. They flew him into Children's by helicopter that first day and he never regained consciousness. Debra was a zombie. And then her mother came out and Tony's parents came out and there was all sorts of shit about when do you pull the plug."

"*Did* they pull the plug?"

"No. You'd have to check with the doctors or the lawyer who handled the lawsuit to get all the medical details. I think he got some kind of secondary infection and that was what killed him. The weird thing is there was never a mark on him, anywhere, except for the surgery."

"You said both their parents were here. Did they get along?"

Nan laughed. "Hardly. Debra's mother is a small-town Midwestern lady. She's a nice woman, but very provincial. About the most provocative thing about her, at least from the smalltown Midwest viewpoint, is that she's a devout Catholic. The kind who still eats fish on Fridays, just to be on the safe side. She's been widowed, oh, maybe five or six years now, I'm not sure. Her husband, Debra's father, was a very take-charge type. Some women really blossom when a guy like that dies and they get to take over their own lives, but I don't think Mrs. LaRoche is one of them. Anyway, LA totally freaked her out. And Tony's parents—" Nan chuckled. "She thought they were some kind of Jersey Mafioso or something."

"Were they?" Rosalie O'Brien asked matter-of-factly.

"Hardly. They were just middle-class Italian people with a Jersey accent. Tony's mother wears a lot of makeup and his father talks too loud. But that was enough. The Fontaines and Marie LaRoche didn't get along at all. They'd never met before, and they were all busy pointing fingers about whose fault the accident was."

"Wait a minute," the detective said. "They didn't meet at the wedding?"

Nan laughed again. "Debra and Tony got married one weekend in Las Vegas on the spur of the moment. Anyway, Tony thought it was the spur of the moment. I know Debra wanted to get married in the worst possible way."

"She was pregnant?"

"No, just anxious." And not for the first time, either. Nan didn't feel ready yet to talk to this detective about Debra's miserable experiences with men. It had been hard enough to tell her about trying to find the old boyfriends and visiting Papillon, even in the most general and neutral terms. Somehow with Debra dead, Nan felt an urge to protect her reputation. No, that wasn't it exactly. To not have the police automatically assume she was some kind of sleazy tramp.

Rosalie O'Brien pushed away the remains of her chef's salad and drank some iced tea. "So back to Timmy. You mentioned a lawyer. They filed against the driver?"

"And collected big. Here's where it gets interesting, in a sordid kind of way. Are you familiar with Ames and Featherton?"

"The real estate development company?"

Nan nodded. "They put up the subdivision where Debra and Tony's house was, as well as a million other places out in the boonies up there. You can see their full-page ads every Sunday in the *Times* real estate section. Well, it happens that John Featherton, a nice respectable family man with a picture-perfect wife and a couple of kids, was having an affair with a decorating consultant in their Saugus office. They were on their way to her place for a nooner when he hit Timmy."

"And his insurance paid?"

"His insurance paid something, I'm not sure how much. But in order to avoid an even bigger scandal than it was turning out to be, Ames and Featherton coughed up a three-quarter-million dollar settlement."

Rosalie O'Brien whistled. "That's a lot of money for a little kid."

"Way out of proportion," Nan agreed. "The cold hard fact is that a dead baby isn't worth a huge amount in the insurance world. A dead wage-earner with big projected earnings, yeah. Or somebody who's severely injured and requires lifelong medical care. If somebody else had been driving that car, Debra and Tony would have had to wait years to get any kind of settlement. As it was, they collected fairly quickly."

"Who was their lawyer?"

"Jane Walinski. She has a plaintiff's P.I. firm with a couple other people down in that insurance ghetto on mid-Wilshire. I referred Debra to her. Jane filed a lawsuit, but the settlement offer came fast and they were smart enough to take it."

"In a lump sum?"

Nan shook her head. "Structured. A big chunk up front and the rest to be paid out over the next fifteen years."

"Divided equally between Debra and Tony?"

"Yeah." Nan stopped suddenly. "Oh."

"Oh indeed," said Rosalie O'Brien. "Will it all go to Tony on Debra's death?"

"I don't have any idea," Nan admitted. "There wasn't a will in her personal papers when I looked through them last week. But I don't know if she could assign that anyway. It would probably revert to Tony as the other parent. You'd have to check with Jane."

"I will," Detective O'Brien said. "Now I want to go out to your place and pick up the things you removed from her house. But first let me just make a phone call." She picked up the check as she rose gracefully from the table, then walked to a pay phone in a back corner by the rest rooms and spoke for about five minutes.

While Nan thought about three-quarters-of-a-million dollars as a motive for murder.

Tony Fontaine looked like he'd been rode hard and put up wet.

It was against Nan's better judgment to see him at all,

but he sounded so distressed on the phone, so lost and horrified, that she reluctantly agreed to meet him at the Red Onion in Marina del Rey.

She arrived just after nine P.M. The mood in the bar was festive, the music lively, the margaritas sloshing merrily away. Nan sipped a cappuccino as Tony downed a double Scotch and bemoaned his five hours of police questioning.

"I can't figure out why they think I'd want to kill her," he said. "I loved that girl. I wanted her back. I'd have done anything to get her back, but I wouldn't kill her, for God's sake. How can they think I'd hurt her?"

"Tony, you *did* hurt her," Nan reminded him. She spoke gently, but she wanted it clear that she knew just exactly what had happened during his brief and painful marriage. "You beat her up. I saw her after she left you. She had bruises on her arm and her jaw."

He buried his face in his hands. "If there were some way I could take that back . . ." He looked up, anguished. "When she told me she was leaving, I lost it. I don't know what happened to me. It was bad enough losing Timmy, but I thought we could have another baby, we could make it better somehow. Then when she said she was going, I couldn't understand. I couldn't handle it."

He stared at Nan for a moment, his dark eyes opaque, unreadable. Then he polished off his drink and signaled for another. "But I didn't *kill* her. I could never do that. I loved her."

Which of course meant nothing. Most murders were committed by someone who dearly loved the victim but just "lost it" for a minute. And most murderers didn't have a three-quarter-million-dollar insurance settlement waiting in the wings, tax free.

"Tony, where were you the week after Labor Day?"

He glared at her. "I just spent the whole goddamned afternoon answering questions like that."

"Then surely it won't be that hard to do it one more time."

"I was in Seattle at a sales program."

"All week?"

He nodded. "I flew up Tuesday morning and got back late Friday. I suppose you want to know my hotel room and all the rest of the shit the cops asked me?"

Nan shook her head. "They'll be checking that far better than I could. What was the conference about? The fall line?"

"Naw. We get all that stuff here. This was something I did on my own, a seminar on salesmanship. I knew somebody who took it the year before and he thought it was really great."

"But wasn't it hard to get away right at the beginning of the new model year?" She remembered the frenzy Robinson Ford had always gone into when the new models arrived in early fall, the late hours her father kept, the excitement of seeing sparkling new cars with dealer plates parked in their driveway, a different one each night.

"Well, it wasn't my first choice of times, but there was a last-minute cancellation. This is a really top program, a lot of folks trying to get into it. The next opening wasn't till December."

"I'm still surprised the agency would let you take off then." A fleeting association with the auto industry was about the only thing Nan had in common with Tony besides Debra. In their rather forced social relationship, Robinson Ford had come up often.

He shook his head. "Things have changed a lot since your dad was in the business, Nan. We sell year-round now. People don't swarm into the showrooms for the new models like they used to, and the start of the new season's staggered more, back into the summer. Everything's a lot more complicated. Folks know if they wait a few months, the rebates will start to kick in, and the cheap financing. Or they've already picked up a closeout from the previous year's models."

"I didn't realize it was so fragmented. So, was the salesmanship program worth it?"

He came momentarily alive. "Nan, it was terrific! I came

back so jazzed you wouldn't believe it. You know, you work in sales for a while and you start to think you know all the tricks. But there's always new angles."

"Hmmm," she said. "Tony, what happens to Timmy's insurance settlement with Debra dead?"

He banged a fist on the table, furious once again. This man thought he could control his temper? "Jesus Christ, you sound just like the goddamned cops. I told them, I'll tell you, I don't know and I don't care. I'm not some bum's gonna stop working and live off that kind of blood money. That's not why I went to the program in Seattle, why I keep trying to improve myself."

"But you were the one who wanted to pursue the lawsuit, even after the offer."

Debra had come to Nan, distraught, when Tony initially refused to settle the case. He was making grandiose noises about suing Ames and Featherton for ten million dollars, suing the auto manufacturer for lousy brakes, suing the city for allowing the developers to curve the street, suing everybody but the maker of the ball Timmy chased down off the lawn.

"Only till I realized what it was doing to Debra, having it all drag out that way. Fifty bucks, fifty million, it wasn't going to bring back Timmy. But I thought if we let it go, maybe that would at least bring back Debra."

He looked up in despair. "Her mother's coming tomorrow, Nan. What can I possibly tell her?"

Nan had been wondering the same thing herself.

CHAPTER 10

Marie LaRoche arrived exhausted at noon on Saturday. She looked like Debra might have, if her daughter had lived through another thirty-five years of continual adversity: wizened, skittish, frail, and thoroughly beaten down.

It was the resemblance to Debra that distressed Nan the most as she and Tony Fontaine shepherded the tiny frightened woman down the long airport corridor toward the baggage claim. Somehow, in the past week, Nan had lost track of just what Debra looked like.

She had dug out the few photos she had of the girl: a grinning wedding shot from the Chapel of Eternal Love in Las Vegas; a Polaroid somebody took at work the day she came in with turquoise hair; the picture from Nan's Third-of-a-Century party that she'd shown around at Papillon; and two heartbreaking shots of Debra with Timmy, first as an infant and then in bright red overalls for his first and only Christmas.

But Debra looked different in every picture and none of them really were the way Nan remembered her. Debra had a rubber face, one that changed to meet each new circumstance, and while she never photographed poorly, none of the shots was really accurate.

Marie LaRoche, however, was the original mold from which Debra had been stamped. The molten gold eyes, the high narrow cheekbones, the thin nose, and surprisingly full lips—all were the same as her daughter. The hair, of course, was different, a utilitarian dark brown pageboy. But despite the age difference, her body was remarkably similar, minia-.

ture and lithe. Though she moved wearily, she kept her shoulders squared and walked with Debra's determined stride.

Except for the period around Timmy's death, all Nan's memories of Marie LaRoche were from two decades earlier, when the woman had been younger than Nan was now. Back then, adults all seemed impossibly old. They also seemed *big*, even when, like both Debra's parents, they were physically slight. It was hard to reconcile those memories with this frail woman.

Mrs. LaRoche said almost nothing, deflecting Nan's attempts at small talk and all but ignoring Tony, who looked even worse than the night before. There were bags under his bloodshot eyes and he was vaguely disheveled. Nan didn't like to think about the drive from the Marina to the Valley he had insisted on making after all those double scotches last night.

They waited at the baggage carousel like three strangers, watching matched sets of designer suitcases and knock-off bargain bags whirl by, seeing duffel bags smashed by cardboard cartons careening down the luggage chute. Finally, Marie LaRoche pointed at an ancient tan leather two-suiter, scuffed and battered and, judging from the shocked look on Tony's face when he hefted it, lined with lead. He hauled it to the curb and walked blindly into traffic, crossing to the parking garage. Nan gasped as a car-rental shuttle honked furiously and barely missed him.

While he was fetching the car, Nan broached the question of accommodations. Mrs. LaRoche listened poker-faced to the various options. Tony was prepared to give her the bedroom in his apartment and sleep on the couch, Nan had a daybed in her second bedroom, Jonathan Henley had offered one of the PLI's guest cottages. Debra's house in Hollywood was under police seal, but the place in Canyon Country was unoccupied. If all else failed, there was the Holiday Inn.

"I'll stay with my son-in-law," she said finally, just as Tony pulled his silver Accord to the curb in front of them.

Nan was mildly surprised, being under the impression that Mrs. LaRoche didn't like Tony at all. But she'd never accepted the impending divorce, and must have considered the appearance of family unity more important than her prejudices. Debra's mother had always been a great one for keeping up appearances. Obviously it hadn't occurred to her that Tony might have killed her daughter. What would she have to say after she'd talked to the police?

Back at Nan's condo, they all picked at a light lunch from Gelson's deli: fresh sourdough baguettes, cream of broccoli soup, an assortment of salads carefully placed in proper serving bowls. Nan's mother was always sending hostess paraphernalia, and Marie LaRoche was an appreciative audience for the nicely set table even if she only nibbled halfheartedly at a slice of bread.

Now Nan noticed another detail of Marie LaRoche's appearance, one that tore at her heart and brought a momentary well of tears to her eyes. Debra had been a nail biter, forever gnawing on a stubby pinky nail or worrying a jagged cuticle.

And here sat her mother, with ten fingernails chewed to the quick and a bleeding hangnail.

While they pretended to eat, Nan told Mrs. LaRoche what little she knew, and explained that Tony would take her to meet with the homicide detectives later that afternoon. When the time seemed right, she brought up the subject of Debra's letters, which she had specifically asked the woman to bring.

"The police will want to keep them, I'm sure," she said. "They like to hang on to everything in a situation like this until they figure out what is and isn't important. But before you turn them over, I'd really appreciate a chance to look through them. I don't think Debra would mind."

Mrs. LaRoche, who had made no gesture toward being addressed as Marie, fixed a hard gaze on Nan. Nan felt suddenly thirteen again, being chewed out for letting Debra skin her knee while roller-skating. The woman's eyes were like topaz marbles. "Debbie's wishes," she said sternly, "don't seem to matter much anymore. And I thought you were cooperating with the police."

"Why of course I am!" Nan answered indignantly. "I was the one who filed the missing persons report, after all, and the one who kept trying to find her. Believe me, Mrs. LaRoche, I'm doing everything I possibly can to help them."

"Then I have no objection," she said wearily. "Tony, if we have to meet with the police so soon, I think I'd rather just freshen up here and go there directly. I haven't ... I haven't had much sleep for the last week and I'm starting to feel a little woozy. My doctor gave me some pills to take to sleep, but I'd like to get all this over with first."

She stood slowly and crossed to her purse, a decoupaged picnic basket. From it she took a packet of letters held together by a length of pink ribbon, the thin crinkly kind used for wrapping gifts.

"Thanks," Nan told her. "I appreciate it. Now here, let me get you some towels." She showed Mrs. LaRoche the bathroom leading off from her bedroom, then hurried back to the living room.

"I'll be right back," she told a confused Tony, picking up the letters and dashing down the hall. Her neighbor James was home as promised and answered her knock instantly. James was tall and thin and pale, a melange of elbows, knees, and angles, with a long, prominent nose. He brought to mind an albino stork.

"Such intrigue," he murmured, as Nan crossed his living room and began photocopying the letters. "I trust you'll tell me everything at some propitious date."

"Of course," she answered, pushing Print.

James was an economic analyst who worked out of his condo and had, so far as Nan could determine, no personal life whatsoever. His living room looked like an office products showfloor: Xerox machine, fax, computer, Dow-Jones and Associated Press wire service printers. The D-J machine was quiet for the weekend, but the AP machine clattered merrily away and the computer printer spit out copy. James was a handy and interesting neighbor, always ready to discuss fluctuations in the world gold standard or the latest skinny on the yen.

She had the letters copied and was back in her own place, curled by the window reading, by the time Marie LaRoche emerged from the bedroom. Her hair was freshly combed and she'd applied red lipstick, but the effort only pointed out how tired she appeared.

"I called Detective Bennett," Tony told her. "He's waiting for us whenever we arrive."

"Then let's get it over with," Marie LaRoche sighed. "Thank you for your hospitality, Nan. I'm sorry I wasn't more hungry after you went to so much trouble."

"No trouble at all," she replied guiltily, gathering the letters again and retying the ribbon carefully.

After they left, Nan sighed and sank into the armchair, relieved that Mrs. LaRoche was staying with Tony. She wanted to help, but the weight of the woman's grief was palpable and Nan felt she was carrying quite enough burden already.

There were too many things she could have done, should have done. She was there, of course, when Debra asked for anything, but it wasn't in Debra's nature to ask for much and Nan had hardly gone that extra mile. What had she done, all told? Set up the girl with a couple of attorneys, met her for a couple of meals, brought a paltry little house-warming gift to the place in Hollywood.

She should have been in closer contact. She should have been more available, seemed more open, been more receptive. Then Debra would have shared both her pain and her attempts to deal with it through the Past Lives Institute.

Yeah, right. And how would Nan have reacted? If Debra came to her with talk of past life actions resulting in Timmy's accident, Nan would have hooted. Gently, she liked to think in retrospect. *Chose* to think.

Well, it was too late to change that now, but there was still one thing she could do for Debra. She could help find out who had killed her and see that whoever it was paid dearly for the act.

Jonathan Henley called just as she was finishing her third reading of Debra's letters. The detectives had been up at the

PLI all morning, he said, close-mouthed and prying. Everyone was in a swivet, first at the shock of Debra's death and now at this police intrusion.

"But never mind all that," he said. "How's her mother doing? Did she get in all right?"

Nan reported on Marie LaRoche's arrival and her decision to stay with Tony. "They're off seeing the police right now. I can't say I envy her the experience."

"She won't have to identify the body, will she?" he asked anxiously. "That could be pretty horrible for her."

"Tony's already done the ID. They let him do it on closed circuit TV, so it wasn't as bad as it might have been. He said she was ... sort of shriveled up. I guess the heat in the car trunk must have mummified the body or something." She hadn't spoken these thing aloud since learning them from Tony last night, found them harsh and difficult to articulate.

She heard Jonathan's breath suck in. "Must have been rough on him. And, Nan, this must be pretty rough on you, too."

"It is," she agreed. "I just can't fathom Debra being dead. She was always so totally alive."

"And so young."

"I suppose this is all really easy for you," Nan heard herself say with surprising bitterness. "You can just say, well, she's off to another life. Happy karma to you."

He was silent a moment. "No, it isn't easy, Nan. I guess maybe it should be easier, feeling certain that this is all part of some larger karmic scheme we don't totally understand. And in a sense that does soften the impact a little. But hell, she was young and sweet and I liked her a lot. From a purely selfish viewpoint, I hate to have her gone from my life."

"Me too," Nan said, dissolving into tears.

"Are you alone now?" he asked gently.

"Um-hmm." Monosyllables. She didn't want him to hear her crying. It was a holdover from childhood: keep it in, control the pain, harness the emotion.

"Why don't you come on up here? There's nothing going

on, no seminars or anything. It's just me and April and Bartholomew and we're all a little bit droopy, too, to tell the truth. You could take a swim, or just sit by yourself in the Serenity Garden. Then later we could fix some dinner here or go out, whatever you want."

"Oh, Jonathan, I don't know. I was thinking of maybe just asking for a rain check on the whole thing."

"I can't let you do that," he said beseechingly. "It might not rain for *years*!"

She chuckled despite herself. "Oh, I really don't know. I was just going to—"

"Sit around and mope and think of ways you could have kept this from happening. Don't you think we're all doing that? Misery loves company, Nan."

"Mine doesn't."

"Then just come sit in the corner of the garden and cry. This is a good place to remember Debra, Nan. She was happy up here, and we all cared about her deeply."

"Did anybody ever suggest that you might try a career in sales?" she asked after a moment. The tears were bitten back now. "All right, I'll come up for a while. But no promises on tonight, or even how long this afternoon."

"Bring your suit and take a swim," he suggested. "Cooling and cathartic all at the same time."

Traffic was horrible on Pacific Coast Highway.

The third week of the heat wave had created a mass exodus from the broiling canyons and flatlands. Cars were parked every which way on both sides of the road, and young people in gaudy bathing suits darted across the highway constantly, utterly oblivious to traffic. Fortunately, nobody was moving fast enough to hit them.

As she fumed in traffic, Nan wondered about the letters from Debra to her mother. There were only about a dozen, dating back to a few months before Timmy's accident. Marie LaRoche explained that Debra didn't really like to write at all, that the letters were a concession because she had pleaded with her daughter for something she could hold in her hands.

"I told Debbie, I love to hear your voice, but when I hang up that phone, it's gone. A letter I can read over and over again. I never dreamed it was all I'd have left of her."

It wasn't much, either. Seldom more than a page, often scribbled on a sheet torn from a legal pad, each was fairly simple and formulistic. The two before Timmy's accident were almost exclusively about the boy, detailing a trip to the Griffith Park Zoo and his enthusiasm for playing catch. The latter might be construed as a portent, Nan supposed, but only by really reaching. Little kids all liked to play with balls.

The ones after the accident were briefer and darker. *I'm getting by from day to day,* she wrote at one point, and *sometimes just from hour to hour. My life feels so empty and Tony's away so much at work. Maybe I should go back to work myself. I could probably get my job back at the State Bar. But I don't think I have the energy for the commute or the job. I think about a new job in a place where I don't know anybody, part-time maybe, but I'm not ready for that yet.*

She prepared her mother gingerly for the divorce she knew would be so shocking. *Things have been difficult between me and Tony for a while, and we've decided to take a little time off from each other and think things through.* By then, according to a check of Nan's back calendar for lunches with Debra, they had already been separated for at least two weeks. Then, later: *I realize this is hard for you to accept, but like I told you on the phone, I really think that it's better for Tony and me to call it quits and stop hurting each other. It was probably a mistake for us to ever get married in the first place.*

The Past Lives Institute made only a brief appearance, in midsummer. *I guess I didn't put it very well when I told you about the PLI and what I've been thinking about reincarnation. Don't worry, I haven't gone off the deep end.* Marie LaRoche's reaction—and apparently it was a strong and enduring one, given her own letter to Debra—had evidently been discussed by phone.

Certainly Debra steered clear of it in what little remained

of her correspondence. There were only two letters after that, one of them wholly inconsequential. The other, at the end of August, had a cryptic reference Nan found troubling. *Something kind of strange has happened recently,* Debra wrote, *and I'm not sure what to do about it or who to tell. Oh well.*

That was it.

By the time Nan got to the PLI, she was hot, sticky, and irritable. The parking lot was empty and the place seemed eerily deserted. She found Jonathan and April and Brother Bartholomew in the gazebo of the Serenity Garden with a pitcher of margaritas.

"What'll you have first, a drink or a swim?" Jonathan asked, getting up and pulling out a chair for her beside his own.

"A drink, definitely," she said. "God, the traffic down there is miserable."

"God had nothing to do with it," said Brother Bartholomew with a bit of a twinkle. It was the first evidence Nan had seen of a sense of humor. "Blame Karl Benz and Gottlieb Daimler, those good Germans who invented the internal combustion engine. And Henry Ford, for bringing it to the masses."

"They seem kind of far removed from Malibu a century later," she said, sipping the margarita that Jonathan set in front of her. It was cold and tart and delicious. "But I don't know who else to blame. I don't suppose you can hold it against the dipshits who do the TV weather forecasts. Listen, this drink is wonderful. Who's the bartender?"

Jonathan smiled and bent forward with a small flourish. "Thank you kindly, ma'am. We just made a distressing discovery, however. We're out of limes."

"And I lost the toss," April said, rising. "I have to go down into Malibu Hell and get some more." She wore running shorts with a tank top cut off raggedly below her small, firm breasts. She looked stunningly healthy.

"I could—" Nan began.

"Don't be ridiculous," Jonathan told her. "You just got

here. Now sit, relax, get a little smashed. We've been talking about having a memorial service for Debra. What do you think?"

"I think that sounds like a really nice idea," Nan answered. Inside the oversized gazebo, the temperature was a good twenty degrees cooler. The surrounding Serenity Garden was shaded by a combination of tall shrubs and latticework.

"I'll be back as soon as I can," April said. She walked down a back path and a moment later whizzed by on a mountain bike.

"She'll broil on that thing," Nan said in surprise. "Why on earth didn't she drive?"

Jonathan laughed. "April doesn't drive."

"Not at all?" The notion seemed outrageous. *Everybody* in Los Angeles drove.

"Nope. Not for years. She was in a bad auto wreck and after that she decided it was bad karma to drive. Hasn't been behind the wheel of a car since. That was ... oh, before we moved up here, anyway. Years."

"But Malibu's so far out from everything! How on earth does she get around?"

He shrugged. "She takes cabs, or catches rides with people going into town. Carleen's husband has a limo service we use for our out-of-town VIPs. Most of the time she just stays up here. We keep a small condo down in Century City, and sometimes she spends the night down there if she's going to a movie or something."

"Incredible."

"Not really. At least it doesn't seem that way to us."

"Let's talk about Debra's service," Brother Bartholomew suggested. Even outdoors in this heat he wore long, flowing robes. But maybe they weren't as hot as they looked. Jesus and the disciples were always pictured in similar garb, and Jerusalem had a climate not unlike Southern California.

"Her mother won't be happy about the idea," Nan said. "I didn't even bring you guys up, to tell the truth. Except to offer her lodgings, and I kind of skated around that.

She's a pretty hard-core Catholic, and I know she was un-happy about Debra being involved here."

"A lot of people we see here are Catholics," Jonathan said, "some of them still very active in the church. But I know what you mean. Still, even if she doesn't want to be involved, I'd like to go ahead with it for Debra's other friends. And for us. Is her mother planning some other service?"

"I don't have any idea. But if she is, I can't imagine her doing it here. My guess is that she'll want to ship the body back to Indiana, where her husband is buried. Tony says he'll go along with whatever she wants. Of course he's in a kind of funny position, being halfway divorced from Debra. And for that matter, I don't know how soon they'll release the body, what kind of tests they do."

"I'll talk to Debra's mother," Bartholomew said. "Per-haps if she understands that what we have in mind is a cel-ebration of Debra's life more than a mourning of her death, she'll be more inclined to go along with us."

"Maybe," Nan said doubtfully. "But even if Mrs. LaRoche doesn't want to come, or be involved, I think you should still do it."

"What about Tuesday morning?" Jonathan asked.

"Fine with me. I'll tell people from work, and whoever else I can find. I don't guess there'd be a real crowd."

"We can do it right here," Bartholomew suggested, "in the Serenity Garden. There's a canvas tent top that can cover the whole area if the heat doesn't break."

"Whatever." Nan suddenly realized she was drinking te-quila while she planned a dear friend's funeral. It should have seemed cold, but it actually felt rather nice.

The rest of the afternoon and evening was nice, too, somehow restorative. April brought back an enormous sack of limes and Nan whirred the citrus juicer in a big kitchen as her contribution toward more margaritas. They swam lazy laps in the palm-circled pool, a real treat after the noisy crowded community pool at the condo. April built a salad and Jonathan grilled steaks and enormous shrimp over mesquite. Brother Bartholomew, whom Nan would have pegged as a diehard vegan, ate a good pound of rare sirloin.

During dinner they reminisced about Debra and planned the Tuesday service. Bartholomew would speak, they decided, and anyone who wished to share memories would be welcome to do so. The music was a problem, since Debra's tastes had been so avant-garde and none of them were sure exactly what or whom she'd liked lately.

"Listen to us," April laughed at one point. "We sound like a bunch of old fuddy-duddies talking about how rock and roll is going to undermine society as we know it."

"I've been waiting thirty years for that to happen," Bartholomew complained, "and before it did, I turned into an old fart myself."

"Old maybe," April said. "Old fart? Never."

Bartholomew laughed. "Oh, sweet flattery. I suppose that means I get to wash the dishes."

Which, indeed, he did. April disappeared then into her little house out back, and Nan and Jonathan walked around the buildings to a viewpoint overlooking the ocean far below. The first hint of a night breeze was beginning to waft up off the water.

"There's something I need to know," Nan said hesitantly. "Did you . . . did you have an affair with Debra?"

He turned and looked at her. Even in the darkness of the overcast night, she could feel his intense eyes boring into her. "No, of course not. Debra was like a lost child to me, a baby sister. It never occurred to me. Why do you ask?"

She ignored his question. "What about Bartholomew? Was she sleeping with him?"

His silence answered the question before his words did. "I think so," he said finally, "but I couldn't tell you for sure."

"Doesn't this place have some kind of, oh, I don't know, code of ethics or something?"

Jonathan smiled. "We're all adults here, Nan."

"Sleeping with clients got at least one of your people into a whole hell of a lot of trouble before."

He looked at her, shocked. "You mean Carleen?"

"Of course I mean Carleen. Why, is there somebody else that applies to, too? Is Bartholomew a lapsed social worker or something? A defrocked rabbi?"

As she spoke, she realized just how much Bartholomew bothered her. Of course this whole PLI setup was screwy, but Jonathan and April had a sense of just folks to them. And Carleen, appallingly unprofessional though she might be, seemed genuinely warm and caring.

There was something *wrong* about Bartholomew, though. She'd grown increasingly certain of it through the course of the afternoon and evening. He seemed comfortable in his current role as resident guru, utterly sincere about his beliefs, kind, friendly, thoughtful, all those Eagle Scout virtues. Certainly he looked the part. Nan could also easily picture him as a rebellious teenager slicking back his hair, chomping a burger and fries at some soda shop, playing a little air guitar while he sang along to Elvis and "Blue Suede Shoes."

What she couldn't figure, however, were the intermediate steps that had led him from there to the Malibu mountains and the Past Lives Institute.

Jonathan seemed mildly insulted. "Nan, I don't worry too much about what people have done before they come here. We're all capable of change and growth. I've made enough mistakes in my life that I know I don't dare punish anybody else for theirs. Let he who is without sin and all that."

"It just seems to me that if you're dealing with people in a spiritual realm, there ought to be a higher standard."

"Than what?"

"I don't know. Than if you were selling them shoes or cars." She thought fleetingly of Tony Fontaine. How were he and Marie LaRoche getting along in what had to be an impossibly cramped bachelor apartment?

"All you can ask of anybody," Jonathan said, "is that they do the best they can with what they have available right now. For instance, at hand right now we have a really nice little hot tub, set in a private grotto with some really nice smelling plants around it—jasmine, I think. I was

thinking it would be nice if you and I were to go get in it
for a while. What do you say?"

"Why not?" she answered, turning and heading back toward the house. He followed with a hand placed lightly on
her shoulder.

It was very dark in the little grotto as Jonathan began casually stripping to the buff. Nan realized that she had made
an unconscious decision, when the second bottle of wine
was uncorked at dinner, not to drive home. Skinny-dipping
in a hot tub followed logically enough from that. She hesitated only a moment before slipping out of her own clothes
and into the warm water.

She could hardly act surprised, then, when Jonathan put
his arm around her and kissed her, gently at first, then with
increasing passion. She felt herself melting into the water,
twisting and arching her body to meet his. It was a long
time since she'd gotten randy in a hot tub and she'd forgotten what a deliciously sensual experience it could be.

"You know what would be really wonderful," he murmured softly, running his hand along her thigh under the
water, "would be if you could spend the night."

This was not what she had in mind when she drove up
here, Nan realized. It was contrary to her customary caution. It was because she was drunk. It was disrespectful, if
not to Debra's death, to her family's mourning. It was . . .

As Jonathan kissed her again, she stopped analyzing,
stopped worrying about what it was or wasn't. "I'd like that
too," she whispered.

The floral scents were rich and sweet in the dark night
air. She'd been through a hell of a week and she liked Jonathan a lot and now he was doing something with his fingers that made her quiver in a way that she hadn't for a
long, long time.

They left the hot tub in a hurry, moved swiftly across the
darkened garden through the French doors that opened directly into Jonathan's bedroom.

It occurred to her, very briefly, that Debra would probably have considered making love a rather nice memorial.

CHAPTER 11

The heat wave finally broke Monday night, and the Tuesday of Debra's memorial service dawned cool and overcast. Nan drove up early to the Past Lives Institute, partly to help and partly because she didn't want to wait one minute longer to see Jonathan Henley again. It had been a very long forty-eight hours.

He looked even better than she remembered, in a pale gray suit with a soft pink shirt and deep rose-colored tie. There was something different in the way one viewed a new lover, a shift in focus that made even the most familiar person seem irrevocably altered. In the case of Jonathan, a veritable stranger anyway, the process was even more confusing.

He greeted her with a warm hug and a whispered declaration that he'd missed her greatly. As she whispered back, she felt his arm tighten around her, a very pleasant sensation, and felt the eyes of Détective C. J. Bennett on them both, the psychological equivalent of an ice-cold shower.

Detectives Bennett and Rosalie O'Brien had already been there over an hour, Jonathan told Nan. April had arranged for plainclothes security men at the PLI gate and inside the grounds, mostly to keep out the media.

Debra's body had been found on a slow news day and her death had gotten more coverage than it might have otherwise. Even the stodgy *Times* had run a tear-jerking Metro story under the headline "Tragedy Stalked Murder Victim." It wasn't the screaming sensationalism that the old *Herald-Examiner* might have provided, but it was a lot more attention than Debra ever got alive. Enterprising reporters had tracked down real-estate magnate John Featherman, his ex-wife and the Other Woman. Channel 4 had shown film of Timmy's grave in Forest Lawn's Babyland. The memorial service was a logical follow-up in a week short on political scandals and international crises.

Uniformed police officers were also stationed down at the gate, and at least one putative paparazzo was a plain-clothes detective. His assignment was to photograph every-body who entered and left—the media horde and other gawkers in the outside crowd.

Tony Fontaine arrived with his mother-in-law and imme-diately asked Nan where they could wait in private. Both of them looked dreadful. Nan shepherded them inside to the apricot rattan therapy room, wondering as she did so whether Debra ever had sessions in there and whether Tony and Marie had figured in those sessions.

Marie LaRoche, in stark black, was stony-faced. "I am absolutely appalled," she announced, "at the very notion of such a paganistic ritual. If my husband were alive, he'd put a stop to this nonsense, I can tell you that."

"There's no ritual involved," Nan told her, for at least the tenth time. Marie LaRoche was not interested in explana-tions, having firmly, if erroneously, made up her own mind. Still, Nan felt obliged to try. "Some of the people here have beliefs I don't personally share, but there's nothing really pa-gan about them. Their spiritual beliefs are entirely sincere."

"They're blasphemous!" Mrs. LaRoche shot back. "It's an ungodly desecration of my daughter's memory."

Nan looked at Tony. His apparel was as spiffy as ever, his suit stylish and darkly appropriate, his tie properly somber, his Italian loafers perfectly shined. But the circles under his eyes were deeper and darker, and he moved in a sort of half trance that seemed ironically appropriate to the location.

"You don't need to be at the memorial service if you don't want," Tony told his mother-in-law shortly. "You can wait in here, or we can probably arrange for you to leave right now."

Nan nodded. "One of the people associated with this place

has a limousine service," she said carefully. "I believe there's a limo here on standby, in case anybody needs it for any reason. You'd be more than welcome to take it back into town."

Mrs. LaRoche's eyes widened. "Having made the commitment to attend this blasphemous affair, I have every intention of staying. You won't get rid of me quite that easily." She wasn't making much sense, but that wasn't surprising. It had taken hours of Tony's rather considerable persuasive capabilities to get her to attend at all.

"Of course not," Nan soothed her. "If you'd like to wait inside here, I'll come and get you when the service is about to begin."

With Marie LaRoche's huffy dismissal echoing in her mind, Nan went back outside and watched as four dozen or so people filtered into the Serenity Garden. White padded folding chairs were set up, and a string trio played softly in the gazebo. Wherever Debra was, she was probably guffawing at the musical selection.

Nan shook herself. The question of immortality was very much on her mind, and this was a logical place to ponder it. But that could come later. If Debra had moved on to a better life, as both her Catholic mother and these reincarnation devotees believed, then there was nothing to worry about. If she hadn't, if there was no life after death, it was too late to help her.

But it wasn't too late to nail her killer. Nan cast her eyes carefully around the crowd.

She recognized many of the mourners. Violet Thomas, Danny Harrington, and a half dozen others from the State Bar huddled together, clearly bemused by the entire place, trying to fit their Debra into this lush setting: part spiritual enclave, part goofy California theme park. She could hardly wait till Danny got a gander at Brother Bartholomew.

The gang from the State Bar looked far more comfortable, however, than the delegation of three from McSweeney Lane: two youngish secretaries and Norman Metcalfe. Nan was surprised to see Norman. They'd started out together in the litigation department at McSweeney Lane, sharing Debra's secretarial services for a while. Norman later moved into Corporate and was fabled for his airtight, unbreakable contracts, some barely shorter than the *Warren Report*.

He crossed to her and spoke solicitously. "We're all so terribly d-distressed."

Nan shook Norman's outstretched, faintly damp hand. "It's a horrible thing, Norman. Nobody can believe it."

As he spoke further of the shock and mourning pervading the firm's halls, Nan swallowed a smile. She remembered how perfectly Debra had mimicked Norman once safely removed from the McSweeney Lane payroll. Debra had him down cold: the slouching walk, the nervous finger drumming whenever his hands weren't occupied, the faint vestiges of the boyhood stutter which sometimes showed up on his dictation tapes. The Great Dictator, Debra called him, in reference to the astonishing amount of paperwork he generated.

Norman was hardly a face man. Indeed, he was the epitome of the back room drone whose billable hours financed all those firm retreats to Maui and the Ahwahnee Lodge. He would beat a hasty exit once the service ended, Nan was sure, anxious to get back to the sanctity of his oaken office, where section III-C-(2)(j)(iv) of some epic undoubtedly awaited a polish.

"Leon asked me to convey his c-condolences," Norman went on, blushing slightly. Interpersonal relationships were not his strong suit. "He's in Washington this week, or he'd be here himself, of course."

"Thanks, Norman. Give him my regards."

"The firm would like to make a small, er, memorial. Was there a particular charity Debra supported?"

Nan almost laughed out loud. The Society for Handsome Indigent Actors, maybe. Punk Musicians United Against Everything. "I'll check with her mother," she promised. Marie LaRoche would probably suggest something like the building fund at St. Ignatius Church in South Bend. "If you would excuse me, now."

Norman moved away and took a conspicuous seat at the

front, while Nan sighed in relief that Leon hadn't come. Of course he never knew Debra well, but she *was* working for Nan at the time of both their marriage and divorce. Debra had given them a pair of chunky glass candleholders, very sleek, very trendy.

It was a lucky break that Leon was out of town. She wondered vaguely what her ex-husband was doing in Washington, besides salivating from his proximity to power. Leon had grown up in Sacramento, the son of a lobbyist, and since boyhood had been fascinated with political movers and shakers.

Nan often wished she could be blasé about her divorce. Others seemed to have little trouble; some, like Shannon, had it down to an art form. For Nan, however, divorce represented an intense personal failure, and all her therapy and ACA camaraderie had only blunted that sense, never eliminated it.

She shook off the self-pity and wandered toward a group of floral displays beside the gazebo. Debra's tenant, Marty, was just coming in, looking a little stoned. He nodded vaguely at her. He stood with several other young men who bore the unmistakable stamp of rock and roll, including the two fellows he'd been with the other night at Papillon. The items of mourning dredged from their various wardrobes were rather touching, clearly parts of performance costumes: black T-shirts, leather pants, a black velvet vest on a skinny young guy with a long single braid and an eyepatch. Nan had somehow expected Linny to be with them, but the delegation from Papillon was exclusively male.

Tom Hannah came up behind Nan. "How are you holding up?" he asked.

"I'm fine," she told him. "You didn't need to come, you know. I told you that."

"I'm a bad listener," he answered, untruthfully. "Who are all these people, anyway?"

Nan pointed out the people she knew. There were others that she didn't have a clue about. Neighbors, perhaps, from Canyon Country, or friends from the grief support group

Debra had belonged to briefly after Timmy's death. Probably a few curiosity-seekers who had talked their way in, claimed some tenuous connection. And quite a few people from the PLI: Carleen McIlheney in severe navy blue, young Marsha bustling around straightening chairs, a bearded, middle-aged male therapist Nan hadn't met before. There were also a dozen or so PLI clients, people from Debra's group sessions.

"So where are her girlfriends?" Tom asked, finally.

Nan frowned. "You know, it's strange. She didn't seem to have any. I never really thought about it till I started looking for her, and even then I didn't stop to wonder about it till we saw Linny. Of course Debra was a loner. She called herself a man's woman one time, which I thought was kind of silly and pretentious."

"Women always have girlfriends," Tom insisted.

"Almost always. I'm beginning to wonder if Debra was ever really close to anybody."

Jonathan Henley came up. "Nan, we're about to begin. You want to get Debra's mother?"

Nan grimaced. "Not really." She introduced Jonathan and Tom, noting in amusement as she left that they circled like suspicious tomcats, each trying to figure out the other's role in her life.

Once Debra's sullen kin were settled in their front row seats, Brother Bartholomew emerged in blindingly white robes and gently convened the gathering. Marsha moved around the garden distributing fragrant long-stemmed coral roses from a white basket. The PLI regulars settled in easily while friends from other parts of Debra's life clustered together in their subgroups, trying not to look uncomfortable. Except Danny Harrington from the State Bar, who was trying not to laugh.

The two detectives remained standing at the rear. Rosalie O'Brien fit in perfectly, might have been one of Debra's co-workers or an old family friend. C. J. Bennett, on the other hand, would probably only blend into a convention of mercenaries or survivalists. Now he swept his head from side to side with a consistent rhythmic motion that suggested a motorized neck.

"We are brought together today by a shared sadness," Brother Bartholomew began, "and by a shared joy at having known a lovely and remarkable young woman. She was taken from us far sooner than we would have hoped, her work in this lifetime finished before we expected."

As Bartholomew's soothing voice continued, Nan looked around. From her seat between Tom and Jonathan, off to the side, she had a clear view of almost everyone. Several people were unabashedly crying, not at all ready to let the joy supersede the grief. One of them, interestingly, was Carleen McIlheney, whose tears streamed down her face. Her frizzy red hair seemed even wilder and more out of control today, further proof that Alistair hadn't yet returned.

Where on earth *was* Alistair, anyway? Since learning he was a longtime PLI associate Nan had redoubled her efforts to find him, leaving half a dozen more messages with each of his numbers. Nobody knew where he was, and she seemed to talk to different people every time she called.

Which would have been bad enough, except that Alistair had actually returned Nan's call on Saturday night when she was up here with Jonathan. He had left a cryptic message on her machine: "Alistair, sweetie. I'll try you later."

Somehow it didn't make her feel better that the police couldn't find him either.

After the service, while the guests milled around eating pastries and drinking lemonade and coffee, Detective C. J. Bennett appeared at Nan's elbow.

"Very touching what you had to say," he told her.

Nan reflexively bristled. C. J. Bennett wouldn't know "touching" if it gnawed his ears off. He wore an ill-fitting navy blazer today, with a white shirt and a shiny navy tie that didn't come close to matching the blazer. The tie bore a stain the shape of Australia, and his shoes looked like he'd found them in a Dumpster.

"Thank you." All she'd said was a couple of sentences—

how Debra had brightened her life and how much she missed her. It was, truly, almost nothing.

"I need to talk to you later today," Bennett declared, with a slight hint of menace.

"How about right now?" Nan wondered if Bennett had studied Nazi SS training films. She didn't feel like talking to him now, or ever. Still, he was like an abscessed tooth, something that didn't get better when you ignored it. She took him inside and into the same therapy room where she had earlier left Tony and Marie.

"Know your way around here pretty well, don't you?" he said, smirking.

"I've been up here a few times," she answered evenly.

It did not seem to be Bennett's business that she was sleeping with Jonathan Henley, and she didn't like the idea that he might know. Might? Was she crazy? C. J. Bennett would *make* it his business to know, had probably already checked the trash for Jonathan's condom brand.

"Marty Mitchum says you broke into Debra's house the first night you were there," the detective announced without preamble.

Damn! "Does it really make any difference how I got in?"

"Does it make any difference, she wants to know? You're the lawyer, I'm just the dumb cop. Mitchum says the door was locked; he tried to get in himself a few times. Then the next thing he knows, you're inside, telling him you busted in."

"I told him no such thing," Nan replied indignantly, trying to remember just exactly what she *had* told Marty. The little fink. Had Bennett caught him holding? By now the police had certainly visited Papillon, were nosing around in Debra's night life.

"California has this thing called a Criminal Code; you might have heard of it," Bennett noted laconically. "A lady like you, holier than thou, working to keep lawyers pure, wouldn't seem to me she'd like to violate that code."

"Is this supposed to be some kind of a threat?" Nan asked irritably. Would it hurt to take the offensive? She was already screwed. Breaking and entering was beyond mere impropriety. It was grounds for summary dismissal from a job as sensitive as hers.

He gave a little half smile. "Not at all, not at all. A guy like me, he runs across a lot of things might not quite be legal. I spent all my time following up that stuff, there'd be no chance to do my real job."

"And?"

"And I want to know how you got into that house. You're straight with me now, it goes no further. You jerk me around any more, I might get annoyed."

"So it *is* a threat. Oh, what the hell." She told about the Visa card and where she'd found the key. He didn't need to know that it had ruined the damn credit card. "You know why I did it. I filed with Missing Persons the next day. I had no criminal intent and I only took things that might help me find her. As you're well aware, my concern was justified. Book me, Dan-o."

He laughed, the first time she'd heard him do so.

"My God, you get feisty! You get underfoot, too. It was one thing you mucking around when it was just your friend missing and the cops maybe not too interested. But meddling in a criminal investigation, that's obstruction of justice."

"Yeah, right," Nan answered grimly. "Listen, if you want to do something constructive, try checking into Brother Bartholomew. I can't quite put my finger on it, but there's something wrong with him." Watching him through the service had made the back of her neck itchy.

"You think so?" Now he sounded doubtful, but it was probably only a reflex. C. J. Bennett would have to find Brother Bartholomew personally repellent.

"Yeah, I think so. But, hey, I wouldn't dream of telling you how to run your investigation. Obstruction of justice and all that." She smiled ever so sweetly at him. "If you'll excuse me now, I'd like to talk to Debra's mother. She's going back home this afternoon."

Bennett swaggered back outside, listing slightly to his

gun side. Nan kicked a rattan loveseat, but it didn't make
her feel any better. It just scuffed her shoe.

Nan made no attempt to go back to work that afternoon.
She drove instead to Venice, to Glorioso Way and the little
house on the walk street across from Shannon's.

She parked and walked under the sprawling bougainvillea toward the front of the house. It would be nice to be
in a house again, she realized. She and Leon had lived in
a Spanish bungalow in Brentwood, in a neighborhood of
young families.

The little house behind the FOR SALE sign was tightly
sealed, a small plaque by the front porch warning it was
protected by Westec. Shannon had pointed out the alarm
system, how easy it was to operate, how difficult to circum-
vent. Two doors down, a dog barked, probably the best security system of all. There seemed to be quite a few big
dogs on these walk streets.

This was a far cry from Brentwood, no matter how expensive the property. Venice between here and the ocean
had a decidedly funky flavor. Would moving here represent
a step forward or backward? Hard to tell, really. But it
would certainly be a change, and that she was ready for.

On impulse, she crossed the sidewalk and rang Shannon's bell. A massive Harley-Davidson was parked in the
side yard. After a minute or two, Shannon's daughter,
Becky, opened the door. Behind her a character who had to
be the biker boyfriend, Rick Oleander, was sprawled on the
bright blue and yellow couch in grimy jeans. He held a can
of Schlitz and sported a Fu Manchu mustache. Nan had, at
Shannon's request, asked Danny Harrington to check his
record; astonishingly, he didn't have one. Perhaps he was
just another Hollywood poseur, which somehow didn't
seem much better.

Nan remembered to call the girl Rebecca, and in turn
Becky had the good grace both to recognize Nan and apologize for her mother's absence. She never got around to in-
troducing her boyfriend or inviting Nan to come inside,

however. Nor did she explain why she wasn't in school. Nan asked her to have Shannon call, then walked back across the street. From somewhere down the block, she could hear an old Bob Dylan album playing.

Twenty years of schooling and they'd put her on the day shift.

There was nobody playing any old Dylan in her condo building, for damn sure. Everybody was looking straight into the future or relentlessly seizing the moment.

And history was last season's swimsuit styles.

That night she made a pot of tea and curled up in bed with all the reincarnation books and materials people had been thrusting on her. Most of it she set aside fairly quickly: implausible personal tales of glamorous previous lives, florid New Age treatises, ponderous tomes on Eastern religion. She lingered a bit longer over some fairly interesting anecdotal books, full of intriguing but unverifiable hypnotic regressions.

The one she finally settled in with was an academic volume with the ever so cautious title of *Twenty Cases Suggestive of Reincarnation*. Written by a University of Virginia professor, Ian Stevenson, the study used scientific methodology to examine cases of children who reported "memories" of previous lives.

These were mostly kids living in isolated villages in cultures where reincarnation was an accepted belief. They gave detailed accounts of recent lives and deaths, which were often violent and/or premature. Researchers then corroborated the material by accompanying the children to locations they described but had never seen in this life. In case after case, the detail was specific and accurate. The kids would lead researchers directly to former homes, pick former friends and relatives out of crowds, sing songs in languages they didn't know, ask why furniture had been rearranged. Sometimes they had birthmarks or birth defects that corresponded to previously fatal wounds. The cumulative effect of all this minutiae was compelling.

Still, Nan decided as she drifted off to sleep, she wasn't

quite ready to sign on as a true believer. How could she accept the notion that she had multiple lives, when it was all she could do to handle one?

On Thursday afternoon, Nan was wading through a mountain of neglected paperwork in her office when Rosalie O'Brien arrived unannounced. The detective wore a simple beige dress today, low comfortable shoes, and an intricately braided gold belt.

"I hope this isn't a bad time," Detective O'Brien said. "But I have a feeling your job is a lot like mine and there's never a good one."

Nan shoved the papers to one side and sat back. "How about that," she agreed. "I'm so far behind everything that I'm mostly just sticking my fingers in some of the leakier spots, wishing I had more than ten of them. It's always tough to keep up, but these last couple of weeks, well ..."

"I won't keep you long then. But I wanted to ask you something. You told me earlier that you didn't know of Debra using drugs."

"Yeah."

"Tell me again."

Nan considered. "I don't know if she ever messed around with anything before she came out here, and initially my relationship with her was kind of strained, really. I was ..." She paused. "I was a nervous young associate and I wasn't used to having subordinates. Debra was an inexperienced secretary who wasn't sure she liked the idea of working for a woman. If we hadn't had that shared history, back in Illinois, I'm not sure it would have worked at all. She made me uncomfortable, somehow."

Rosalie O'Brien grinned. "I get the picture."

Nan had a feeling that under other circumstances, she and the detective might well become friends. Nan had come onto the legal scene after the nastiest spadework for women in law firms was finished, decades after Sandra Day O'Connor completed law school and was offered a job as a legal secretary. There hadn't been many female partners in big firms yet, but women were pouring out of law schools and it was clear they couldn't be ignored indefinitely. Rosalie O'Brien, on the other hand, had fought her way up in the police force. Nightmare time.

"Anyway," Nan went on, "we were very polite in the office, but we didn't see each other socially at all. We certainly weren't sharing any confidences about drug experiences. Then, about a year or so after she moved out here, one of Debra's friends OD'd. A drummer, I think. I don't think he was actually her boyfriend or even that she'd ever dated him. But it happened at a party she was at. Debra found him in the bathroom with a needle sticking out of his arm and called the paramedics while everybody else hauled ass out the back door. That was a real turning point for her."

It had also been a real turning point for Debra and Nan's relationship. Nan recalled Debra sitting ashen at her word processor the following Monday morning, jumping a foot when Nan asked if everything was all right, suddenly crumpling into tears. Nan brought her across into her own office, closed the door, and got the whole awful story out of her. It was the first real glimpse she'd had into Debra's life, and it both fascinated and horrified her.

"And after that she stayed away from drugs?"

"She always said so. I believed her, though I guess you never can really know, particularly about somebody you only see at work."

"But you did see her socially a little."

"Not on any kind of regular basis. And except for when she got married, and had the baby and all that, it was always on my turf."

"I see. When you went through her house, did you take away anything, paraphernalia or pills or grass or coke or whatever?"

"Of course not," Nan answered indignantly. "There wasn't anything like that there. And why would I take it if there were?"

"To protect her?"

"From what? I didn't know she was dead. I wasn't even

sure she was genuinely missing. Are you accusing me of something?"

"Whoa, whoa. Of course not. I'm just asking. You're sure there wasn't anything there? Think about it. Change your mind if you'd like."

"What *is* this? I can't change my mind. There wasn't anything there. I turned over everything I took away to you that first day."

"And as far as you know, Debra wasn't doing any drugs?"

"As far as I know. She didn't even like to drink. It was something about the birth control pills she was taking, I think, that messed up her tolerance for alcohol. Two drinks and she'd pass out. So she didn't do that either."

"But it's possible that after Timmy's death, she might have, oh, say, started taking antidepressants."

"Look, anything's possible. Why don't you ask somebody who knew her socially?"

"We have," Rosalie O'Brien said, "and they all give us the same answer you do. They say she was a real straight arrow, didn't touch anything."

"So why are you asking?"

Detective O'Brien smiled. "C. J. probably wouldn't want me to tell you this, and it's not for general knowledge yet, but we've gotten a preliminary toxicology report. There was methaqualone in Debra's body."

"You're kidding!"

"Not at all. The question is how it got there. And why. Any ideas?"

Nan hesitated. "You might ask Tony," she said finally.

"Oh?"

"Yeah. Oh, I don't think Tony's any kind of hard-core druggie, but I remember Debra talking about how before she started going with him, he used to do a lot of downers."

"Which he stopped?"

Nan shrugged her shoulders. "Who knows? Tony and I have never been what you'd call tight. Even after he married Debra, I mostly just saw her either at work or at lunch or something. Until this past week, most of the times I saw

Tony were when Timmy was in intensive care. We weren't discussing recreational drugs."

"We'll have to check on that," Detective O'Brien said. "Thanks."

"Wait a minute. I thought Debra was beaten to death."

"She was."

"So you're not saying that the drugs killed her?"

"Oh, no, not at all. It wasn't anywhere near a lethal level."

"But if . . . oh, never mind."

"If what?" Rosalie O'Brien seemed genuinely interested in Nan's opinion, a pleasant change from her partner.

"Tony wasn't even in town that week."

"We still don't know exactly when Debra was killed, and we can't really pin it down very precisely. The last time she was seen was leaving the Past Lives Institute on Monday night. Tony didn't go up to Seattle till Tuesday morning. He could have met her on Monday night."

"And what? Drugged her and beaten her to death? Why on earth would he do that?"

"If she wasn't used to the effect of the drug maybe she'd have a funny reaction. Paranoiac, accusatory, who knows? She starts accusing him of being responsible for their little boy's death, say, and he gets mad and hits her."

Nan was silent. It could have happened that way. But the part that didn't fit was Debra taking the Quaalude. Nor did it seem likely there was any new accusation she could hurl at Tony. Every possible ugly utterance had already spewed forth a hundred times.

"You really think Tony could have killed her?"

"I don't have an opinion yet," Detective O'Brien said. "But you've got to admit you find the idea plausible. It was you who first brought up Tony when we told you Debra was dead."

"Yeah," Nan said slowly. "It was, wasn't it?"

"I'll let you get back to work now." Rosalie O'Brien stood up and turned toward the office door. "Oh, by the way. You were right about Brother Bartholomew."

Nan smiled and gestured toward the empty chair. "Then sit right back down and tell me."

"It won't take that long. His name is really Albert Foster and he grew up in Terre Haute, Indiana. His juvenile record there is sealed, but I'm told it takes two people to lift it. He worked as a welder for a while and did some time on misdemeanors. Receiving stolen goods, unlawful entry. When he came up on grand theft auto, the court gave him a choice between enlisting in the army or hard time. He took the military."

Nan shook her head. "And we wonder why the armed services are in such a mess."

"Yeah. Well, he served two tours in Vietnam and his military record's clean. When he got out of the army, he went back to Asia and bummed around there for years."

"Is that when he was supposedly studying with the masters of Eastern mysticism?"

"Indeed it was. And he did study Eastern religion, apparently. But he was also studying Western capitalism. The DEA was never able to pin anything on him, but they say he had a nice little smuggling operation going for a number of years."

"Drugs?" Nan asked.

"You were thinking maybe Nepalese carpets? Yeah, drugs. The IRS tried to get him on tax evasion after he came back to the United States, but his assets were gone by then. Anyway, there's no indication he's dirty now. The DEA doesn't have anything current on him, and our own narcotics people never heard of him or the Past Lives Institute."

Rosalie O'Brien looked at her watch. "I think," she said, "that I'll go meet C.J. and we'll have another chat with Tony Fontaine."

"Don't tell him I told you he did downers," Nan said.

"Why? Are you afraid of him?"

"Of course not," she answered, not hearing much conviction in her voice.

Was she really afraid of Tony Fontaine?

Had Debra been?

CHAPTER 12

The killer had watched Tony Fontaine, the grieving widower, at Debra's memorial service. An arrogant little shit, full of bravado and self-importance. Not too smart, either. Debra never thought so, and she was no brain trust herself. A tenacious snoop, maybe, but not innately clever. The miscalculation had been in assuming that she could be fooled indefinitely, could be put off by casual lies, would accept disappearing information.

Too bad for Debra that hadn't been true.

Too bad for Tony, too. Because the best and easiest way to get rid of her meant ultimately sacrificing him as well. Some sacrifice.

It would probably have been better to wait a bit longer before having the grieving widower take drastic repentance for his sins. But the cops were too persistent, too nosy. They'd tumbled to the missing tape, though there was no indication that anybody realized what it meant or that it was significant.

Now they were asking pointed questions about Debra's drug use, which meant they knew about the Quaalude. Everybody was so shocked at the idea of Debra doing dope, and so adamant in their denials, that it only made sense to have the one person with a history of downers feel he'd come to the end of his tether.

Which he had, though he didn't yet know it.

Here came the car lights now, curving around the bend, slowing. Was that Tony? Yeah, it was his car. A nice victory, being able to get him to come out in the middle of the night in response to a cock-and-bull story about Debra confiding unnamed concerns, things that Tony needed to know about.

And a pleasantly ironic touch that the meeting was taking place at almost exactly the same place where Debra had died. Too bad there was no way to let Tony know that.

Too bad that all this couldn't be shared with *somebody*.

The killer stepped into the road, waved the car to a stop. There didn't seem to be anyone following Tony. The jerk wasn't bright enough to tell the cops where he was going.

"What's going on?" Tony asked, blinking. What a dolt. Good looking, but the IQ of a garbanzo bean. "What are you doing here?"

"I need to show you something," the killer said quietly. "I didn't want us to be observed." Be gentle, be persuasive. Don't raise his suspicions unnecessarily. And whatever else, don't get him mad.

"I don't get it," Tony complained.

"Trust me." Was that going too far? "Just park over here and come with me for a minute."

Tony frowned, but he pulled to the side of the road and switched off his engine. He got out and peered around suspiciously. "There's nothing here," he said.

"Over there," the killer pointed, beyond him.

As Tony turned, the killer pulled the short solid length of pipe out of a back pocket and swung hard. The pipe came down heavily above Tony's right ear with a loud and satisfying crunch. Tony crumpled to the ground without a sound.

Blood.

That was the next worry. The killer pulled out a small canvas bag hidden by the roadside and took out a small flashlight. When the beam was fixed on Tony's head, a definite dent showed, but not much blood. His breathing was light and shallow.

Perfect.

A few twists of the Ace bandage around Tony's head held the wad of paper towel in place. Not much of a bandage, but it was only temporary anyway.

Now to get him into the trunk. It would be easier to keep

track of him in the car, but far too risky if he came to before they reached the final destination. Just so he didn't
leave some kind of clue in the trunk. Have to double-check
on that later.

At least this way he wouldn't be able to get out before
it was time. And he probably wasn't coming to, either. Already his breathing was fainter. Have to move quickly.
Wouldn't want him dead too soon. That could screw up everything pretty royally.

The killer pulled on gloves and took the key from the ig-
nition, closing the door to cut off the interior light. The
trunk was empty.

Perfect. It took only a moment to spread plastic garbage
bags across the bottom of the trunk. No point in leaving
any dangerous stains that some smartass evidence techni-
cian might identify.

The car drove smoothly, had only 3,900 miles on it. It
was an odd feeling moving into traffic realizing what was in
the trunk, but there wasn't the frantic anxiety of the first
time.

Experience made anything easier.

The metal pipe went into a Dumpster behind a fast food
restaurant just before the freeway entrance. It was a temp-
tation to get rid of everything else now, too, but there was
no telling what might be called for later. Where they were
heading, there'd be no 7-Elevens to pick up a spare roll of
paper towels or a giant Hefty bag.

The San Diego Freeway was almost hypnotic as it
coursed north through the San Fernando Valley. Tony had
the radio set to some contemporary rock station; silence
was preferable. Would he wake up in the trunk, realize
what was happening? The killer hoped not. That contingency was covered, but it might get messy.

At last the car pulled off at the Canyon Country exit,
headed away from civilization down a rough secondary
road. No point going any farther than necessary now.

Tony seemed heavier than he had when he went into the
trunk, but he was still unconscious. More important, he was

still alive. At last he was out. It was possible to half walk him, keep his clothes clean. Finally he was propped against a boulder, looking just as if he'd sat down to collect his final thoughts.

The bandaging came off his head easily, slipped into one of the garbage bags retrieved from the trunk. Now came the tricky part.

Tony's hand was limp. It was harder than it should have been to curve his fingers around the trigger of the gun. They kept slipping off as his hand was raised to his head.

But there could be only one shot and it had to obliterate all traces of the crease above his ear.

Finally his hand was in position. The killer smiled as Tony's finger, with a bit of help, tightened around the trigger. Now.

The gunshot exploded into the quiet night, taking with it much of Tony Fontaine's head. The killer gagged reflexively, swallowed deeply, and stepped back, allowing Tony's hand with the gun to fall at his side.

There were blood spatters on the garbage bag carefully tucked around the killer's own clothing for protection. Within moments, the bag was wrapped up, tucked inside the canvas sack with all the other odds and ends.

Then, with one last look around, the killer walked away.

☀

On Saturday morning, Nan met Shannon and took another look at the house on Glorioso Way.

It still seemed mighty small, but it was starting to feel familiar and friendly. There were quite a few people outside, and today's soundtrack wafting down the block was from Linda Ronstadt's country rock period. Two little boys played in a front yard next to Shannon's house, and an older man on hands and knees diligently weeded a vegetable garden that filled most of his front yard. A guy in running shorts jogged past with a smile and a wave. Down the alley, a man in his thirties lovingly massaged a coat of wax into his Miata.

"So here's the deal," Shannon said, back at her place. Shannon's T-shirt read: ALL THOSE WOMEN MOANING ABOUT FINDING HUSBANDS HAVE OBVIOUSLY NEVER HAD ONE. "We make an offer on this place contingent on selling your condo within say, ninety days. They'll probably want to cut that down to sixty, but that's all right. Then we put the condo on the market and push the hell out of it."

"But the real estate market's so soft," Nan protested. "There are at least a dozen condos for sale in my complex alone, and nobody's buying them."

"Because the owners aren't realistic about the prices they want. Listen, Nan, I'm not doing this to make money. I'll cut my commission on selling your condo to the bone. But dammit, I sure think it would be fun to have you in the neighborhood."

"I like that part just fine too," Nan agreed, "and as far as the commission goes, I know you have to make a living."

The offer brought up contradictory emotions in Nan. That part of her which automatically perked up at the mere whisper of the words *sale, bargain, cheap*, was on red alert. On the other hand, the part of her that supported friends and other women in business, a part she refused to label feminist but liked to think of as simple integrity, was appalled. On balance, she suspected saving a buck would win out over philosophy.

Nan made perfunctory arguments, but she could feel herself wavering. Well, why not? Seize the moment, grab the gusto. Debra, she knew, would have said to go for it.

"But what happens if I can't sell the condo?"

Shannon smiled, showing off the deep dimples which had made her so appealing on *Our Family*. "You lose a little earnest money, that's all. Maybe not even that." She crossed to the stereo and popped in the *Hotel California* CD.

"Living in this neighborhood would be like being trapped inside an oldies radio station," Nan said, with a wry smile.

"It's our only block regulation. No music recorded less than ten years ago. Think you could live with it?"

"I'm sure I could. But Shannon, give me another couple days to think about the house, all right?"

Shannon showed her dimples again. "So long as you aren't saying no outright, take as much time as you need."

On her way home, Nan ran all the errands that pile up in the course of a normal work week, miscellany she'd been neglecting for several weeks now. She wandered through Builder's Emporium looking at patio furniture that might be appropriate for the house on Glorioso Way, then drove down to Culver City to Trader Joe's and stocked up on exotic beers and cheeses. She went to Savon for shampoo and more industrial strength sunscreen. Out on Lincoln Boulevard, the beach-bound tied up traffic in all directions.

Idly she switched channels on the radio. On the all-news station, a national roundup was just ending.

"Locally, the body of car salesman Tony Fontaine was found this morning in Canyon Country, an apparent suicide," the impersonal voice reported.

Nan's hands began to shake uncontrollably and she was grateful to be stopped at a red light. She pulled to the curb when the light changed and sat trembling through the rest of the report.

"The thirty-three-year-old Fontaine had been considered a suspect in the death of his estranged wife, Debra LaRoche, whose body was found September twenty-eighth in the trunk of her parked car. Police refused to comment on Fontaine's death. . . . Angry shopkeepers in Downey, protesting—"

Nan snapped the radio off.

Tony.

Suicide.

She could not imagine Tony Fontaine, he of the quick temper and slow Mediterranean charm, taking his own life. Tony was a fighter. If he had killed himself, it could mean only one thing, that he had also killed Debra.

The long halls of Nan's condo were wallpapered in a banana leaf pattern, a low-grade imitation of the Beverly Hills Hotel. As she dug for her key outside her unit door, her phone began ringing. She hurried to get in before the machine picked it up. She was sick and tired of message machines, tired of hang-ups and people who didn't call back and messages that never seemed to get picked up or relayed.

It was Jonathan. "Have you heard?" he asked neutrally.

"You mean Tony," she said, kicking off her sandals and taking a cold Molson Golden out of the refrigerator. "On the radio just now. What do you know?"

"Probably less than you, if you heard it on the news. I got it second-hand from Carleen. She just called up here a minute ago."

"I . . . I'm kind of shaken up," she said. "I suppose the thing to do would be call the police, but I don't imagine they'll be in any hurry to talk to *me*. Jonathan, I'm all . . . I don't know."

But she did know. *Tony!* It was much easier to picture Debra killed by some stranger, even some horrible smooth-talking serial murderer, than to believe that Tony would kill her.

Jonathan's voice was slow, soothing. "Nan, why don't you just take it easy this afternoon. Take a nap, a swim, whatever. Then later I'll come down and maybe we can get a quiet dinner somewhere."

"Right now, I really don't feel like going out tonight."

"Then we could stay in," he said softly. "I promised April I'd drive her into town late this afternoon anyway. So how about if I pick up some Chinese food and we can eat at your place. You like Szechuan?"

"Sure."

"Then it's set. Listen, I've got a call coming in from one of our tour guides in the Middle East. I've been trying to get in touch with him for two days."

"Take the call," Nan said. "But about tonight, I don't know."

"Then turn me away at your door," he said, and hung up.

It took Rosalie O'Brien four hours to return Nan's call.

"I'm sorry I didn't get back to you sooner," she apologized, "but I'm sure you understand how busy we've been."

"I don't understand anything," Nan complained. She caught herself. There was no reason to whine at Rosalie.

"Well, make yourself comfortable," the detective said, "and I'll fill you in as much as I can. This morning about seven o'clock a couple of guys came across Tony Fontaine's car out in Canyon Country, a few miles from where Debra and Tony lived. They stopped to take a look and found Tony sitting just off the road with his head blown off."

Nan inhaled sharply. "You're sure it was Tony?"

"Oh yeah. His car was right there, his wallet was in his pocket, the fingerprints match. No question of ID at all. Fortunately somebody out there made the connection right away and called us."

"Was there a note?"

"Nothing. We checked his apartment and the Honda showroom and the house in Canyon Country. Everything came up empty. Of course he might have mailed something, but if he did it could be weeks before it gets here."

Nan gave a little chuckle despite herself. There was something appealing about the detective's black sense of humor. It was probably essential in her line of work.

"It was definitely suicide?"

Rosalie O'Brien hesitated a moment. "There's no reason to rule suicide out," she said finally. "His prints are on the gun, a .357 that's never been registered anywhere we can find. The gun was in his hand. We'll have to wait for forensics to see if he fired it, but my guess is that'll come up positive."

"You don't sound entirely convinced."

There was a long silence. "C.J. considers the case closed. I can't say that I entirely agree with him right now, but I'm thinking about it."

"It would be tidy, wouldn't it?"

"That it would."

If they really considered the case closed, there was something Nan had to know. "Listen, this may be none of my business, but don't you get a little tired of always playing Good Cop to his Bad Cop?"

Rosalie O'Brien chuckled. "What makes you think I always do?"

"Well, you certainly did it with me."

"Because of who and what you are. It can work just as well in reverse. If we're talking to some tough guy, sometimes I'll come on as a real brass-balls bitch and then C.J. takes him aside, one macho buddy to another."

Nan hadn't thought of that. "Hmmph," she answered. It was depressing to think of the kind of suspect who'd consider C.J. Bennett a buddy. "Is that what you did with Tony?"

"Not really."

Well, what did it matter now? "After you came to see me about the drugs, you talked to him . . . when? Thursday?"

"And yesterday, both. He was very huffy about the idea that we thought he'd been doing drugs, and since we'd already searched his places with permission and not found anything, there wasn't much more we could do with that."

"How did he react to the idea that he'd drugged Debra?"

"First he laughed. Then he got really angry. That boy sure had a powerful temper," Rosalie O'Brien said.

"Yup. But you know, it's that temper that makes it so hard to believe he'd kill himself. I could never bring myself to think he'd kill somebody he loved as much as Debra, but I can almost picture him doing that more easily than shooting himself."

"You really can't see him as a suicide?"

"No," Nan said firmly. "I can't. Besides, there are too many other things I don't understand. Like whatever happened to Debra's past lives journal?"

"Does it matter?"

Nan hesitated. "I'm not exactly sure. But it strikes me as very strange that it hasn't turned up. If Debra was as dedicated to writing in it as Carleen McIlheney says, it should have been with her things. I know it wasn't in her house, and Carleen says it's not at the PLI. You're sure it wasn't with her stuff in the car?"

"All there was in the car was her purse and a little tote

bag with a change of clothes and some makeup, toothpaste, overnight things. No journal."

"But if she never got home from the PLI on Labor Day night, what happened to the journal?"

"I know what C.J. would say"—Rosalie O'Brien chuckled—"and it wouldn't be printable. He isn't too terribly taken with the gang up at the Past Lives Institute, including your boyfriend."

"Jonathan isn't my boyfriend," Nan answered shortly.

"Sorry. I had the impression—"

"I think," Nan said more slowly, "your impression is wrong. But even if it isn't, that doesn't have anything to do with Debra's missing journal. Listen, what happens to the insurance settlement with Tony dead too? Does it go to Tony's and Debra's parents?"

"I'm checking on that, but you'd probably have a better idea than I would. You're the lawyer."

"Not that kind of lawyer. My guess is that it becomes part of their estates, and if Tony died without a will the way Debra did, then it would be covered by the state intestacy provisions. It could also depend on how the settlement was worded. *Somebody* must be entitled to that money now. It doesn't stand to reason that a legitimate settlement would be nullified just because the principle recipients died. Otherwise, you'd expect insurance companies to have hit men skulking around taking out anybody who ever got a cent, State Farm and Allstate running classified ads in *U.S.A. Today* for mercenaries."

Detective O'Brien laughed heartily. "What a great image! C.J. will love the idea."

"Yeah, a new line of work if he ever leaves the force. Rosalie, your best bet is to call Jane Walinski again and see. Could you let me know when you find out?"

"Sure." The detective hesitated for a moment. "Perhaps I put this badly before. Am I mistaken in thinking you're likely to spend more time with Jonathan Henley?"

Nan laughed despite herself. "How diplomatic. No, I

don't think you're mistaken, but don't exaggerate the relationship."

"I wouldn't dream of it. But if you run across anything up there you think I ought to know about, I'm counting on you to tell me."

"But of course," Nan promised.

Jonathan arrived with a brimming bag of white waxed cartons at seven-thirty.

By then Nan knew she wouldn't turn him away at the door. By then she had, in fact, taken a long walk down to the beach, soaked in a hot bubble bath for an hour, washed her hair, dressed in a long dress printed with birds-of-paradise, and set a table for two with the Fiestaware she had collected during her marriage.

"What a nice place," Jonathan said, walking out toward the minuscule patio, admiring the framed tryptych above her white Haitian cotton sofa. He seemed slightly distant and distracted.

"It must seem like slumming to you," she demurred.

His laugh was hearty. "You're talking to a guy who grew up in a four-room shack behind a gas station, remember?"

"But that was a long time ago."

"Not so long that I'll ever forget it. Nan, don't sell yourself short, or your place. So, are you feeling better now?"

She nodded. "And I think I can keep on feeling better if you'll promise me one thing."

"It's yours," he answered without hesitation.

She laughed. "You don't know that I'm not planning to ask for a Rolls Corniche convertible."

"You want it . . ." He waved a hand magnanimously.

"Golly," she vamped, batting her eyes wildly. "Actually, what I'd like is a lot simpler. I'd like to try to forget about Debra tonight. And Tony."

"I think that's a swell idea," he said, putting his arms around her and kissing her.

By the time they got around to the Szechuan dinner, it was stone cold.

CHAPTER 13

Nan woke to the sound of Jonathan's deep breathing and water rushing through pipes in the wall just behind her head. Jonathan stirred beside her, opened one eye, and reached for her with a slow, lazy smile.

"What a nice way to wake up," he said, much later. "I'm going to miss you."

"Oh?" She kept her tone low and neutral.

"I have to go back East," he explained. "It's a PLI grand tour. I'll be leaving late this afternoon and be gone almost two weeks."

"Oh?" she said again.

"Goodness, you sound suspicious." He chuckled. "It's no big deal. I do this two or three times a year. You know we have permanent regional offices in Houston, Atlanta, and Boston."

April had explained all that. Each eastern office was staffed by hypnotherapists and spiritual folks who taught meditation techniques, people Nan thought of privately as Om-makers. "So what happens?"

"The local people set up special programs. Dinners, seminars, promotions for the regression tours. We're pushing those hard right now. They're scheduled to run through the winter below the equator and right now they're undersubscribed."

"I'm amazed anybody goes at all," Nan told him. "I can see maybe wanting to do something like that on your own, but what's the point of going along on somebody else's trip?"

He swung his legs out of bed and walked to the window. He moved easily in the nude, and it was a pleasure to watch his body. Nan had seen plenty of movies where some narcissistic actor's rear end had a more prominent role than most of the supporting cast. Jonathan's butt was equal to any of them, better than many.

"You'd be surprised," he said, fiddling with the blinds. "There's a lot of genuine camaraderie. We try to pin everything down as precisely as possible in advance, but a lot of times we're trying to find an area where somebody lived hundreds, even thousands of years ago. People really get into the hunt, working together on location, so that even if we aren't always successful, at least the client comes away with the sense that a whole lot of really dedicated people gave it their all."

It seemed like a gargantuan rip-off to Nan, who kept the opinion to herself. "You ever go on those?"

He shuddered and sat down in the armchair by the window. "Not on your life. I went once and hated it. I'm not much of a traveler, to tell the truth. I don't even like going back to visit the regionals. The thought of being stuck in some Sicilian *pensione* gives me the willies. Most of our clients weren't thoughtful enough to live their previous lives in areas where there are first-class hotels today. Fortunately, I've got a staff of intrepid travelers who thrive on that sort of thing."

Enough of this nonsense. "When will you be back?"

"A week from Friday. After I go to the three regionals, some of the Boston staff and I are going to conduct special programs in four more cities. New York, Philadelphia, Washington, Chicago. We're looking to open two more regional offices this year and we have to decide which cities to target."

"How do you go about it?" Customary market research techniques somehow seemed grossly inadequate to the task.

"April sets it all up in advance. Basically, we blow into town and razzle-dazzle them out of their minds." He grinned. "Group regressions, intensive workshops, testimonials from satisfied previous clients who live in the area. A lot of people have come out here or visited one of the regionals for prolonged work, and they're thrilled at the idea of having a PLI office near their homes."

He stood up and walked back to the bed, sitting beside Nan and kissing her lightly. "I'm starving," he announced. "Let's shower and go out for some breakfast."

Upstairs, loud music began reverberating. The ceiling started to shake in rhythm. An aerobics workout for a small herd of rhinos, it sounded like. "What?" Nan asked. "And leave paradise?"

He laughed. "After that, I'd like to take a look at that house you're thinking about buying."

Shannon was waiting in her living room, fully made up and in her best summer silk slacks. Nan watched Jonathan as she introduced them, saw his eyes narrow slightly and a smile begin.

"Shannon Revell," he said slowly. "Shannon Revell. I don't believe this. When I was ten years old, I had the most amazing crush on you."

Shannon stared for a moment, and Nan would have sworn her friend started to blush. "Oh, come on," Shannon simpered. She gave Nan a look of mild accusation. Normally Shannon didn't like to dwell on her showbiz background, though she *had* retained her stage name through four marriages and countless careers.

"I didn't say a word," Nan told her. "Honest."

"She's telling the truth," Jonathan assured Shannon. "Out where we lived when I was a kid, we could only get reception for one TV network. Yours. *Our Family* was the highlight of my week."

"He's a salesman," Nan told Shannon. "Pay no attention to anything he says."

"Don't be absurd," Shannon shot back. "He just made my week, and there's still six and a half days to go. Now. Anybody want to see a charming little bungalow for sale at a terrific price in a wonderful neighborhood?"

By the time they left, Jonathan seemed ready to call Bekins on Nan's behalf. "I love Venice," he said, pulling out of the alley behind Shannon's house. "When I lived down on the Strand, I used to sit at the Ocean Front Café for hours at a stretch and watch the madness."

"This is pretty far away from there," Nan pointed out.

"These days that's not such a terrible thing. All the homeless down at the beach, it's pretty depressing. Dangerous, too. I don't know if I'd think you were safe at the beach."

Nan was surprised to find she rather liked the idea that Jonathan was worried about her safety. The truth was that the incident with the flea bomb in her car had shaken her badly. Had Tony done that? He knew where she worked and he certainly was familiar with the Mustang. But it seemed wildly out of character for him to call in the middle of the night to tell her to bug off.

As if, Nan realized suddenly, she had any idea what was actually in character for Tony Fontaine, a virtual stranger.

Now a dead stranger.

They drove to Century City to pick up April, who had met friends in town the night before for dinner and a movie.

"It must be really rough to maintain any kind of decent private life," Nan suggested, as they swept along the curves on Motor past big, comfortable family homes, "when you live way the hell out in Malibu with your brother, for God's sake, and you don't even drive."

"Not really," Jonathan replied. "Of course it was easier when she lived in Santa Monica and took the Big Blue Bus everywhere. It's really not that hard to get around LA by public transportation if you put a little thought into it."

"Oh yeah? When was the last time *you* rode the bus?"

He chuckled. "High school. It was big and yellow and stopped right out front of the house."

"Does April have a boyfriend?" Nan asked.

"Not that I'm aware of," he answered.

"Has she ever been married?"

"My goodness, you're a nosy little thing."

Nan smiled. "I ask questions for a living. And you didn't answer my last one."

"Yeah. She was married in Denver a long time ago to a guy named Will Domanick. The Henleys have a way of marrying the wrong people when we're too young."

Nan didn't feel quite ready to get into that one. Apart from his public statements at the introductory seminar, Jonathan had said nothing to Nan about his failed marriage, and she'd been equally mum on the subject of Leon. "What happened to her husband?"

Jonathan shrugged as he turned onto Pico. "I suppose he's still in Denver. To tell the truth, I haven't thought about him for years. April never talks about her marriage. She's a pretty private person."

The private person was waiting, in running shorts and shoes, outside a high-rise condominium. Beside her stood a doorman dressed like an organ grinder's monkey. April climbed into the backseat.

"Thanks," April said. "Boy, I'm glad that heat broke. I just had a great run. Hope I'm not too gamy. I didn't think I'd have time to shower before you got here."

"You run every day?" Nan asked.

"Just about," she answered. "I really love to work out."

That seemed a bit of a conversational dead end to Nan, who worked out mainly because her body began to sag and pooch in all the wrong places when she didn't.

"How was the movie?" Jonathan asked.

"Overrated." April sighed. "I don't understand how you can start with so much talent and end up with such a lousy movie. More and more, I wonder why I bother to even go."

"We're too old for the movies they make today," Nan agreed.

"Please," April moaned, "don't remind me. It's like Bartholomew was saying the other day—we're all turning into old farts. I never dreamed I'd turn into the kind of person who bitches about the good old days."

"None of us did," Nan said. "But here we are."

"You girls want to stop by the Senior Citizens' Center for a little light lunch?" Jonathan asked. "They're having tuna puff today, easy to chew."

Everybody laughed and Nan sat back, feeling much more comfortable. In the normal course of events, there'd be no occasion to meet a new lover's family until the relationship was on fairly stable ground, and even then it was always awkward. Having Jonathan's sister on the scene, actually sharing the same address, was an unorthodox variation on the theme. But Nan recognized the melody.

"Carleen's bringing her kids to use the pool today," Jonathan said. "I forgot to tell you she called yesterday afternoon."

"How nice," April answered, a bit grimly. "I was just thinking what fun it would be to watch Jamie pull the wings off flies while Allison colors on the wall."

"Oh, those kids aren't so bad," Jonathan protested.

"Ha!" April snorted. "Nan, how do you feel about children and discipline?"

"I don't think I want to get in the middle of this one," Nan answered carefully. "All I know about kids is that whenever my friends have them, I never see them again. My friends, that is."

"Raising children is all-consuming if you do it properly." April sniffed.

Nan remembered the drawing of the dragon devouring the red-haired lady on Carleen's office wall. It would probably be very instructive to see the little McIlheneys in action.

"What's that place?" Nan asked as they passed a dilapidated stone structure on one of the sharper bends in the road leading up to the Past Lives Institute. It appeared uninhabited, appeared, indeed, not to even have a roof. "I always wonder when I go by, and then I forget to ask."

"It belonged to some early settler," April answered. "Some eccentric who wanted to get away from it all. As far as I know, it's been sitting there empty for fifty years. I don't see why somebody doesn't tear it down."

"I'm surprised there aren't a couple dozen homeless people camped out in it," Nan said.

"Please." Jonathan grimaced. "Don't even suggest it." He spoke over his shoulder to April. "Nan's thinking of buying a house on one of the Venice walk streets."

"Mentioning the homeless brought that to mind?" Nan asked.

"Hardly," he answered. "It's a great little place," he went on, "and it's also that much closer to here."

Nan laughed as they rounded the final turn and the Past Lives Institute spread out before them. A white stretch limo was parked outside the front entrance. "The distance between that place and here is measured in a lot more than miles."

"Hey, we're just folks," he replied with a grin, pulling his eighty-thousand-dollar Mercedes into the garage beside a Jeep Ranchero that could probably climb Mount McKinley.

Loud shrieks and splashes came from the pool. Wrinkling her nose, April disappeared inside her bungalow while Jonathan and Nan went to meet the McIlheneys.

"Hey!" Carleen said cheerfully. "How are you guys doing?" She wore a gauze caftan, wide-brimmed hat, and a smudge of zinc oxide on her nose. This was a woman engaged in mortal combat with the sun. She introduced Nan to her husband, Len, a broad soft fellow ineffectually supervising two small children in the shallow end of the pool. The little boy was systematically trying to overturn the inflated Snoopy seat his sister rode in.

By the time Nan and Jonathan had changed into swimsuits and returned to the pool, the kids were separated and Len was giving Allison a swimming lesson. Jamie had a fleet of little cars and trucks engaged in a sprightly demolition derby at his mother's feet.

"What have you found out about Tony?" Carleen asked. Nan reported most of what she'd learned from Rosalie

O'Brien the afternoon before. Carleen listened carefully, nodding and making occasional "hmms" and "ohs."

"Poor Tony," Carleen said finally. "He had such a terrible childhood."

"Oh?" Nan asked. Once again, Carleen was skating on ethical thin ice. On the other hand, Tony *was* dead and if Carleen could help explain that, Nan was willing to forgive a broached confidence or two.

"Let's go get some cold drinks," Jonathan suggested to little Jamie. He had wiggled restlessly through Nan's recital of the Tony story. "Would you like some juice?"

"Soda pop," the little boy said firmly. "And I don't wanna go."

"I can't carry everything myself," Jonathan explained with a disarming smile.

"Tough," Jamie answered. He picked up a small airplane and began flying it around the pool deck. Jonathan shrugged and took drink orders, then disappeared inside.

"Tony was adopted," Carleen explained. "His parents had tried to get pregnant forever and then they finally adopted Tony, which should have been a happy ending except his mother got pregnant then and had what they always called their 'real' son."

"How unfair," Nan murmured sympathetically.

"His father used to beat him when he was a kid, for no reason at all."

Remembering Tony's scorn for the PLI and his story of driving up just to take a look at the place, Nan realized that Carleen's information was at best multiple hearsay. Still, it was all that was available.

"Was that why Tony beat Debra?" Nan asked. Two could play the pop psych game.

"Oh, certainly. But their relationship also had really tangled roots in their past lives together."

"Lives plural?"

"Uh-huh. They'd been together in, oh gosh, I think it was three different lives."

Nan decided to play it straight. "Tony just mentioned one

to me that Debra told him about, where they'd neglected a child together." She had meant to ask him more about that. It was odd to think that it was too late now. Too late forever.

"That was the most dramatic," Carleen said. "The poor child was sick and they didn't get any kind of medical help until it was far too late."

"What made them think the baby could have been saved?"

"They didn't realize it at the time, perhaps, but after the life was ended and they evaluated it with their higher selves, that information became clear. In a regression, you don't just get the facts, you get the full story."

By Looney Toons. "What were their other lives together like?"

"One was relatively innocuous," Carleen said, frowning slightly. The white goo on her nose wrinkled. "They were something like brother and sister, or good friends. Then there was another where he was killed in a war before they had a chance to really spend any time together. Before this life, the last one was the one we've already talked about as French peasants in Marseilles."

"Where the child died?"

"Yeah."

Nothing Carleen said made any of this seem a bit less wacky. Still, Nan's curiosity was getting the better of her. A lifelong control freak, she was not about to let anybody hypnotize her personally, not even Jonathan whom she felt fairly certain she trusted. But more and more the idea of delving into one's past through hypnosis intrigued her. Even the malarkey about long-dead French peasants.

"You told me once all these hypnotic regressions were taped. Do you still have Debra's tapes?"

"Oh sure," Carleen answered. "We keep all of them. I think that Debra transcribed some of hers, too."

Somehow that wasn't surprising. Miss Perfect, typing a hundred odd words a minute, would consider that a perfectly reasonable task.

"Would you have the transcripts?"

Carleen frowned, then jumped as Jamie raced at her from behind and crashed his airplane into the back of her head. "Now, Jamie," she said gently, "let's not have any more of that or we'll have to have a time out."

At the California Youth Authority, Nan thought grimly. She understood now why April had made herself scarce.

Jamie stuck his tongue out at Carleen, then raced down the length of the pool to attack his sister. Carleen shook her head. "Where was I?"

Maternal la-la land. "The transcripts of Debra's regression tapes."

"Oh, right. I don't know if those are here or not, but I'm sure the tapes are. The police took the originals, but I have copies."

"Do you suppose I could listen to some of them?" Nan asked. The very notion was a gross invasion of privacy, but all the invadees were dead, after all.

"Listen to what?" Jonathan asked, returning with a tray of assorted drinks.

"Debra's regression tapes," Nan answered, taking a tall piña colada in a frosty glass. "I thought they might be interesting, give me a little insight. Is there a problem with that?"

Jonathan stared at her strangely. "I guess there's no reason why not," he replied after a moment.

From the far end of the pool Allison let out a wail they could probably hear down at the Zuma lifeguard station. Jamie had her pinned to the pool deck and was sticking his fingers in her eye. Len had disappeared.

"Oh my," Carleen murmured helplessly. She fluttered a bit, but didn't quite make it to her feet.

Instead it was Jonathan who pulled the little hellion off his sister. Nan, hesitantly moving closer, could hear him speak softly to the little boy.

"Do that again," Jonathan said in a pleasant, soothing tone, "and I'll put *my* fingers in *your* eyes."

Nan had never admired him more.

* * *

Later, when Carleen took the kids inside to change, Nan found herself alone for the first time with Len McIlheney. He was a little bit smashed and had a rising bruise on his shin where Jamie had kicked him when told it was time to get out of the pool.

"It must take a lot of energy keeping up with those kids," Nan said carefully.

"They're frisky," he agreed. "But Carleen mostly does that. And her mother takes care of them when we're both at work. I can be pretty flexible about my schedule, though." He chuckled. "That's one advantage to having your own business."

"You've had the limo service for a long time?"

"Just a couple years. It started as an offshoot of a car rental operation I had, specializing in exotics. Convertibles, old Jaguars, fifty-seven T-birds, that kind of thing."

"How interesting!"

Len groaned. "You could put it that way. It ended up being more trouble than it was worth. You've got to keep the cars in really great shape and people drive the shit out of them. The insurance was killing me."

"So you gave it up?"

"It kind of gave me up. Some joker rented a sixty-three Vette and took it out to Palm Springs so his kid could be cool over spring break. The kid gets it out on a desert straightaway and rods the shit out of it. It blows a tire at ninety-five, and then they turn around and sue me for not maintaining it properly."

"Surely your insurance would cover—"

"By that time I was already spending more time with my insurance adjustor than my family. I figured the hell with it and unloaded the car rentals. Took a loss, but tough. The limo service was already set up, but I hadn't done much with it yet. That was all I kept."

"And you made an arrangement with the PLI?" Nan asked.

Len smiled. "Jonathan was really great—gave me a nice

boost when I really needed it. Allison was born with a hole in her heart, had three operations before she was one. The medical bills were killing us. Jonathan set it up so we'd do all the transportation for the PLI. It helped us hold things together there at the beginning."

A shriek behind Nan announced the return of Len McIlheney's family. His face brightened as Allison, in a little red-and-white polka dot sundress, hurtled onto his lap and wrapped her arms around her daddy's neck. He hugged her tightly.

A baby needing heart surgery would be an incredible financial *and* emotional drain on a family. Was Carleen expecting some kind of financial help from Debra, who would obviously be sympathetic to a baby with health problems? That could be a motive for murder, but only if an arrangement had been made, and there was no sign of one. No will, no transfer of funds, nothing obvious.

Apart from that, however, Nan realized how hard it would be for Carleen to leave her kids to come up here each day. And what would she find when she got to the PLI? The frivolous worries of rich people who thought they'd be happy if they knew they'd been spittoon polishers at the Continental Congress. While her own kids, far more needy of her attention, were cared for by somebody else. Perhaps the awareness of their fragility explained why Carleen was so overindulgent to her children.

On the other hand, Nan thought, heading indoors to find another drink, it could be as simple as the old adage about the cobbler's children.

Two piña coladas later, Nan knocked on the door of Brother Bartholomew's cottage.

He swung the door open, dressed in faded cutoff Levi's and a T-shirt that announced ELVIS LIVES over four renderings of the King in various disguises. It was the first time Nan had ever seen him in anything but his robes. In mufti, he was just another aging hippie.

He was clearly startled to see Nan there. Sandalwood incense was burning, with a faint underlay of marijuana. The Moody Blues' *In Search of the Lost Chord* played at high volume.

"Could I talk to you for a minute?" she asked.

"Sure," he answered slowly, "come on in."

The interior walls of his little house were white, the floor a gleaming polished hardwood. A large and complicated woven hanging in earth tones covered much of one wall. A couch and two armchairs were fashioned from huge chunks of redwood burl, and a glass slab topped another piece of redwood as a coffee table. Apart from the stereo, that was it.

"Musically I guess I'm living in the past," he said, turning down the volume.

"Actually," Nan said, "I always really liked that album, and I haven't heard it in years. Besides, isn't the past the raison d'être for this whole place?"

He grinned suddenly. Nan realized that she'd never seen him give a truly big smile. It changed his face, altered his entire countenance. But before she got sucked in by his charm, there was business to take care of.

"Was Debra in love with you?" she asked abruptly, sitting unbidden on one of the redwood chairs. It was spectacularly uncomfortable.

He opened his eyes wide and sat down on the couch across from her, picking up a half-finished joint from a small ashtray and lighting it. "You don't beat around the bush, do you?"

"Oh, I can," Nan told him airily, "but sometimes there doesn't seem any point."

He took a long toke on the joint and offered it to her.

"No thanks," she said, twisting to see if there might be a more comfortable position in the chair. There wasn't. Maybe it was part of a program of mortification of the flesh. Somehow, though, she didn't think flesh was frequently mortified around Bartholomew's house, unless maybe he was into spanking.

He inhaled again deeply and set the joint down. He

leaned back. "Why do you think Debra would be in love with me?"

"Because she fell in love easily, for one thing." The piña coladas had really loosened her tongue. "Because she'd been through a helluva year. And because you're the type of man she'd fall for."

"A man of the cloth?" he asked with a twisted smile.

"No," she answered shortly. "An ex-con."

His reaction surprised her. He burst out laughing, laughed so hard that he began to cough. When he recovered, he gave that big grin again. "You really *don't* beat around the bush. Well, my past isn't something I talk about a lot, but it's not a secret, either."

"Did Debra know about it, Albert?"

He made a horrible face. "No," he said, "and please. I think it was being named Albert that drove me to crime in the first place. I was called Al unless you wanted your face rearranged. And I haven't been called that for a long, long time. I have a new life and a new name."

"I guess this isn't really relevant, but why 'Bartholomew'?"

He raised both hands, palms up. "Why not? Bartholomew was one of the lesser disciples, only mentioned once in the New Testament. But later on, he was a missionary to Asia and found his true calling there. There's a parallel to my own life, a little shaky maybe, but I liked it."

Nan tried to remember her disciples, without success. "How did Bartholomew end up?"

"Sainted for martyrdom in Armenia. The accounts vary. Some say he was crucified, others have him beheaded or flayed alive."

"Couldn't you regress yourself and find out for sure?" Nan asked.

He laughed. "That would only work if I'd actually *been* Bartholomew in one of my own past lives. Which I wasn't. You're laboring under a common misconception about past lives. They aren't what you'd like them to have been. They're what they were."

"Whatever," Nan said. "But we're getting a little far afield of Debra here. Was she in love with you?"

"Probably," he admitted. "No, that's not really fair. I'd say she almost certainly was. And no, I wasn't in love with her, even though I loved her. You understand the distinction?"

"Of course. Don't patronize me."

"I didn't intend to. Debra . . . Debra was a drifting soul, and she just happened to pull into this harbor. She was looking for answers, trying to make sense of things, looking to nourish her spiritual side. Adversity often brings people to religion, of course."

Nan nodded, with greater understanding than she'd have been willing to share with this ersatz holy man. During her adolescence, when her father's drinking and its impact on the entire Robinson family came into real focus for the first time, Nan had taken refuge in the First Methodist Church and the memorization of scripture. Once she'd even gone to McCormick Place to the Billy Graham Crusades.

"She was terribly vulnerable," he went on, "and I think it was fortunate for her that she came here. Believe me, plenty of worse things could have happened to somebody in her state."

"She ended up dead," Nan reminded him.

"But that had nothing to do with us."

Nan wasn't so sure. Tony, already frustrated by his inability to regain Debra's affections, had been outraged at the idea she was being exploited by these people. And Debra, in an attempt to convince Tony their marriage was truly over, might well have mentioned her affair with Brother Bartholomew.

"Maybe not directly," she said finally. "But are you trying to tell me it was healthy for her to have an affair with somebody who wanted her to think that her problems were a result of all this past lives business?"

"I'm thirsty," Bartholomew said, rising abruptly. "Would you like something to drink? I have beer and lemonade."

"Lemonade would be nice." Frustrated, Nan followed him to his kitchen.

It didn't look like a place where complicated culinary activity—or any activity at all, for that matter—went on. The counters were totally clear, the stove spotless, and the refrigerator empty except for a couple of sixpacks of Dos Equis and a Rubbermaid pitcher. He took glasses from a cupboard and filled them with lemonade, then walked back into the living room. The album had ended, and he turned it over.

"Let me explain something to you," he said. "Nobody from the PLI sought Debra out. We didn't know who she was or what her problems were. She came up here one day with that goofy hairdresser—what's his name?"

"Alistair?"

"Right. Alistair. She came up here with Alistair, and it felt right to her. She told me she thought she was coming home. She loved the idea of hypnotic regression and she was fascinated by what she was learning about herself. As far as any physical relationship I had with her, it was totally unrelated to her own quest for self-knowledge. She's the one who came on to me, and to be perfectly honest I was reluctant to get involved with her. You know—never eat at a place called Mom's and never sleep with anybody whose problems are worse than your own."

"But you did."

"But I did. I made it clear from the very beginning that I wasn't in a position to make any kind of permanent commitment to her and she said that didn't matter."

If he'd known Debra as well as he purported, he must have realized that would only make him more appealing. Debra, the eternal romantic, would be sure she could change him.

"When did it end?" Nan asked.

His eyes widened again and bored into her own.

"It never did," he answered. "That was why I was so certain something was wrong when she disappeared. She

didn't even come by to say good-bye the last night she was
here."

❋

The killer lay awake late into the night. It seemed that the
police were satisfied with Tony Fontaine's "suicide."

That was nice.

But there was something strangely upsetting about having everything over with. Let the police close the file, by
all means. Let everybody go back to their normal routines.
Let time settle things down.

But there wouldn't be any of that heady excitement for
a while, none of the adrenaline surges that accompanied
even something as simple as hearing Nan Robinson gasp in
the middle of the night at an unbidden phone call. The odd
satisfaction of so harmless an act as slitting the canvas convertible top and pushing the button on the flea bomb in her
car.

It would be hard to give all that up.

Of course everything would be disrupted again later,
when the big shock came. It would only be possible to
imagine what was happening then, of course, not to witness
it personally. Would that prove disappointing, diminish the
pleasure somehow?

Perhaps, but probably not for long.

But there was no need now to hurry that, and every reason to wait. If not patiently, at least with the semblance of
patience. It had been a long time coming, and it would last
a long time once it happened.

They'd be sorry then.

Sorry? Maybe.

Baffled? Certainly.

For now though, there was still this curious letdown. Perhaps this was the way that military leaders felt on successfully completing an offensive.

Did they also wish that it didn't have to end?

Of course, maybe it didn't. . . .

CHAPTER 14

Debra's voice in Nan's living room was jarring, spooky, with that odd sense that comes from knowing the speaker is gone and won't ever be heard alive again. It wasn't Martin Luther King vowing, "I have a dream," or John Kennedy announcing *"Ich bin ein Berliner,"* or even John Lennon burbling about starting over.

But it was deeply unsettling.

After two false starts, Nan found herself manufacturing small chores to be completed before actually getting down to the business of listening to Debra's hypnosis tapes. She freshened her glass of iced tea, wiped off the glass top on her coffee table, emptied the dishwasher. She set out the clothes she'd wear to work the next day, changed her sheets, and started a load of laundry.

She even read once more through the copies of Debra's letters to her mother. Aside from the reference in the last one to something troubling Debra, they remained as unenlightening as ever. By then Nan needed more iced tea.

Finally, there was no getting around it. She pushed the Play button and sat back to listen.

The first tape began with Carleen McIlheney's soothing explanation to Debra of what she intended to do, her exhortations to the subject to lie back and make herself comfortable.

CARLEEN: *Are you ready to begin?*
DEBRA: *Yes.*
CARLEEN: *Take a nice deep breath now, close your eyes,*

and begin to relax. Begin with the top of your head and let waves of relaxation sweep gently down toward your toes. As the waves lap down the surface of your body, you will feel each muscle loosening and you will feel more and more comfortable. Listen to your breathing as you inhale and exhale. Now relax your breathing. Let it grow slower, rhythmic. Notice any normal sounds around you and realize that they are unimportant. Ignore them, let them drop away like petals from a flower. Begin relaxing your face now, with the muscles in your jaw going loose, your teeth separating. . . .

Carleen went on in a similar vein for several minutes, to the point where Nan suddenly realized she was going slack and limp on her own couch. Startled, she switched off the tape recorder and paced briskly around the room a couple of times. Then she sat down in a deliberately less comfortable position, turned the machine back on, and waited for Carleen's lengthy induction to end.

CARLEEN: *We're going to move backward through time now. I want you to move back across the years and find a time in your childhood when you were totally happy and relaxed. When you reach that time, tell me.*

DEBRA: *I'm there.*

CARLEEN: *Where are you?*

DEBRA: *Down by the lake with Angela and Jimmy.*

CARLEEN: *Who are Angela and Jimmy?*

DEBRA: *Friends. They have the cottage next to us.*

CARLEEN: *How old are you?*

DEBRA: *I just had my ninth birthday last week.*

CARLEEN: *Tell me about what you and your friends are doing.*

DEBRA: *We're collecting fireflies. Angela's mama gave us Mason jars and we're trying to fill the jars. It's a contest and so far Jimmy's got the most. He always wins, but that's 'cause he's older.*

CARLEEN: *Where do you live?*

DEBRA: *Spring Hill, but we're at the lake right now.*
CARLEEN: *What lake is that?*
DEBRA: *Just the lake. We come here in the summer every year.*
CARLEEN: *Where is the lake?*
DEBRA: *Way far away from home, a long ride.*

Carleen moved Debra through fifteen minutes or so of reminiscence about her childhood. There were familiar settings: the nearby park in Spring Hill where neighborhood kids went to play; Queen of Martyrs, the Catholic elementary school Debra had attended. Nan had a sudden memory of Debra, pig-tailed in her ugly gray plaid school uniform.

Then Carleen asked her to move backward through time again, back before she was born, to find another happy moment. Nan was startled by Debra's sudden laughter.

CARLEEN: *Where are you now?*
DEBRA: *At the Masons' house-raising. Everybody's come from all around the county. Old Miltie's playing his fiddle and Granny Hopkins is dancing the funniest jig. I can't believe Granny's being so silly.*
CARLEEN: *Where do you live? What county?*
DEBRA: *Why, Clay County, of course.*
CARLEEN: *Where is that?*
DEBRA: *Kansas, along the Republican River.*
CARLEEN: *Can you tell me what year it is?*
DEBRA: *Why, 1872.*
CARLEEN: *And who are you? Tell me about yourself.*
DEBRA: *I'm Catherine Wood. My husband, Henry, and I came here from Indiana three years ago and we live in a soddie about four miles downstream. Next year we plan to put up a house of our own aboveground. We were planning to build this year, but then we lost most of our hay and cattle in the fire.*

Carleen asked Debra a lot more questions about this life. Nan was intrigued by the differences in Debra's speech patterns as she took on this other identity. It was the same voice, but the language and cadence differed, almost as if it actually *were* some other entity.

Debra/Catherine detailed a family in Indiana, spoke glowingly of her Kansas children, sketched a portrait of a placid and unremarkable relationship with her husband, Henry. Then Carleen startled Nan by telling Debra she wished to speak with her superconscious mind.

CARLEEN: *How does Henry relate to your life as Debra?*
DEBRA: *Henry is my father.*

Uh-huh. Nan's skepticism Geiger counter started clicking merrily away. Next Carleen led Debra through a lengthy list of the people she had mentioned in the story of this Kansas life. Debra identified many of them as people from her current life, mostly from her early years in Spring Hill. Nan heard about Debra's parents, her grandparents, her teachers, and her best friend as a child, Megan Malone. Nan hadn't thought about Megan in decades.

Suddenly there came a shocker.

DEBRA: *And there's Nan, of course.*
CARLEEN: *Who's Nan?*
DEBRA: *Nan Robinson, my old boss. And of course my babysitter in Spring Hill. She was my mother in Indiana.*
CARLEEN: *You didn't specifically mention your mother earlier. Was there a particular significance to the relationship?*
DEBRA (laughing): *Yeah. She didn't want me to go to Kansas. And she hated Henry, said he wasn't good enough for me.*

Nan abruptly switched off the tape and went to find herself a beer. This was clearly preposterous. Debra was claiming that Nan had been her mother in Indiana during the Civil War. Sure. And they had front row seats together for the Gettysburg Address.

Of course it was no goofier than to assume that Megan Malone had been there, or Debra's mother and father from this life.

But the weird and truly unnerving part was that Debra was so matter-of-fact about the statement, her laughter so achingly familiar. It was the same laugh she'd always used when Nan suggested, ever so politely, that one of Debra's boyfriends should be allowed to crawl back under his rock, or that the cost of a bottle of Elizabeth Taylor's Passion might better be invested in groceries.

Did this mean that Nan had been looking out for Debra through the ages, and that Debra had found it amusing for millennia?

Hold on. Did this mean that Nan herself was buying into this folderol, embracing this tomfoolery?

Of course not. What Debra had believed was precisely that: what Debra believed. It had no demonstrable basis in fact, no more than any of the reincarnation literature Jonathan and Shannon had thrust upon Nan in the past few weeks. She had read some of it, sure, was convinced that these authors genuinely believed themselves to be dealing with sequential lives. Some of their "evidence," particularly the University of Virginia studies of children, was curiously compelling.

But that didn't mean that Nan had to go along with it.

It would be nice to feel a sense that there was some kind of order to the universe, that life and death weren't merely haphazard. But it was tough to square that notion with the fact that Milton Berle and Dean Martin had lived twice as long as Gilda Radner and Steve Goodman. Or that Adolf Hitler had lived at all.

On the other hand, if the notion of reincarnation was all balderdash, then why was it so damned unsettling to listen to Debra's tapes?

Nan finished the beer and started another, wishing she had the transcripts Debra had supposedly made. Carleen hadn't been able to find them anywhere, belatedly remembered that she'd already looked once at the cops' request.

The absence of the transcripts meant that Nan needed to listen to something like thirty hours of this poppycock. At this rate, it would take till Christmas.

Of course she didn't *really* need to listen to anything. It was all over, finished. Debra was buried in South Bend, Tony down in the morgue. Nan's lingering doubts probably didn't mean anything. Tony was capable of violence, probably capable of slipping Debra a Quaalude in hopes it would mellow her out. And if he could kill his one true love, he could certainly kill himself.

She shook her head. It felt too neat.

Somehow she was sure she owed it to Debra to listen to the rest of the tapes. And there was another consideration. Nan Robinson had made one cameo appearance already. Even if the whole thing were hogwash, her curiosity would never permit her to stop listening now.

She started the tape again and listened for another five minutes with no major revelations before the session ended. She started a second tape and listened to Carleen induce Debra again, tell her subject to move backward through time until she found a lifetime where she and Tony Fontaine had previously been together.

This was more like it.

CARLEEN: *Where are you?*
DEBRA: *Marseilles, near the docks.*
CARLEEN: *What is your name?*
DEBRA: *Anne-Marie. Anne-Marie Broussard.*
CARLEEN: *Tell me about your life.*
DEBRA: *Louis and I . . . we are terribly poor.* (Long silence.)
CARLEEN: *Are you happy?*
DEBRA (hesitantly): *No.*
CARLEEN: *Do you know what year it is?*
DEBRA: *It is the year of the new pope.*
CARLEEN: *I see. Is Louis your husband?*
DEBRA: *Yes.*
CARLEEN: *Do you have children?*

DEBRA: *Seven.* (Defiantly). *We have seven children who survived, Louis and I. Seven.*

CARLEEN: *You seem upset discussing your children. Is there some reason for that?*

DEBRA: *It ... it is Jean-Paul. Jean-Paul is our oldest son, but Louis says ... sometimes he says he is not the father of the boy.*

CARLEEN (very gently): *Is Louis Jean-Paul's father?*

DEBRA: *Of course he is. A thousand times I have told him that, but always he doubts me.* (Rising urgency.) *When Louis and I were betrothed, he was still able to go out on the fishing boats. There was a boy apprenticed to the tailor, Pierre, who was fond of me. But I never, never ... Pierre was my friend, that is all ... and then Jean-Paul was born early, and Louis, he said ...*

The distress in Debra's voice was unmistakable. As Carleen eased her through the story, Nan ached for the girl. Something was happening here, and Nan wasn't qualified to say what it was. Maybe it was Debra's too-vivid imagination or some kind of semiconscious dream or a mutant form of schizophrenia. Maybe, though Nan wasn't ready to believe this just yet, it was actually a past-life experience.

But whatever it was, it was clearly devastating to Debra. When Carleen spoke again, her voice was firmer.

CARLEEN: *Anne-Marie, this is obviously very painful for you. I want you to understand that nothing you are telling me now can hurt you. You are safe and protected. Do you understand that?*

DEBRA: *Yes.*

CARLEEN: *Do you love Jean-Paul?*

DEBRA (hesitates): *Yes. Yes, of course I do. But my life, it would be easier if he had never been born.*

CARLEEN: *I understand. Tell me about Louis, now. Does he work?*

DEBRA (bitter laugh): *When he can. Louis ... he makes people angry sometimes. And he is not a healthy man.*

When we were first married, he worked on the docks, selling fish. Always he smelled of fish. Our house, it smelled of fish. But Monsieur Richard, he made Louis leave, he said Louis was stealing. After that, Louis could find no work for a long time, almost a year. Father Bernard, he let Louis work in the stables at the church, but Louis hated it. It made his coughing worse, he said.

CARLEEN: *What does Louis do now?*

DEBRA: *He cleans fish on the docks when he can. It is hard for him to work. He has a terrible cough all the time.*

CARLEEN: *That must be very difficult for you. Does Louis treat you well?*

DEBRA: *He is my husband.*

CARLEEN: *I understand that. Does he love you?*

DEBRA: *He is my husband.*

CARLEEN: *You're very loyal, Anne-Marie, and that's good. But what I'm hearing suggests that perhaps Louis takes out his frustrations on you somehow.*

DEBRA: *(Silence.)*

CARLEEN: *Anne-Marie, does Louis ever hurt you?*

DEBRA: *Only when I behave stupidly.*

CARLEEN: *What do you mean by "behave stupidly"?*

DEBRA: *(Silence.)*

CARLEEN: *All right. If you'd rather not talk about that, why don't you tell me about your son Jean-Paul, then. How old is he?*

DEBRA: *Twelve. (Defensively.) Louis says Jean-Paul should go to work, but Jean-Paul is not well. He has never been well.*

CARLEEN: *What's the matter with him?*

DEBRA: *He is lame, he was born with a twisted leg. He has always been weak, always. Louis calls him lazy, but that is not true. Jean-Paul is not strong, that is all. He is very smart. But he is not strong.*

This was mean, heavy stuff, and Nan felt uncomfortable and queasy, the way she had the semester in law school when the couple in the next apartment were going through a loud and messy marital breakup. But now, as then, she couldn't stop listening.

Carleen, with a lilt in her voice that suggested she'd hit paydirt, next flashed Debra/Anne-Marie forward, telling her to move to a time or event that was particularly significant in her family relationships. Debra/Anne-Marie detailed a terrible argument with Louis about whether Jean-Paul should be sent out on a fishing boat. The argument ended with Anne-Marie's arm broken. She attributed the broken arm to her own intractability.

Louis won the argument and Jean-Paul went to sea. Carleen instructed her subject to move forward in time again.

DEBRA: *Jean-Paul is quite sick now, but it is all right, he will soon be better. He merely caught cold from the storm they were in coming back from Naples. I am not worried. The money from when he went to sea helps—we have shoes for the children now. Louis was right, Louis always is right.*

Or maybe not.

A few months later, Jean-Paul lay dreadfully ill while Anne-Marie prayed for his recovery and Louis cursed that the boy wasn't out swabbing decks and making a decent wage. Jean-Paul had missed out on another chance to sail to Italy and it was wreaking havoc in the economics of the Broussard household.

Nan was startled to find herself, the dispassionate listener who didn't believe in reincarnation, wanting Louis himself scuttled at sea.

DEBRA: *Mama says Jean-Paul must see a doctor, that he must have a bloodletting, that it is his only chance. She does not understand that the boy will be well soon and able to go out again on the boats, perhaps on the next boat for Naples. We must have his wages. Louis's cough*

*is much worse and he can no longer work on the docks
for more than an hour or two at a time.*
CARLEEN: *Are the other children healthy?*
DEBRA: *Except for little Genevieve, but she is like Jean-
Paul, always sickly. Louis says, and he is right of course,
that it would be foolish to have the doctor come, that we
have no money for a doctor, that then no one could eat.*

Shortly thereafter, Jean-Paul stopped eating for good.
Debra/Anne-Marie's voice was dull and uninflected, full of
stifled pain and defensive resignation.

DEBRA: *He is not the first one I lost, after all. There were
the babies who died at birth, the two little boys, and the
first Genevieve who died as a baby.* (Defiantly.) *It was
not my fault, nor the fault of Louis. This is the will of
God.*
CARLEEN: *Do you miss Jean-Paul?*
DEBRA: *Do I miss him?*
CARLEEN: *Yes.*
DEBRA: *He was my oldest son, my first-born. Louis is still
coughing badly, but he is not so angry all the time. Jean-
Paul is with God.*
CARLEEN (insistently): *But do you miss Jean-Paul?*
DEBRA (softly, after a long silence): *No. I am glad he is
dead.*

There it was, the bombshell.

Carleen brought Debra out of that miserable lifetime, had
Debra's superconscious self identify Louis and Jean-Paul as
Tony and Timmy, respectively, of the late twentieth century.
Then, with exhortations that Debra was not to feel guilt or
anxiety about the experience she had just undergone,
Carleen brought her subject back to real life.

Whatever that was.

Nan turned off the cassette player, shaking.

This was what had so upset Debra, had led her to believe
that little Timmy's death was a karmic payback. Listening

to the tape, Nan could understand perfectly how deeply affected Debra would have been by the experience.

But Nan couldn't quite picture Tony Fontaine sitting in a fancy restaurant, trying to woo back his true love, listening to Debra tell this horrendous story. Tony would want to talk about having another baby, moving back to Canyon Country, putting Timmy and his terrible accident behind them, pretending none of it had ever really happened. While Debra wanted to wallow in some wretched Marseilles slum where babies died as a matter of course and a first-born son went neglected to his death because she, the boy's mother, was afraid to defy her husband, Tony, and seek medical help.

Tony would not have wanted to hear any of it.

Hearing the tape accomplished one thing, however. For the first time, Nan was able to seriously entertain the possibility that Tony had killed Debra.

It was almost a week before Nan got back to the tapes again.

She went in early to work and stayed late, throwing herself into the familiar routines that had always structured her life. On Wednesday night before her session with Moira Callahan, she went by the house on Glorioso Way again, liking the way it looked in the waning evening sun, sitting cross-legged under the bougainvillea, not even minding that she was grinding permanent dirt into a perfectly nice dress. The house felt good, and she was almost—*almost*—ready to tell Shannon to go ahead and set the whole scary process into motion.

Moira had fixed dinner for Nan, as was their custom, fricasseed chicken with dumplings and orange Jell-O with canned pears marching in military precision around a circular mold. Moira's meals reminded Nan of the Midwest, even though Moira herself was Brooklyn-born and bred. They all seemed to leap from the pages of a fifties women's magazine.

Moira had heard about Tony's death on TV, had even

bought a newspaper so she could read about it. Nan found that detail wonderfully touching. Moira generally showed little interest in current events and almost never bothered with a newspaper. "What's the point?" Moira would ask, and Nan was hard-pressed to find an answer. What Moira did genuinely enjoy was the large-print *Reader's Digest* subscription Nan had given her for her birthday.

"So tell me about this new boyfriend of yours," Moira said, over apple pie and coffee. Moira's pies were legendary, in great demand for bake sales and church fundraisers. "This Jonathan."

Nan was stunned. "What makes you think he's my boyfriend?" she parried. First Rosalie O'Brien, now Moira. Was she really that transparent?

Moira laughed. "A mother can tell these things. You get sort of fidgety when you talk about him, and you look at your plate like you're expecting the raisins in your pie to start dancing."

"He's away on a business trip," Nan said, examining the raisins in her pie for tap shoes.

A limousine from McIlheney Moves, Carleen's husband's company, had dropped Nan off late Sunday afternoon as it took Jonathan to the airport. Nan felt rather like the giddy new girlfriend of some hot rock star off on tour, performing nightly before huge adulatory crowds. That was *her honey* out there, wowing those crowds, packing them in, getting them to throw their Visa cards at the stage.

Throw those cards they would, make no mistake. People were paying good money for the simple privilege of being in Jonathan Henley's presence.

"And he doesn't call?" Moira wondered.

Nan laughed. "He calls, Moira, he calls. He sends flowers, too." It was starting to be an embarrassment. Every day a floral delivery arrived at work. They were enormous, an outrageous extravagance. Today's offering had required a wheeled cart. Nan's romance had become the talk of the California State Bar.

"Ooh." Moira sighed appreciatively. "Flowers. He's been married?"

"Once," Nan admitted.

"That's good," Moira stated firmly. "A man gets to a certain age and he's never married, you should wonder a little. A mama's boy, or worse. He has children?"

"No." Nan realized suddenly that she had never specifically asked Jonathan about children, that he had never volunteered any information. But of course he didn't. He'd have said something. He was quick enough to trot out his ex-wife in introductory seminars, after all. Surely he'd use the kids, too, if there were any.

"You get moving now, you can do something about that."

Nan laughed nervously. "What are you suggesting, anyway?"

"That you marry this boy and have some babies. You're not getting any younger, you know."

"Did my mother put you up to this?"

Moira frowned. "You know I don't know your mother. I just see a girl like you, so much to offer, and it makes me mad you're not raising children." She held up a hand at Nan's nervous chuckle. "Don't laugh, it's not funny. There's babies having babies all over the place today, girls too young to know what to do. And then somebody like you, smart and pretty and so much to offer, you're all by yourself. It just seems wrong."

Nan hesitated. "I don't know what to tell you," she said finally. "I didn't plan for my life to be the way it is. But Jonathan isn't asking me to marry him and have his children. And neither is anybody else."

Moira stood up and began clearing the dessert dishes. "Well, don't be so quick to let him get away," she cautioned. "Even if he does have that cockamamie business."

Which was probably the best and most succinct description yet of the Past Lives Institute.

* * *

Later, driving home, Nan thought about Moira and her sweet concern. She thought about Jonathan, too, already feeling her pulse accelerate in anticipation of the call she knew would come later that evening.

She didn't think she was in love with him. She'd been in love enough times to understand that there was something overwhelmingly mystical and chemical about the experience, a decided loss of control, a heady recklessness that she wasn't even close to experiencing yet.

But she sure liked him a lot. As a girl she would have written Jonathan's name a hundred times on a sheet of paper entwined with hearts, would have fabricated excuses to walk by his house or altered her course between high school classes so she might meet him in the hall and brightly say hello.

Now, of course, she was a grown-up, far too cool for such nonsense.

Uh-huh.

Jonathan called every night and they talked for hours. When he finished his East Coast programs it was still early in California, still light in Nan's living room as she lay on the sofa and listened to him complain about the humidity in Atlanta, describe a funny old lady covered with emeralds in Houston, confide in a low impassioned voice just how much he missed her.

On Friday, after Jonathan had been gone five days, Nan began listening to Debra's regression tapes again. She played them in her car as she drove to and from the office, used them as a sound track as she puttered around the condo at night. Over the weekend she stayed home and listened some more, taking a break only to go with Tom Hannah to a film screening in Culver City.

On Sunday she went back to the tapes. Debra moved in and out of different entities, the only constant being Carleen's soft concerned voice.

Now and then Nan made an appearance, twice as a sister, another time as a child. Each time it happened she expected to hear the theme music from *Twilight Zone*. She found herself rewinding the tapes to listen more closely for details of those relationships, annoyed that Carleen hadn't further pursued them. Always, however, they proved to be minor, relatively insignificant.

It was a little scary how much that disappointed her.

When she picked up the phone on the second Thursday night of Jonathan's absence, she expected to hear his voice, to have him tell her how the day's program had gone in Philadelphia. But it wasn't Jonathan at all.

"Sweetie?" The voice cut through her, catapulted Nan into an entirely different level of reality. She was suddenly in a Hollywood kitchen that smelled of permanent wave solution while a couple of women with fumes rising from their heads chattered about bikini waxing.

"Sweetie, it's Alistair. I was just passing through town on my way to San Francisco and I simply can't believe what I'm hearing about poor little Debra."

CHAPTER 15

Alistair was sipping sake in the Silver Lake sushi bar when Nan arrived for lunch on Friday.

It was several years since she'd last seen him, but he looked very much as she remembered: slight and insouciant, with close-cropped dark brown hair, chocolate-brown eyes, long black lashes. His features were even and patrician, like the male models suffering terminal ennui in *Esquire* clothing pictorials. He normally alternated between graceful languor and volatile kineticism. During the latter periods, he seemed to carry about his own field of crackling energy. Nan suspected that in absolute darkness, visible charges would pulsate off Alistair like miniature lightning bolts.

Today was one of the frenetic periods. He jumped up to greet her with an extended hand that practically trembled. That was another thing about Alistair: his manners were astonishingly good, and he knew exactly what level of physical contact each of his clients was comfortable with. Nan had watched him sweep clients of both sexes—folks with whom he presumably had no relationship beyond an occasional shampoo and blow-dry—into torrid embraces suitable for the covers of bodice-ripper romance novels. But he'd never offered more than a handshake to Nan, nor had she ever wanted more.

"You must tell me everything," he told her, as a young Japanese man in impeccable chef's whites set a plate and sake cup before Nan, then placed a small platter of sushi between her and Alistair. "Thanks, Kenji. Just keep interesting things coming, all right?"

Kenji nodded with a brief flash of pearly teeth and moved down the sushi bar to another customer. Most of the other customers, Nan noticed, were Japanese businessmen in dark suits. Quite a few had cigarettes smoldering at their elbows.

Nan looked at the plate of sushi. It was beautiful, unusual, and probably authentic enough that a prudent diner wouldn't want to precisely identify all the ingredients. The place was a hole-in-the-wall suggested by Alistair, and it was obvious there'd be no avocado-filled California Roll here, none of the bastardized junk found on wall-menu photographs at shopping mall McSushi joints.

She took a tentative nibble and found the morsel delicious. "Mmmm," she said. "Incredible. How did you ever find this place?"

"I used to live up the street."

She laughed. "Of course. You probably know more neighborhood restaurants from having lived in the neighborhood than any ten other people I know put together."

"I've gathered little moss," he agreed. "Now tell me about Debra."

"After you tell me where you've been and why it was so damned hard to get in touch with you."

"Fair enough." He poured each of them some sake. "But it's not a pretty story."

"I'm a big girl. I can take it."

"It wasn't you I was thinking about." He grimaced. "It's me. To make a long story very, very short, I have AIDS."

Immediately she felt like a total jerk. "Oh, Alistair. I'm so sorry to hear that."

"Well, thanks. Not nearly as sorry as I am to tell it, not that I can say it's any kind of extraordinary surprise. I always had what you might call a bit of a life-style."

Nan couldn't help laughing and knew instinctively that Alistair wouldn't mind. He laughed with her, even as she apologized.

"Well anyway, I haven't given up yet. I'm trying a lot of stuff the AMA would probably be afraid to test on dogs, and who knows? I may lick it yet. But anyway, I found out about six weeks ago. I knew I was HIV-positive, of course, but then I got this . . . oh hell, I'll spare you the medical details. We're eating. Once I found out I actually had it, I knew there were some things I had to take care of, some extremely unfinished business. My family."

Nan listened silently and kept eating as Kenji delivered another plate. This she did recognize, lustrous slices of yellowtail and rich purple tuna.

"Where do you think I grew up?" Alistair asked.

"I haven't the vaguest idea," Nan admitted.

"Would it surprise you to learn I'm a scion of the Deep South, a son of the Confederacy?"

She considered. "Yeah. You don't have any kind of an accent."

"Ah don't?" He switched effortlessly into a molasses-thick drawl. "My daddy down in Vicksburg, Mississippi, would be mighty pained to hear you say that."

"Mississippi?"

"That's right, sugarplum." He dropped the accent then and continued a tale Nan wasn't really sure she wanted to hear. But she couldn't very well cut him off. She'd asked. No, she'd *insisted*.

"My full name—and listen closely, 'cause this isn't something I'm in the habit of revealing—is William Alistair Weddington. Billy Al, they'd call me in certain circles, but the Weddingtons did not and do not move in those kinds of circles. The Weddingtons are lawyers and the Alistairs are bankers and between the two families, there isn't much goes on in the Mississippi Delta doesn't bear the thumbprints of one side or the other."

He ate a piece of yellowtail and smiled. "I was a grievous disappointment to my daddy, let me tell you. I knew from the time I was ten I was different and I think he probably did too, but we both kept up a real nice fiction clear through when I got kicked out of Ole Miss for moral turpitude."

He rolled the syllables and momentarily reinstated the drawl. "Moral Turpitude. I love the way that sounds. I always thought it would make a fabulous name for a rock band. Of course Daddy wasn't too pleased about my little episode at Ole Miss. I was supposed to come home and go to work in one of the Alistair banks, but instead I decided to go to Atlanta and start some serious flaming."

"There was a big gay community in Atlanta?"

"It was no Castro Street, but we had our moments. I started cutting hair mostly 'cause I knew it would make Daddy crazy, and it came as a real surprise when I found out I liked it and had a talent. Then I met this fabulous voice coach who helped me lose my accent. By the time I got to San Francisco, only somebody else from below the Mason-Dixon line would ever guess where I was from, and then only in the heat of passion."

"Did you stay in touch with your family?"

"More with Mother than Daddy. I even went back a few times, but they were not exactly slaying fatted calves in my honor." He giggled. "I brought a drag queen to my sister's wedding. As my date."

Nan chuckled at the image. "Did they realize?"

"Daddy did, but there wasn't much he could say without making a scene he *really* didn't want. Laura Lee, my sister, suspected. 'Will,' she told me, 'Anna seems a trifle, well, *coarse*.' And Mother still wouldn't believe it if I swore on the Alistair family Bible. Mother has a strong sense of decorum. I believe she's already worrying about how to phrase my obituary so as to make no mention of opportunistic infections."

"Oh, Alistair, it sounds awful." The communications problems Nan had experienced with her parents suddenly seemed paltry and inconsequential.

His smile was gentle. "It's not so bad. I was just back there for more than a month, working things out. With a side trip to Atlanta and a little R & R down in New Orleans when things got too heavy once or twice. It wasn't my parents' fault that I am what I am. They tried to do right by me, and I wanted to do right by them before it was too late. I'm hoping to get out of this lifetime carrying as little bad karma as possible."

Karma. There it was again. Nan had gotten so caught up in Alistair's tale of woe that she'd almost forgotten why they were meeting in the first place.

He seemed to realize it too. "So tell me all about Debra, now."

Nan did, through six or seven more plates of sushi. Alistair was an appreciative audience, nodding and murmuring and periodically widening his eyes in horror. When she had finished, he buried his face in his hands.

"If only I'd known," he said.

"I tried to get a message to you," Nan said, "but nobody ever knew where to find you or how to get in touch or anything. The cops even tried to find you, Alistair."

"Really? How intriguing. And what a scene that would have made if they'd tracked me down in Vicksburg. I'm sorry, Nan. I've gotten so used to being secretive, having the parts of my life compartmentalized, it's just a habit." He frowned. "You know, Debra seemed worried the last time I saw her. I asked her what the problem was, but she said it wasn't important. That Tony was such an asshole. If he were still alive, I'd have to kill him." He smiled and one corner of his mouth turned up, the other down. "I haven't got much left to lose."

"I still can't believe Tony killed her."

"And Mother still can't believe I'm not a Mississippi judge."

"No, Alistair, this is different."

"Is it?"

"Yeah, I think it is. Tell me what you mean when you say she seemed worried the last time you saw her."

"I cut her—let's see, it was right before I left town—at the end of August. I usually did her once a month and it had been a little longer that time—I forget why. She was complaining that she was just a mess, but of course she was beautiful. We talked about doing a body perm but she wanted to let it grow out a bit first. It was real short."

"She seemed worried," Nan prompted.

"Preoccupied, more, I'd say. I asked her what was wrong and she said nothing, she didn't think. Something didn't make sense, that was all. I asked her if it had anything to do with Bartholomew—you know Brother Bartholomew, that gorgeous guru?"

"I sure do."

"Then you know she was seeing him. I didn't really approve, but at least he was kind to her. She said no, it wasn't him. Then I don't know—the phone rang or something and that was it."

It wasn't much. Nan sighed. "I understand you're the one who took Debra up to the Past Lives Institute the first time."

"Well, of course I did! The poor girl was a basket case, and I just knew it would help her to find out why something so horrible had happened to her. She didn't want to go at first. I practically had to kidnap her. But then, when she started to put everything together, she was so thankful. I knew it would work out for her."

"Yeah, it worked out just great."

He stared at her, shocked. "You surely don't mean to imply that Tony killed her because she found out he'd been a brute in Marseilles? Why, that was *centuries* ago!"

"So you know all about her supposed past lives?"

"Why, of course I do! She told me hers and I told her mine. It was wonderfully cathartic. I suppose now you're going to tell me you don't believe in reincarnation," he accused.

Nan smiled. "I was going to put it a little more equivocally than that, but yeah. You're right. I don't."

"Oh, sweetie," he sighed, "you should. You could save yourself so much grief."

"It didn't save Debra much grief. And if you don't mind

my being blunt, I don't see how it's going to help you stay healthy."

He shook his head. "But that's not the *point*. You know, I went through this whole business with my father and he was exactly the same way you are."

"You said he was a lawyer, didn't you?"

"Is that supposed to mean you think better than we mere mortals?"

Nan felt momentarily guilty. "Of course not. But we're trained to be skeptical."

"Well, if you don't want to believe, I can't make you. But let me just tell you something I learned in my own regressions, and you'll see I'm not doing this to make myself look good."

Kenji appeared before them, looking quizzical.

"No, I think we've probably had enough, Kenji," Alistair said, "and it was fabulous. Are you still hungry, Nan?" Nan shook her head and stifled a burp. "Let's just get a check then."

Kenji had it ready. He bowed slightly and set the check discreetly between them. Alistair protested feebly for a moment before Nan prevailed. She wondered for a moment what he would have done if she'd agreed to let him pay it.

"Now where was I?" Alistair asked, as they walked out into the bright noonday sun.

Nan shrugged, hoping he'd forget, and unlocked the Mustang a few doors down from the restaurant.

"What a fabulous car!" he gushed. "But don't think you're getting away just yet. I need to tell you about my most recent past life."

Nan leaned on the Mustang's front fender and smiled politely.

"I was killed in World War II," he told her, "and I wasn't one of the good guys. I was a rabid young homophobe from Frankfurt who helped round up sexual criminals for mein führer."

Nan gaped. This was even more ridiculous than the story of Louis and Anne-Marie and little lame Jean-Paul. Alistair clearly believed it, because there'd be no other reason for telling her something so outrageously damning about himself. But just because he bought it didn't mean she had to. She rearranged her face into a noncommittal, nonjudgmental expression of mild interest.

"I was killed fairly early on," Alistair continued, "during the invasion of Poland. I had what you might call a bit of a temper, you see, and got into a spot of trouble in Frankfurt. I was sent to the front. For which I should probably be grateful, because I was terrifically ambitious and at the rate I was going, I'd have probably ended up running a concentration camp. I'd be working off *that* karma for millennia."

"Very interesting," Nan told him politely.

"You don't get it, do you?"

"Well, I suppose . . ." she faltered. No, she didn't get it.

"It's very simple, sweetie. This time out I had to learn just what it was like to be a homosexual in an intolerant world, and Vicksburg, Mississippi, wrote the book on intolerant. I got beaten up on the playground for being a sissy and I was too skinny to play football. I loved taking piano lessons and I hated hunting. I figured I'd just be a miserable misfit my entire life. Then I went to Ole Miss and discovered there was another world out there, full of people just like me. Of course we were all hideously discreet, miles into the closet. Moral turpitude notwithstanding."

Nan kept smiling. Was this leading somewhere? Alistair seemed to think so.

"Then just when I'd finally gotten my own life more or less together, blam-o, along came AIDS. A visitation from God, Daddy calls it. My just desserts for defying the natural order of man. Supportive to the bitter end, that's my old man. But he'll bury me in the manliest casket he can find, solid mahogany, with a shotgun cradled in my arms and burly pallbearers singing 'Stout-Hearted Men.' "

Nan, for once caught utterly speechless, simply stared.

"I won't force any more of this on you," Alistair said with a sudden grin. "I just wanted you to understand how real it is to me. How real it was to Debra."

"I've listened to her regression tapes," Nan told him. "I know it was real to her."

"You should read her past lives journal too, then."

"I'd love to, but nobody can find it. It's disappeared."

His smile was long and lazy. "No it hasn't, sweetie. You just haven't been looking in the right place. I've got it."

"*You've* got it!" Nan jumped forward and grabbed him by the shoulders. "Why on earth didn't you tell me before?"

"I didn't realize you cared."

Nan walked away a few steps, then turned and faced him. "Alistair, I've been going crazy trying to find that damned thing. Why on earth did she give it to you?"

"She didn't. She left it behind by accident when I cut her hair. It fell out of her purse. She was going to come back and get it, but then something came up and she couldn't come, and then I had to go somewhere. I'd just gotten diagnosed and, to tell you the truth, it didn't seem very important to me. I left it with Dale and she was going to pick it up, but she didn't. It was still there when I got back."

"Alistair, I *need* that journal."

He batted his eyelashes provocatively. "Then come on up and see my etchings."

"But you're supposed to be on the plane!" Nan exclaimed when Jonathan's voice came through her phone receiver later that afternoon. She'd already called the airline three times to track the progress of his flight.

"I *am* on the plane." He laughed. "Surely you've heard of air-to-surface phone service."

"Well, yeah, but I thought it was just used by people whose corporations were about to be seized in unfriendly takeovers."

"Hey, I'm calling my lawyer. Isn't that good enough?"

After she hung up, oddly thrilled by what was basically a very decadent abuse of technology, Nan stared at the purple grosgrain cover of Debra's past lives journal.

On the whole, it was curiously disappointing.

It was a small hardbound book with heavy unlined pages, the kind sold by stationers for gifts when you haven't a clue what somebody might like. Inside the front cover, Debra had neatly written her name and address, with the underlined admonition: *Private and Confidential*. She used only the right-hand pages and began each new entry on a fresh page. She favored purple ink.

There didn't seem much point in reading through the whole journal right now. Most of it was already familiar from the tapes. Debra had written in the book after each session, simple synopses with brief comments on how the revelations made her feel. Astonished, mostly. The comments were longer after the sessions in which past incarnations of Tony Fontaine figured. Notations like *I just can't get over this* or *Now I think I understand* appeared often. And there was a lot of cloying philosophy that sounded suspiciously like Brother Bartholomew.

The only mildly discordant entry was in the last few written pages, dated August nineteenth:

Boy, everything seemed to go wrong today. The cat pooped in my shoe and I had a flat tire at Ralphs. Then the darned hard drive was supposedly full and I *knew* that couldn't be. It took me all morning to remember how to use the directory search program and then it turned out to be just like the other time. Very weird and I don't know what to think about it all. And then, as if all that wasn't bad enough, my regression turned out lousy. I was *really* hoping we'd track down a new life today, but nothing much happened. I was sure there'd be something there, but I guess not. I have the oddest feeling that something *is* there, that something *did* happen and it's important, but whatever it is must be really blocked. Maybe not even there. And to top it all off, the tape recorder went on the fritz. Oh, well. Bartholomew says I worry too much and maybe he's right.

Following that entry came reports on two more sessions, neither involving Tony. Blank pages followed.

As Nan closed the book, she saw writing on a page near the end, a list of pencilled notations:

BUDGET1.DAT = ALOHA.1?
BUDGET2.DAT = ALOHA.2, etc.
CURREV.JUL = PIESKY.JUL, etc.
ATLAREV.JUL = TARA.JUL, etc.
HOUREV.JUL = HOWDY.JUL, etc.
BOSREV.JUL = TEAPARTY. JUL, etc.
TRIPREVS.1,2,3 = JOKER.1,2,3
LITLIST.1,2, etc. missing
MAILLIST.1,2, etc. missing
????????
Check all figures again!

She closed the book and picked up a file. Two more hours.

LAX on Friday afternoon was a nightmare, and getting there from downtown was no picnic either. But Nan didn't care. She had a hard time keeping her hands off Jonathan in the airport, and he didn't help by standing behind her at the luggage carousel with his arms wrapped around her waist. They drove directly to Nan's condo and barely made it inside.

"This could be habit-forming," Nan sighed afterward, looking at the trail of clothing leading toward the hall door. She and Jonathan lay in the middle of the living room floor.

"Don't worry, I have experience in addiction control," Jonathan murmured, reaching for her again. "You think we could try this again in the bedroom?"

Later they stopped for Mexican food on the way to Malibu. By then it was dark, and traffic on the Pacific Coast Highway was light. At the PLI, she and Jonathan adjourned to the hot tub after he popped in briefly to tell April he was back.

In the morning, the place hummed with activity. April and Bartholomew had a workshop in full swing and Carleen was conducting a group therapy session. Marsha scurried about with armloads of paper and brimming pitchers of iced lemonade. The lot was jammed with expensive late-model cars, and Nan hadn't seen so many people at the PLI since Debra's memorial service. They all looked earnest or dazed or both.

Nan and Jonathan slipped into the dining room and filled plates from a dazzling seafood buffet set out for workshop participants. They took the food out to the gazebo, where Bartholomew, Carleen, and April were already eating. Everyone wanted the details of Jonathan's trip, which he dutifully reported.

"I'm sold on Philadelphia as one of the two new regionals," he concluded, "but I can't decide whether the other should be in New York or Chicago."

"The overhead would be terrific in Manhattan," April cautioned. "Plus you know how cynical New Yorkers are about anything metaphysical. We're based in Malibu, remember. They all hate California."

"Tell me about it," Jonathan answered. "I was having breakfast in a coffee shop, talking to the guy sitting next to me, telling him why I was in town, trying to explain the concept of reincarnation. 'Forget it,' he says. 'You can't spread it on a bagel, it ain't really there.' But I'm not sure Chicago's that much better. Chicagoans have that Midwestern suspicious streak, begging your pardon, Nan."

"You've totally ruled out D.C.?" Carleen asked.

"Everybody there's too nervous about appearing different. We had our lowest turnouts there, and the folks who did come all had permanent cricks in their necks from looking over their shoulders. You've got to remember that people with political ambitions—which means everybody in town—don't want to be associated with some crackpot spiritual movement. It might, pardon the expression, come back to haunt them later."

"Yeah," grunted Bartholomew. "Like all those hypocrite

politicians who want to run for president, but first they make this statement: 'Hey, back in the sixties in a moment of madness I took one teeny tiny little toke on a joint'— only they call it a puff on a marijuana cigarette so they won't look like they really know what they're talking about—'I must have been temporarily out of my mind, 'cause I hate drugs, I really do. They're destroying society. And anyway, I really didn't like it at all and I didn't inhale and it didn't do a thing for me and of course I didn't get stoned.' Like it's something they should be sorry about. Me, I don't trust anybody who was young back then and *didn't* do a little dope. What's the point in being young if you're too chickenshit to try something new?"

Everyone chewed in silence for a moment. Then Nan turned to Carleen. "You remember we were wondering what happened to Debra's past lives journal? Well, I found it."

"You did?" Carleen sounded genuinely shocked. "Where?"

"Alistair had it. I had lunch with him yesterday."

"Alistair? You found him too?" Carleen's hands automatically flew to her hair and pushed her unruly red bangs away from her forehead. "Where on earth has he been?"

This was not Nan's tale to tell. "Out of town. He's been ill."

"I didn't realize you were looking for the journal," April said.

"Yeah, why?" asked Bartholomew.

"Initially I was hoping there'd be something in it to help figure out who killed her."

"It's a little late for that," April noted dryly. "RIP Tony."

"Well, yeah. But it's interesting just the same, particularly since I've been listening to her regression tapes."

"I'd really like to see it," Carleen said.

"It ought to be burned," Bartholomew put in suddenly, "out of respect for Debra's memory."

"Aren't we locking the barn door a little late on that one?" Jonathan asked lazily.

"If I could just make a photocopy?" Carleen persisted.

"Sure, why not?" Nan told her. "It's over in Jonathan's house. I'll get it for you."

"It's wrong," Bartholomew insisted. "Debra never meant for anybody else to read that. It held her innermost thoughts."

"We all know her innermost thoughts by now," Nan said. "I don't see what harm there is in sharing them."

Nan finished her lunch and retrieved the journal. It passed around the group, each person handling it gingerly, as if it had some mystical power. Or as if, she realized suddenly, it were too hot to handle. Perhaps they weren't as sophisticated as they believed.

Carleen was turning its pages, unconsciously running her tongue over her upper lip, when Nan and Jonathan left to take a long leisurely swim. Somehow or another, the swim necessitated yet another hasty adjournment to the bedroom. They were acting like a pair of teenagers, Jonathan said, but Nan didn't remember her teen years being nearly so much fun, or a fraction so sexually active.

❋

The killer fought panic. This couldn't be happening. That damned Alistair!

"He's been ill," Nan had said. Well, everybody knew what *that* meant. There was only one thing that young faggots got sick from these days, and the only bad part was that it hadn't killed him already.

Was he going to ruin everything? And *then* die?

Stay calm. There had to be a way out.

First of all, the damned journal had to go, had to be destroyed. It wouldn't be easy, now that everybody knew about it, had pawed through it. But it was absolutely essential to get rid of it once and for all.

It was all there, the information that meant destruction and failure. The worst was on only a few pages and they could be ripped out. Then the photocopies could be destroyed, at least the ones of those pages.

But how? When?

Deep breathing. Stay *calm*!

There wasn't time to stay calm. Wasn't time, period.

Nan Robinson would have to go, too. No question about it. She'd had the damned journal for twenty-four hours, had plenty of time to go through it. Had plenty of time—heart-stopping thought—to make copies of it and leave them at her office, her home, wherever.

She might be playing dumb about it now, or maybe she didn't realize yet what she had. Maybe she was so horny that she honestly didn't know yet.

But she'd figure it out. She was sure to. And then everything would be ruined. It would all be over, before the good part even began.

It was so incredibly *unfair*.

So what now?

Speed was critical. She'd be leaving soon and she couldn't be allowed to get the journal to anybody else. Particularly not the cops. That greasy little shit C. J. Bennett might not realize how important it was, but his dyke partner was sure to.

An accident. That was it.

Nan Robinson would have to have a tragic accident.

CHAPTER 16

Before Nan even realized, it was nearly four, time to leave the PLI if she intended to make it to the dry cleaner's before they closed. Tonight Jonathan was taking her to Antonelli's, a new West Side restaurant recently opened by a pair of famous young chefs. Antonelli's was the kind of fantastically hip place where reservations were required weeks in advance, and Nan presumed Jonathan had crossed someone's palm with quite a lot of silver to get in.

Carleen was gone, but she'd left Debra's journal on her desk. Nan stuck it in her purse and walked around to the side parking area with Jonathan. He helped put the convertible top down on the Mustang and then kissed her goodbye. "I'll pick you up at eight," he told her. "Bring your toothbrush."

She headed down the hill, absentmindedly wondering about this unaccustomed life-style she had gotten caught up in. Reincarnation wasn't even the half of it. There was also lots of cold hard cash, and big chunks of it were being spent on her. Flowers, phone calls from airplanes, French silk negligees Jonathan brought her from New York, outlandishly expensive dinners at posh eateries—it was all rather new and overwhelming, though undoubtedly something Nan could get used to.

She rounded the first bend coming down the narrow two-lane stretch of the road leading from the Past Lives Institute down to the Pacific Coast Highway and touched her brake. It caught for a moment, then suddenly her foot smashed clear to the floor.

What in the . . .

She was gaining momentum fast as she careened down the steep road, frantically pedaling the useless brake. How on earth could she stop?

Of course. The emergency brake.

She yanked on it and felt it pop in her hand, useless. Now what? She forced herself to remain calm. Downshift, that was it. She downshifted into low, listening to the engine complain, fighting to stay on the road.

There were no side guardrails to rub against, no parked cars to smash into, just a lot of rocks and chaparral and the occasional celebrity gate. Even that was no help. The next gate, belonging to a reclusive retired actor, was nearly a mile farther down the road.

It was like some amusement park thrill ride, except this was for real. There were no safety features here, no centrifugally engineered curves, no artfully hidden rails. There was just one terrified woman in an open convertible headed down a winding mountain road at breakneck speed.

She had to somehow stop the car.

She tried to rub it into the rising side of the hill, but the slope wasn't steep enough and she rebounded, almost spinning off the other side of the road. There was quite a substantial drop over there, more than she cared to negotiate in a car with neither roof nor rollbar.

She was on a straightaway stretch now, building up greater speed as she approached that abandoned stone cottage. It sat on a ninety-degree bend that was scary even with a shipshape braking system. After that, she realized with growing terror, came a stretch of hairpin curves.

There was the abandoned cottage now, baking roofless in the late afternoon sun, straight ahead of her, coming up fast. She twisted the wheel sharply to the left to minimize the impact on her side of the car and braced herself on the steering wheel.

The last thing she saw was the stone wall looming up over her right shoulder.

* * *

There were noises, dim and confusing, an urgent voice saying, "I think she's coming around."

Nan opened her eyes cautiously and saw two faces directly in front of her, two IV stands swaying. The faces were both speaking at once, but she couldn't tell what they were saying because tidal waves of pain were rushing through her head. She opened her mouth, to try to speak, but nothing came out.

She closed her eyes and let the pain sweep her away.

When she awoke again, the room was brightly lit and there was only one face over her, a young Asian man in white. Her head felt huge and pain throbbed through it. She tried to look around, to locate the other source of pain. Her arm, that was it. It lay stiff and unnatural in a heavy white cast on top of the sheets.

"You waking up?" the Asian man said. He sounded far away. "Welcome back."

She tried to nod her head, but it hurt too much.

"Just take it easy," he cautioned her. "I'm Robert, your nurse." He reached above her head and did something. "She's awake," he said. Moments later, another white-clad figure was standing over her. This one was a petite blond woman with sharp features and horn-rimmed glasses.

"Where . . ." Nan tried to ask. It was incredibly hard to speak.

"You're in intensive care at Santa Monica Hospital," the woman answered. "I'm Dr. Graybill."

A male nurse and a female doctor. Nan thought vaguely how nice that was. "How . . ." she started to speak again. There were so many questions to ask but the effort seemed too enormous.

She closed her eyes and let the pain carry her off again.

The third time she woke up she could see that it was dark outside her window even though the room was still brightly lit. A large clock straight ahead read 3:19; below it a tear-away calendar announced it was Sunday, October 21.

Her head throbbed resolutely, but the sharp stabbing pain was gone. So was the Asian man. A pretty Latina in a white pantsuit was sitting beside her, reading a fashion magazine.

This time Nan decided to wait a moment, not to try to speak right away. Inventory first. The cast on her left arm, oh yeah. The pain in her head, of course. What else? There were odd aches all over her body.

What had happened?

"Hello there," the Latina nurse said with a smile, standing up and lifting Nan's right wrist to take her pulse. "How are you feeling?"

"I hurt," Nan said. Her voice came out in an odd croak.

"I'm sure you do," the nurse said. Her voice had a light, lilting quality. "Dr. Graybill wanted to see you as soon as you woke up." She reached behind Nan and spoke. "Call Dr. Graybill. She's conscious."

Nan watched the second hand sweep around the clock seven times before Dr. Graybill appeared at the foot of her bed. She looked vaguely familiar. Oh, of course, she'd been there earlier.

Where earlier? What was Nan doing in the hospital and what on earth had happened to her?

Dr. Graybill examined her, shone lights into Nan's eyes and poked her abdomen, flexed her right arm and both legs, stuck painful little pins into her toes. She jabbed and prodded, asked lots and lots of questions. Many made no sense. The date was right there on the wall and who cared who was president of the United States? Did you have to pass a civics test before your health insurance kicked in?

Nan's voice grew stronger as she used it more. When Dr. Graybill had finished and was starting to leave, Nan held up her good hand.

"Wait," she said. "Tell me what happened."

"You were in an automobile accident," Dr. Graybill said. "Don't you remember?"

"No." What *did* she remember? Alistair. Sushi for lunch.

"You've got a concussion," the doctor explained. "It's

not unusual in a case like yours to have a little recent memory loss. It may or may not come back."

"My head . . ."

"You're going to have a whooping headache for a while, and we can't give you too much for the pain till we're sure there aren't any more problems. But your brain scan is fine, no depressed fractures or bleeding. We'll do another one in the morning to be on the safe side. We're going to keep a close eye on you for the present, but I don't think you need to worry about any lasting damage."

Lasting damage. *Brain* damage? A shiver of fear passed through Nan.

"As far as the rest of you is concerned," Dr. Graybill went on, "there's no evidence of any internal bleeding. You've got some pretty stunning bruises, but only one broken bone. That's a clean break of your left ulna. It's been set and it ought to heal just fine. You're right-handed?"

Nan nodded.

"That will help. Now get some rest and we'll give you another thorough check in the morning."

A thought struck Nan. "Did they call my mother?"

Dr. Graybill flipped through the chart. "I don't see anything on here about a next of kin," she said. "Would you like us to notify somebody?"

Nan moved her head slowly from side to side. "No."

Suddenly it was morning.

She awoke as she was being wheeled through the door, bed and all, for her MRI. Outside the door a young uniformed cop stood up and followed at a discreet distance, getting close only during the elevator ride. What was he doing there? There were so many people: nurses, doctors, orderlies, X-ray technicians. Them she could understand, but a cop?

Back in her room, a new doctor appeared. Dr. Anson was thick lidded, frizzy haired. He resembled Garfield the cat. He made bad jokes and terrible puns as he poked and prodded. Sometimes he was even funny, but Nan quickly discovered that laughing really hurt. He also asked a lot of questions, many of dubious relevance. When he was finished, he pulled a chair next to the bed and smiled.

"You're doing real well," he told her. "Your brain scan this morning is beautiful and the rest of you is doing nicely too. You were very lucky."

She was? "Who's the cop?"

"Officer Flannery, visiting from our neighbor to the east, LA. When you feel up to it, he wants to ask you some questions. There's a man named Jonathan Henley here, too. He's been waiting all night."

Jonathan! Was he back? Of course he was. He was coming in on Friday night. She was supposed to pick him up at the airport.

"I'd like to see him," she said.

"I'll tell him that. But the police say no visitors till you talk to them."

"Why?"

"You'll have to ask them," Dr. Anson said. "But don't feel you have to do it right away if you don't want to."

Nan hesitated. The one thing she hated more than bad news was uncertainty. She knew she'd lost thirty-six hours somewhere, and it couldn't be a coincidence that LAPD was sitting outside her door. Besides, until she dealt with them, she couldn't see Jonathan.

"Tell him to come in," she said. "The cop."

Officer Flannery refused to answer any questions and he didn't linger. "Detective O'Brien wants to talk to you," he said. "I'll call her right now."

Rosalie O'Brien was in pale blue tailored slacks and a Fair Isle cotton sweater when she arrived half an hour later. "You had quite an adventure," she said sympathetically. "How are you feeling?"

"I hurt all over."

Rosalie winced. "I can just imagine. They tell me you're going to be just fine, though."

"What happened?"

The detective smiled wryly and pulled a chair close to

Nan's bed. "I was hoping you'd be able to tell me that, but apparently you've got some traumatic amnesia. Why don't we start with what you *do* remember and then I'll fill in the blanks."

"I don't remember much. Lunch on Friday with Alistair. We had sushi."

"And after that?"

Nan shook her head. "I was here."

"Hmmm. You remember getting Debra's past lives journals from Alistair?" Nan shook her head. "Well, you did. Then you picked up Jonathan Henley at the airport and went out to the Past Lives Institute. You spent Friday night and most of Saturday there. You left around four-fifteen and crashed your car into an abandoned stone house on the road down to PCH. That isn't a very heavily traveled road, but fortunately you were discovered almost immediately. Somebody leaving a workshop at the PLI was coming down the road behind you and heard the crash." She smiled. "He had a cellular phone so he was able to call for help before he even reached your car."

Nan shuffled these facts around, but none of them seemed familiar.

"Was I by myself when I had the accident?"

"Uh-huh. Jonathan says you were going home to change for dinner."

That sounded plausible enough, but it didn't ring any bells. Was it possible that this little chunk of her life was gone forever?

"What about my car?"

"It's a mess," Rosalie said, "but it didn't burn. You were lucky."

"Lucky?" Why did everybody keep telling her that?

Detective O'Brien shook her head emphatically. "Very, very lucky. It wasn't just an accident, you see. Somebody sabotaged your brakes."

Nan closed her eyes. What on earth could this mean? Somebody wanted her to have an accident. Somebody wanted to *kill* her? It seemed impossible.

"You're sure?" she asked.

"Absolutely. The rubber on the hydraulic line from your master cylinder to the brakes was shaved very thin in one spot. Probably there was a little pinprick too. You wouldn't have immediately noticed any problem on flat ground, like when you were leaving the PLI. But as soon as you started going downhill, riding the brake, that put a lot of stress on the weakened part. It burst open, your fluid drained out, and your brakes were gone."

"Incredible. But who? Why? I don't understand."

"Well, we're not clear yet on who or why. But 'when' I can give you. It happened while you were parked at the PLI, sometime between when you got there Friday night and when you left on Saturday afternoon. We found some shavings from the brake line on the ground where your car was parked around the side. Problem is, in that particular location, the car was out of view from any of the windows in the buildings, but accessible to anybody on the grounds. It wouldn't take more than a few minutes for somebody who knew what they were doing. And there were lots and lots of people there on Saturday."

"But why would anybody want to . . . kill me?" It was a horrifying thought.

"That's what I'm trying to find out," Rosalie O'Brien said grimly. "It's vaguely possible, I suppose, that some disbarred attorney was up at the PLI Saturday afternoon looking into his past lives and saw an opportunity for revenge, but I'd hate to calculate the odds against that. I'd say it almost certainly has to do with Debra LaRoche's death."

Nan forced a smile. "Well, we know it wasn't Tony."

The detective's expression remained stony. "That we do. Trying to murder you was really a very stupid move on somebody's part. The Debra-Tony case was all neatly tied up, murder-suicide. Now it's wide open again. Even C.J. agrees."

"Damned big of him."

Rosalie laughed. "C.J.'s not nearly as bad as you make

him out to be. But listen, Nan. Until we figure out what's going on, you're in very real danger. The best thing that could have happened to you, from a personal safety standpoint, is your memory loss. I'm hoping like crazy you get that memory back, 'cause I think it will help us. And if you remember anything at all from the lost period, I want you to let me know pronto. But—and this is really crucial—if you *do* remember anything, for God's sake don't tell anybody. *Anybody!* That means your friends, your neighbors, your family." She paused for a moment. "It means Jonathan Henley too."

"Jonathan wouldn't hurt me," Nan protested.

"Maybe not. You know him better than I do and obviously you like him a lot. But I'd hate to find out the hard way that you were mistaken. Everybody who was at the Past Lives Institute while you were there this weekend had an opportunity to sabotage those brakes. Was Jonathan likely to be in your sight every minute?"

"No," she admitted reluctantly.

"Then he's as much a suspect as anybody else. Which means, among other things, that I don't want you alone with him till this gets cleared up. If you want to see him, that's up to you. But Officer Flannery or some other police officer will be in the room when you have any personal visitors. I understand they're planning to move you out of ICU into a regular room later this morning. A private room."

"But my insurance won't cover—"

"Let's worry about that later, all right? It won't matter that you're in good standing with your insurance carrier if somebody kills you, Nan."

"All right, all right." Nan suddenly felt incredibly weak and tired. "I'm kind of . . . fading."

"I'll leave you, then. I'll stop by later this evening and see how you're doing. All right?"

But Nan was already asleep.

When Rosalie O'Brien returned it was dark again and Jonathan Henley was sitting beside Nan's bed, holding her good hand. A police officer stood just inside the door. It was a ridiculous form of chaperonage and Nan hated it.

"I'll run out and get a burger or something," Jonathan told her, leaning down to kiss her good-bye. "Then I'll come back."

"Why don't you just go home and get some rest?" Nan suggested. "You look really wiped out." It was true. Jonathan's skin was gray and his eyes were sunken and he looked like a candidate for a hospital bed himself.

"Are you sure?" he asked. "I can come back."

"I'm sure. Once Rosalie goes, I just want to sleep."

"All right then," he answered doubtfully. He turned to Detective O'Brien. "Don't wear her out."

Rosalie O'Brien's return smile looked a little thin. "I'll be considerate."

When Jonathan was gone and Nan had reported on the state of her body, the detective told her, with a bit of a sigh, that there was no real news at all.

Nan frowned. "Rosalie, didn't you tell me earlier that Alistair had Debra's past lives journal?" The detective nodded. "What happened to it?"

"It was in your car when you crashed. I've got it."

"Can you tell me what's in it?"

"A lot of complicated stories about living other places, other times." The detective's flip tone contrasted with her gentle smile.

"You don't believe in reincarnation?" Nan asked wryly. Rosalie O'Brien had managed to hide any and all details of her personal life and beliefs. Admirable and professional, of course, but annoying just the same.

"Me personally? No. But I wish you'd let us know when you got hold of that journal. We might have been able to prevent this."

"Oh come on. You wouldn't have cared. It would have been Missing Persons all over again. I wasn't really trying to prove anything about Debra's death with it anyway. But I just spent a couple of weeks listening to her regression tapes and I wanted to ... I don't know. I was curious. Nosy."

"Keep in mind what curiosity did to the cat, Nan. When you're feeling better, I'd like you to take a look at the journal. Maybe it will bring something back or explain something." The detective cocked her head quizzically. "You listened to all those tapes?"

Nan nodded. "Didn't you?"

"Some of them. I had somebody else listen to the rest," she admitted. "But as I recall, the only thing out of order was that there was one missing. She was doing two regressions a week except for one week near the end when there was only one."

"I didn't catch that," Nan admitted.

"I don't think it was significant. I asked and apparently there was some kind of technical failure that day with the tape recorder. But then we found Tony's body."

Nan suddenly realized just how poorly she'd been tracking. "Somebody murdered Tony then, too!"

"It would appear that way. We're rechecking alibis right now. Care to comment on your own?"

"If I remember correctly, I was washing my hair."

Rosalie O'Brien laughed. "Ah, the carefree life of the single career woman! Well, that's no worse than anybody else's alibi. They're all lousy. Of course now that this Alistair is back, we can add him to the list."

"Alistair? Come on."

"Well, why not? Everyone says he was very devoted to Debra and apparently she trusted him enough to give him the journal. Say Tony did kill Debra. Alistair might have wanted to avenge her death."

"That sounds so melodramatic. And she didn't give him the journal. It fell out of her purse." Still, Alistair himself had said something about vengeance in the sushi bar. One of the last things she remembered. What *had* happened afterward? "Besides he was in Mississippi, trying to reconcile with his family. He's got AIDS."

"Then I think it's definitely time to meet him."

"Good luck finding him. He was going to San Francisco."

"He may be in danger himself, you know."

Nan hadn't thought of that. "The number where he was going is in my purse, but I don't know what happened to the purse."

"I took it as evidence last night. Tell me where to find the number." Nan did. "I've got a copy of the past lives journal with me now. If your feeling up to it, I can leave it for you. Maybe you can figure out what there was in it that was so threatening."

"You think that's why . . ."

"I don't know what to think. But I do know that right after you got that journal and showed it around at the PLI, somebody tried to kill you. One thing you learn early on as a cop is to distrust coincidence."

Nan sighed, suddenly exhausted.

The detective stood. "I'll go now and let you get some rest. You take it easy, now."

"You make it sound as if I had a choice."

"You know," Shannon said, setting a white wicker bed tray in front of Nan, "this would be a whole lot easier if you lived across the street."

Nan smiled and took a sip of Moira Callahan's homemade chicken noodle soup. She was on a comfort food diet, with a big cinnamon-sprinkled bowl of Moira's best rice pudding waiting in the corner of the tray. Moira herself had clucked and fussed over Nan for an hour before reluctantly going home.

Shannon had brought Nan home from the hospital a few hours earlier and was planning to stay for the next couple of days. Nan's sister, Julie, down in Floritas, had offered to come, but Nan told her not to. Julie hated LA, feared the traffic, was busy running her flower farm. The sisters had agreed that it would be counterproductive to tell their mother about the accident, at least for now.

"Are you trying to take advantage of my weakened condition?" Nan asked.

"Just trying to maximize the use of my time, like they tell you in those professional advancement seminars. Now drink your soup like a good girl while I go see if the officer is hungry."

"He's married, Shannon."

Shannon screeched to a halt. "Well, I guess we'll just have to let that boy *starve*, then."

Alone, Nan dutifully finished her soup, though she hadn't had much of an appetite since the accident. It was going to be crowded in the condo, what with Shannon sleeping on the daybed in Nan's office and Officers Casey and Goodman alternately camped in the living room. She could hear the TV playing.

Tuesday evening now and despite Rosalie's worries, there'd been no further attempts on Nan's life. Nan wasn't seriously expecting one; she was still in heavy denial about the sabotaged brakes. But she was too weak to argue and, perhaps more important, too weak to fight off anybody who might wish her harm.

Jonathan had hovered around her hospital room the past couple of days, haggard and absentminded, seeming a totally different person from the confident charmer she had grown so fond of. It bothered her to think she'd just spent all that time with him and had no memory of it. But it seemed to bother him even more. He kept promising he'd go home and get some rest himself, but every time she saw him he seemed more tired and distracted. She had made him promise not to return until tomorrow morning.

She picked at the rice pudding, then pushed the tray aside and picked up the photocopy of Debra's past lives journal. Somewhere in here was the key to something.

But what?

She read slowly and carefully from the beginning, recognizing the incidents Debra related from her own earlier listening to the tapes. She was just about to set it aside and take another nap—napping being the one thing she did with consummate skill these days—when Detective O'Brien arrived, tailored and crisp in one of those straight-skirted suits she wore so well.

"You look better," Rosalie announced.

"Don't I wish," Nan shot back. A web of nicks and scratches laced her face and a huge bruise splotched her right cheek, color-coordinated to others on her arms, legs and ribs.

"Nonsense," the detective protested, reaching into a bag and bringing out the purple-covered past lives journal. "I'm glad you were already going over this, because I want to show you something here in the original. Toward the back of the book, there are a couple of pages torn out. Whatever was on them didn't carry through to the pages beyond, because Debra wrote in felt-tip. And there isn't anything that corresponds in the photocopies Carleen made. She doesn't remember copying anything at the back of the book. Of course she might not have noticed."

Nan propped the book on the cast on her left arm and flipped to the back. There were indeed missing pages ripped out at the binding: two within the body of the journal and another at the back, amid blank pages. Why would somebody rip out a blank page?

"Did you check the dates against the tapes?" she asked.

"Of course. The day that's missing is the one the tape recorder malfunctioned. Which is the kind of coincidence I don't like very much. April Henley did that regression because Carleen was on vacation. But April says it was an insignificant session. So there we are. What I find more puzzling is that page ripped out in the back."

Nan closed her eyes and tried to remember. For the thousandth time, she failed. The frustration was unbearable. And suddenly she was exhausted again.

"I'm sorry," she told Rosalie, handing back the book. "I really am. And I'm really beat all of a sudden. It's like I've got a finite amount of energy, but no gauge of how much. I don't know how long it's going to last until all of a sudden, *bam*, it's just gone."

"Hey, don't apologize to me," the detective said, patting Nan's shoulder gently. "I'm not the one who crashed into a house."

Nan was asleep before the detective left the room.

She awoke again just before Tom Hannah arrived with an armload of helium balloons and an assortment of pastries from a Viennese bakery he'd recently discovered in the Fairfax district.

Tom's mere presence brought an air of party into what Nan was trying not to think of as a sickroom. Tom was good at that, the kind of guy who knew how to sneak backstage at the circus, belonged to all the art museums, acquired fantastic kites.

The challenge of living in LA on a teacher's salary brought out a natural bargain-hunting capability that had become truly encyclopedic. Tom knew all the Happy Hours with hefty munchie buffets, cut-rate appliance centers, second-day bakery outlets, budget dry cleaners. He was a habitué of the marked-down produce bins at Gelson's and relied on a network of low-level friends in the film industry for passes to free screenings. He had a drawer full of coupons, mostly expired, for products and services he was unlikely to ever need or want. He always knew the cheapest place in town to buy avocados, Levi's 501s, or a toasteroven.

Tonight he brought along a Monopoly game he'd picked up at a yard sale somewhere. Nan and Shannon and Tom played for almost two hours, till Tom put up a hotel on Boardwalk and wiped everybody out.

"Don't ever let anybody know I lost at a real estate game." Shannon grinned, stacking up the money neatly and snapping on rubber bands.

"Hey, this is the only way I'll *ever* own any property," Tom answered. "Nan, you look like you've about had it."

"That's probably the nicest thing anybody's said about my appearance since Saturday," Nan answered. "But you're right. I don't want to—"

"Listen, I've been kicked out of ladies' bedrooms for far less convincing reasons," he answered with a smile. "I know how to make a graceful exit. Ask any of my ex-wives."

Nan dreamed of Debra that night.

Debra with turquoise-streaked hair, laughing as she poured celebrity perfumes over the shoulders of a dozen men kneeling before her: Tony, Bartholomew, Jonathan, guitarist Marty, all the loser boyfriends.

Debra juggling floppy disks in the doorway of Nan's office, wearing her you're-never-gonna-believe-this-one smile.

Debra dancing with white-robed Brother Bartholomew just above the satin-sheeted surface of the waterbed in her little house in the Hollywood flatlands, heavy metal music shaking the walls.

Debra giving Danny Harrington a high five in the hall at the State Bar.

Debra sitting in front of an enormous computer monitor reading a directory that was all question marks.

Debra in Marseilles with hennaed ringlets in a funny old-timey dress, tossing a fish wearing Tony's face high in the air.

Debra writing in a small purple-grosgrain-covered book in the gazebo at the Past Lives Institute while mysterious forms flitted past in the background.

Debra flying down a mountain road on top of a huge computer, pursued by an enormous driverless limousine.

When she awoke Wednesday morning, Nan remembered meeting Jonathan at the airport, remembered going to the PLI, lunching in the gazebo, reading Debra's journal.

She remembered the missing pages and she knew who had killed Debra.

CHAPTER 17

Nan was able to catch Danny Harrington at home before he left for the office on Wednesday morning.

"You remember the Anderson fraud case?" she asked him.

"Uh-huh. You writing your memoirs while you're on sick leave?"

"Not quite yet. Tell me how Debra found the information that clinched the case."

"Let me think." Danny grumbled for a moment, and Nan could hear him slurping coffee. "I think this is how it went," he said finally, and told her.

Nan hung up, feeling deadened. Yes, this was what she'd wanted to figure out, and yes, she desperately wanted Debra's killer apprehended. But it still hurt to know the truth. There was the pain of knowing and the altogether separate pain of realizing that the knowledge would destroy what had seemed a truly promising personal relationship.

Next she tried Detective Rosalie O'Brien. She wasn't in her office yet, but the young man who took the call promised to page her and have her call Nan immediately. Rosalie sounded uncharacteristically out of breath when she phoned six minutes later.

"I was out running," she huffed. "What's up?"

Nan told her. "You did DMV checks on everybody, didn't you?"

"Well, sure."

"Try this name," Nan suggested.

Half an hour later, Rosalie called back. "Bingo," she said. "How on earth did you think of that?"

"I don't really know," Nan admitted. "It just came to me. You can tell C.J. it was woman's intuition. Listen, Rosalie, this is going to be tricky, but I think I know how we can prove it. Did you find Alistair up in San Francisco?"

"I talked with him by phone."

"Did he tell you if he saw or spoke to anybody connected with this case before he left town?"

"I don't think so."

"Then it ought to work. He'll have to come back down here, but I'm sure he'll be more than willing to help." Nan outlined what she had in mind.

"You don't ask for much, do you?" Rosalie asked when Nan was finished.

"I try to keep my needs simple," Nan murmured. "Can you do it?"

"I think so."

"Good. And Rosalie, one thing more."

There was a moment's silence. "I'm almost afraid to ask."

"I want to be there."

"I don't think that's a very good idea," Rosalie O'Brien said slowly, "all things considered. Besides, you just got out of the hospital, remember?"

"Look," Nan answered, "I know what you're thinking. I can handle it, really. And as for my health, well, there's no way we can pull this off before tomorrow. By then I'll be doing cartwheels down the hall here." She deliberately lightened her tone. "And if all else fails, I'm wearing a blunt instrument on my left arm."

❀

The killer glared at the telephone as if it might suddenly explode, erupt in uniformed policemen bearing handcuffs and leg irons and large-bore automatic weapons.

This couldn't be.

That miserable, rotten, abominable Alistair. It was all his

fault, every bit of it. If he hadn't existed, none of this would have happened. It was Alistair, after all, who'd introduced Debra to the Past Lives Institute in the first place. If he hadn't done that, she'd never have discovered the bookkeeping discrepancies that had so puzzled and concerned her.

"I don't get it," Debra had said, in all apparent innocence. She was uncomfortable, but seemed eager to have her suspicions proven wrong, to be mollified and reassured. "I got this error message that the hard drive was full and I knew that couldn't be, so I used the search program you have to check it out. And I came up with this hidden directory. What's going on, anyway?"

Little Miss Anxious-to-Help, signing her own death warrant. Of course, it might not have been necessary to kill her if she'd just let it go at that. But no, she couldn't let it go. She had to keep snooping. Once it was obvious that she'd dipped into the files in that hidden directory, that was it. Debra might not have been a genius, but she'd spent enough time making entries into the PLI records to realize that she'd stumbled on their counterparts.

And then, as if he hadn't already caused enough trouble, Alistair had to show up again with the damned past lives journal. Once it was clear the journal had resurfaced, even getting rid of Nan Robinson wasn't enough, botched though that attempt had been. Nan could be dealt with later, though.

And it would be a pleasure.

Alistair was the problem now. The larcenous little shit, calling up with innuendos and barely veiled suggestions that he desperately needed money to meet his medical expenses. Setting up an appointment to talk about "this terrible misunderstanding," as he put it. What did he think, that they were going to set up some kind of payment plan for him?

Alistair, ultimately, had to answer for Debra's death. He had set her on the road that led to all of this, had put everything in motion initially. He was some kind of hideous nemesis, and he would have to be stopped.

He was dying anyway, right?

Well, he could stop worrying about meeting his medical expenses.

✺

At three o'clock on Thursday, the following afternoon, Nan stared in horror at the ghastly apparition huddled in the wheelchair in front of her.

Alistair looked thirty pounds lighter than he had at lunch the previous Friday. His eyes were dark rimmed, deeply sunk in a gaunt and sallow face, his skin stretched tightly over forehead and cheekbones. Slightly wrinkled striped pajamas hung loose off his shoulders, and a soiled white cotton throw was tossed across his lap. An oxygen tank stood beside him and the room had the sour medicinal odor of terminal illness.

"My God!" Nan exclaimed, sinking into a dirty brown-and-mustard-striped armchair. The Echo Park apartment was tiny and grim, sparsely furnished with the kind of cheap furniture sold in suites on time payments to people whose only other alternative is sleeping in doorways. It hadn't been new for decades, or cleaned ever.

"Welcome to my future," Alistair told her with a macabre grin.

"Don't talk like that!" Nan answered, genuinely distressed.

"Oh come on," he said lightly, "don't be so prissy." He looked at himself critically in a hand mirror. "You don't think the pancake is too much, Jerry?"

The intense silver-haired NBC makeup artist responsible for Alistair's startling transformation leaned forward and stared closely. Jerry was a friend of Alistair's and had willingly volunteered his services. The idea had been Nan's, and the cops came up with the apartment, but it was Alistair who suggested most of the details that lent his appearance such dreadful verisimilitude.

"Not in this light," Jerry told him. "You'll keep the blinds closed?"

"Absolutely."

"Then you're fine at any range up to eighteen inches. Keep the light behind you."

"My wig's slipping," Alistair fussed. "What if the tape gives and I lose my instant face-lift?"

Jerry made an adjustment behind Alistair's left ear. "It won't. You're fine, all ready for the movie of the week." He slipped the clear plastic oxygen tubing carefully over Alistair's head and into his nostrils.

Detective C.J. Bennett walked in, looked around, and closed the dull brown drapes a little farther. They matched his slacks. In fact, the room seemed a perfect natural habitat for C.J., lacking only a layer of crushed Budweiser cans and empty pizza boxes.

"Sound check is great," Bennett announced, stalking the perimeters of the close, crowded room. He maintained a respectful, faintly horrified, distance from Alistair. "We pick up everything from here perfectly next door, but there's no carryover in the opposite direction."

The apartment was borrowed from the DEA, which had used it just a week earlier. The wiring was all still in position, and the bullet holes had been covered by some cheap dime-store prints of hunting scenes. The door was brand-new, intentionally flimsy.

"Remember," C.J. went on, "no heroics. I wish we could risk having somebody actually in the apartment, but that might blow it. The guys upstairs will move onto the fire escape as soon as the suspect enters the building. We've got the exits covered front and rear. Any questions?"

Alistair smiled sweetly at C.J. Jerry had done something to his teeth, too, yellowed and stained them. "Just one," Alistair simpered, enjoying the detective's discomfort. "When this is all over, can we fill this tank with nitrous oxide?"

Twenty minutes later, Nan fidgeted beside the window in the apartment next door, her cast heavy in her lap, looking out the one-way curtain at the street below. A man wearing a massive utility belt perched atop a pole beside a closed Pacific Bell van just down the block. Out back a dissolute "wino" was "passed out" on a scrap of filthy corrugated cardboard in the alley. They had everything but a hovering helicopter, and still she worried about Alistair's safety.

She worried about herself, too. With all these cops around, she wasn't in much physical danger, but emotionally she was hurtling headlong toward disaster. There was no way she could come out of this happy. Ever since she'd realized what must have happened, she'd discovered it was possible to feel simultaneously numb and nauseated. Avoiding Jonathan had been the only easy part.

Just after four, a silver Thunderbird pulled up in front of the building.

"Three-seventy-four . . ." Rosalie read off the license plate. "That's it!" She snapped her fingers reflexively and spoke into a walkie-talkie. "Subject parked outside the front entry."

"Hot damn!" C.J.'s voice vibrated with anticipation.

Just then Alistair's voice came through to the tape recorder. "Have to figure out how to get this thing to do a wheelie," he said clearly.

"Shut up, you idiot," C.J. hissed.

"Love you all, darlings," Alistair said, and was silent again.

Nan had never been in a situation where tension and excitement and fear mingled quite so thoroughly. She could feel adrenaline surging through her body, and she was very much afraid she'd throw up.

The door of the Thunderbird opened, and she held her breath.

✸

April Henley stepped into the fall afternoon and wrinkled her nose automatically at the acrid odor of smog. There was a lot to be said for the fresh breezes coming off the ocean at Malibu. How could anybody breathe in this kind of atmosphere? She could practically see chunks of orange gunk hanging in the air.

Alistair's directions had been easy enough to follow. In fact, the only tricky part was breaking away from Jonathan's latest crisis over the new regional offices in time to catch the cab into town and pick up her car at the Century City garage where she kept it, unknown to anyone. Female problems, she'd told Jonathan. A medical appointment, which was true enough.

Her clothing was androgynous and anonymous, the combination that had worked so successfully with both Debra and Tony. Hell, the drunk who gave her a lift back into the San Fernando Valley after she killed Tony actually thought she was a man, made beaver jokes, and talked about the World Series. Then as now she wore a baggy gray sweatsuit, wraparound dark glasses, and a gray baseball cap pulled low, with her hair tucked up inside it.

The apartment building was a dive, just the sort of place you'd expect somebody like Alistair to end up in. The neighborhood seemed grungy and not particularly safe. She'd have to get in and out quickly before somebody tried to steal her car. *That* could prove a bit awkward.

She looked carefully around. Alistair wasn't the kind of guy who'd have a lot of friends, but it paid to be careful. There was a PacBell truck down the street with a workman up on a pole, probably screwing up somebody's service. She strolled nonchalantly up the side path to the rear of the building, almost tripping over a bum in the parking lot. The guy smelled like dogshit and cheap wine, a real charmer.

LA was really the pits. She couldn't wait to get out of here and never have to come back. Soon, soon it would all happen, maybe even sooner than she'd planned.

She shook herself. Back to now, to reality.

To Alistair, the scum-sucking pervert.

The apartment building seemed almost deserted, which was fine. Obviously nobody would live here if they had any other options. The few cars in the lot at the rear were dented and rust flecked. She walked back to the front and went inside. Two-B, he said he'd be in. She checked the mailboxes. There it was, taped on, the single name. What an affectation! Must have taken the idea from his role model, Liberace.

The inside of the building smelled rancid—old odors of lard and cabbage overlaid with human urine. She quickly scaled the stairs and stood at the top, listening carefully. From the third floor she could hear Mexican music playing faintly, but all was quiet on two. She stepped briskly down the hall and rapped twice on the door of 2-B.

Once April walked in the front door, Nan began reflexively holding her breath. At the sound of the amplified knock, it all came out in a sudden exhalation, as if she'd been suddenly punched.

"It's open," Alistair called out feebly. His voice through the microphones now sounded weak and hesitant.

The door clicked open and then slammed shut.

"Well, well, well." It was the first time Nan had heard April's voice since her visit to the hospital with Jonathan on Monday night. Now she sounded cold and hard and mean. "You don't look too frisky, Alistair."

Nan closed her eyes, hating every moment of this, wanting only to have it over so she could go off by herself someplace and cry. It was no comfort to learn that she had been right. It was, in fact, quite awful.

"Forgive me if I don't stand up," Alistair answered. "What are you doing?" The sound of doors opening and closing came clearly through the microphones.

"Checking to be sure we're alone. It's awfully dark in here," April complained.

"Leave the drapes closed," Alistair whined. "Light hurts my eyes. It's a side effect of some of the medication I'm on."

"Didn't this come on kind of suddenly?" April's voice was crisp and matter-of-fact. "I remember when you came up to the PLI and cut everybody's hair back at the beginning of August, wasn't it? You looked just fine then."

Alistair gave a weak little chuckle. "AIDS never comes on suddenly, sweetheart. I flunked my first blood test six years ago. But I was starting to think of myself as a miracle boy, like those fellows who get their pictures in the paper just 'cause they're still alive. And then it hit me. I'm in a period of what the doctors so charmingly call 'rapid deterioration.'"

"Then how on earth were you able to travel?" she asked suspiciously.

"Well, I didn't have to charter an Air France jet like Rock Hudson," he answered petulantly. "I rode up to San Francisco with a friend."

"And before that?"

"I took a plane back East. Get a note from your doctor and they have to let you fly. But you didn't come here to talk about my travel arrangements, April, and I don't suppose you're here for a trim, either. Do take that silly hat off, though, so I can see your hair." A moment later he spoke critically. "You need more fullness in the sides, sweetheart. Who cut that?"

"What the hell difference does it make?" April snapped.

"Well, if you don't care, I guess there's no reason for me to," Alistair sniffed. "Just trying to observe the amenities."

"Fuck the amenities. I want to know what you were talking about when you called me."

"Why, Debra, of course," he said sweetly. "She told me the whole story, darling, before I left to see my family back in Mississippi."

"What whole story?"

"How you were cooking the books up at the Past Lives Institute."

"Dammit!" April sounded furious. "The little fool. She just couldn't leave well enough alone. I suppose she told you how she found out, too?"

Alistair hesitated and Nan held her breath. They were on shaky ground here.

"Frankly," he said, "I didn't understand it too well. I've always had trouble running my little pocket calculator, and

computers are just too much for me. But I thought it was
something about different sets of figures, only one of them
was hard to find? I may be wrong," he apologized. "I've
never been much good at money management."

"No, you're not wrong," April said bitterly. "She just
couldn't let well enough alone."

"But how on earth did Debra find out?"

Nan looked at the detectives in the room with her.
Rosalie and C.J. both sat mesmerized. Alistair's instructions were to get as much information out of April as he
could. C.J. Bennett had tried to script the whole thing, but
Alistair was adamantly opposed. Too complicated, he ar-
gued. He was obviously right, and he was doing just fine.

"I don't see what difference it can possibly make to
you," April told him impatiently.

"Well, my goodness, if it was important enough to kill
Debra about, you can hardly blame me for being curious.
After all, Debra was just horrified at the idea that you'd be
stealing. Particularly when it was really just stealing from
yourself."

"Not hardly. I'm not the PLI and the PLI isn't me. And
once I take care of a few minor problems, I'll be gone for
good."

April hadn't really explained everything, but she'd said
enough to confirm what Nan suspected—that Debra had
discovered the same sort of computer machination she'd
uncovered on the Anderson fraud case.

Nan remembered that situation well, though it wasn't her
case and the particulars had always been a bit fuzzy to her.
Danny Harrington had hauled Charlie Anderson's computer
into the office, spent days glumly sifting through backup
disks before Debra suggested that what they were looking
for might be hidden on the hard drive. Debra located a directory search program, figured out how to use it, then uncovered the hidden files which nailed Charlie Anderson,
costing him his law license and a few years in Lompoc.

"But why did you have to kill her? I don't understand."
There was genuine hurt and anger in Alistair's question.

"She was a blabbermouth, that's why. It was just a matter of time before she told Jonathan, and I wasn't ready to pull out just yet. For a while there I was terrified that she'd already told Bartholomew, not that he'd have paid any attention, he's so stoned all the time. She couldn't keep a secret, Alistair, you ought to know that. She told *you*, didn't she?"

"But I didn't care."

"Yeah, right. That's why you called me up whining about how much your medical treatment costs."

"I just thought you might be inclined to help."

"Blackmail's so ugly, Alistair."

"And murder's pretty? Where I grew up, we always thought it was kind of wrong."

April snorted. "Right, wrong, what's the difference? It was my money as much as Jonathan's or the PLI's. That place would never have turned a profit if it wasn't for me. *I* made the Past Lives Institute a financial success. Jonathan can't balance a checkbook, and the rest are just bleeding hearts, or else all caught up in the spiritual mumbo-jumbo."

"You mean to tell me," Alistair said incredulously, "that you don't even believe in what the PLI is doing?"

"I believe in making people pay if you indulge their fantasies," April answered. "But the rest of it is just bullshit. You know, Debra kept saying it was bad karma, what I'd done. Bad karma, for God's sake! The little idiot never heard of karma before she came to us. Before *you* brought her to us. As far as I'm concerned, her death is your responsibility."

"That's ridiculous!" Alistair sounded truly angry now. "All I did was try to help her, and all she ever did was try to help you."

"Yeah, she was a swell help. If she'd just stuck to what she was supposed to be doing, none of this would have had to happen. She shouldn't have been able to fiddle around with my computer program that way. She was only a secretary, for God's sake."

Nan felt her anger rising almost beyond control. *Only a secretary.* It was a hell of a death sentence.

"But why did it matter so much?" Alistair asked. "It can't have been all that much."

April's laugh was hard. "Do you have any idea how much money flows through the PLI? With the regional offices and the travel programs and the mail order and everything else? It was plenty, believe me. And it still is."

"But so what? What could you possibly want or need that you don't have now?"

"Freedom." April practically spat the word out. "Freedom. I'm not planning to be around here much longer, see, and I'm not planning to work again once I leave. Ever."

"But where will you go?" Alistair asked.

"You don't need to know. But let me put it this way. There are plenty of places without extradition treaties where a person with enough money can get lost forever."

"Skimming from the Past Lives Institute," Alistair said reflectively. "Debra was right. That's definitely bad karma."

"Spare me the bullshit, please."

"I just can't get over that none of you actually believe—"

"Oh, Jonathan believes, all right, and Bartholomew and I suppose the rest of them. But as far as I'm concerned, it's just a convenient way to separate unhappy rich people from their money. That's it. Oh, don't look so shocked and wounded, Alistair."

"I just . . . I never dreamed. . . ." His voice trailed off.

"I'm entitled to a life, too," April went on defensively, "and I don't plan on waiting for some bullshit reward in some life that supposedly is going to happen down the line. I want mine now, while I can enjoy it."

"You always seemed happy enough to me."

"Well, I guess you're not as perceptive as you think. I've had enough of being fat, ugly April taking care of all those irritating little business details while big handsome Jonathan's out there playing God. He's running around screwing actresses and cruising on yachts out of Newport with soci-

ety bitches, and I'm back at the office setting up hotel reservations for jackasses who think they'll be happy if they
find the exact spot where they were Abyssinian slaves three
thousand years ago. I ask you, is that fair?"

Nan stared at her cast. April's bitterness was frightening,
and her hatred for Jonathan truly malignant. It was astonishing that she had been able to camouflage her true feelings so well. As for the actresses and society ladies, that
didn't bear thinking of right now.

Obviously anything that might have been with Jonathan
Henley would never happen now.

She felt an odd emptiness inside her.

April paced back and forth across the worn shag carpet.
How could anybody live in this kind of squalor, anyway?
Alistair was sick as a dog already. This filthy dive had to
be teeming with germs.

Not that it would matter for long.

Alistair waved an airy hand. "Fair? Well, I suppose not,"
he answered agreeably, "but why couldn't you—" He broke
off, then glared at her accusingly. His righteous indignation
was getting really tiresome. "So you killed Debra and set
up Tony to take the fall for it."

"Why not?" Tony was every bit as much a lowlife as
Debra, the little tramp. A charming pair they made. Her
with the morals of a mink, him a wife beater.

"I don't suppose it really matters, but how did you manage it all?"

April hesitated, then smiled. It couldn't hurt to tell him.
He wouldn't be passing it on. And one of the most frustrat-
ing aspects of the entire thing had been not being able to
tell anybody about it.

"It was easy enough," she said. "Little Miss Motor-
mouth'd been up at the PLI for all of Labor Day weekend.
Everybody knew Tony used to beat her and that he was trying to get back together. She told me he was going out of

town that week, which made leaving the car at the airpor
kind of a nice touch, I thought."

"I hope she at least didn't have to ... suffer," Alistai
said after a moment, frowning.

"Not at all."

"Oh that's right," he said. "You drugged her."

"I hadn't planned to do that, actually. I was going t
hypnotize her instead. Easier, and no toxicological residues
But I didn't think she'd trust me enough anymore to be
proper subject. I'd already tried that, see."

"You had?"

"After she came to me the first time about the hidden di
rectory. I thought maybe I could just make her forget
through posthypnotic suggestion. She was scheduled for
regression anyway and Carleen was out of town, so I of
fered to do it. She was normally an excellent hypnotic sub
ject, just pathetically eager. But she was terribly resista
that day. She didn't trust me anymore. I wasn't able to wip
out the information the way I'd hoped. The best I could d
was try to get her to forget the session and then tell her th
tape recorder had malfunctioned."

"So you gave her a Quaalude instead."

Why was his tone so accusatory, anyway? The Quaalud
had been an inspired touch, actually. "I'd heard her ta
about Tony and his downers. Filched a couple out of Ba
tholomew's medicine chest. Anyway, by the time I offere
to drive her home that night, she was too spaced to even r
alize what was wrong."

"That's right! You don't drive!" Alistair stared at he
stunned. How the hell did he think she'd gotten here toda
anyway? Flying saucer?

She chuckled. "Not officially. Actually I didn't drive
all for a long time, years and years after my accident. B
I never let my license lapse."

"Well, I'm surprised somebody didn't catch on. Dor
the police check that sort of thing?"

"It's in my married name."

"You're *married*?" His shock was naked and unflatterin

"Not anymore," she snapped at him, "and you don't need to act so bloody surprised."

"I just never had any idea . . ." he went on lamely.

"Can it," she ordered.

"But I remember giving you rides, bringing you into town with me because you didn't drive."

"Normally I don't," she agreed. "But a few years ago I got tired of riding the goddamned bus and waiting around for cabs and Len McIlheney's limos. I'd just started my little savings program. My first purchase out of the freedom fund was an Alfa Romeo. I've had six other cars since then. I keep them garaged in town and nobody ever knows. Except Debra again, dammit."

April shook her head. What a jinx that girl had turned out to be! "She saw me driving in West Hollywood one day just after she started coming to the PLI and mentioned it a little later when she found out I 'didn't drive.' Of course I denied it and told her she must have seen somebody else, but that was just one more reason why I couldn't risk having her around any longer."

"But why did you have to kill Tony too?" Alistair asked.

This was starting to get tiresome. The sniveling faggot was just trying to postpone the inevitable. "To close the investigation, of course! I couldn't very well risk having attention focused on me or anybody else at the PLI, and the police were so incredibly dense. I mean, what could be more obvious than a violent ex-husband?"

"But I can't imagine somebody as macho as Tony just letting a girl come up and shoot him," Alistair protested.

"Actually, Tony being macho made it easier. He never had any idea what happened. Fortunately, he was a little shit." April looked at the pathetic, frail figure in the wheelchair. "Kind of like you."

"Hardly like *me*!" Alistair exclaimed indignantly.

"Well, don't worry, I'm not going to shoot you," she reassured him.

"What are you going to do, then," he asked, snickering, "cut my brake line?"

"She should have crashed and burned," April grumbled, "along with that miserable journal. I've had the worst damned luck. And it's your bad luck that Debra chose to confide in you," she went on. "Though the shape you're in, killing you is probably a favor."

"You needn't bother," Alistair said politely.

She had to laugh. "Oh, it's no trouble. You know, a lot of people with terminal illnesses choose not to put themselves and their loved ones through unnecessary pain and suffering."

She reached into her tote bag and brought out a Ziploc bag full of literature from the Hemlock Society. It had none of her fingerprints on it, and Alistair's could be added later. Anybody in the kind of shape Alistair was in—and broke, to boot—was an obvious suicide candidate.

"Listen," he said, starting to look genuinely frightened. His breathing seemed to accelerate. "You don't need to bother killing me. I'm not going to last much longer anyway. I won't tell anybody anything."

"Sorry. I can't risk you getting an attack of conscience and deciding confession will be good for your soul. Don't worry, this won't be painful. In fact, it's the method of choice for folks in your kind of weakened condition." She brought out a white plastic garbage bag now and a precut length of twine.

His eyes widened. "Suffocation!?"

"Don't give me a hard time," she said, coming up behind him and pulling out the oxygen tubing. "You just told me you believe in reincarnation, right? Think of this as an express ticket to your next life." She glanced around the grubby apartment. "It can't help but be an improvement over this one."

When she started to pull the bag over his head, he gave a loud yell. *HELP!*

His hands rose suddenly and grabbed her wrists in a vice lock. Then, before she could realize what was happening, he was up and out of the chair, struggling fiercely with her.

How could anybody so sick be so strong? He had his hands around her throat now, was cutting off her air.

As she fought back, she heard the door crash open and a loud male voice shouted, *"Police, FREEZE! You're under arrest!"*

The pressure on her throat ended, but there were other hands on her now, rough ones.

The little bastard had set her up.

This couldn't be happening. It just couldn't.

Then Nan Robinson walked into the room, that miserable bitch, that rotten scum-sucking buttinsky. She had a big, self-satisfied smile on her face, and April hated her more than she ever had before.

It was all over, and she knew it.

She slumped back against the cop who was holding her, slipping handcuffs on her. It was the telephone repairman, for God's sake, and where in the hell had he come from? The room was full of people now.

But it didn't matter.

Nothing did.

EPILOGUE

Three days later, Jonathan came to Nan's condo in the early evening, announced unexpectedly by the security guard at the front gate.

Nan had wondered if she'd ever hear from him again, knew from Rosalie O'Brien and the *Los Angeles Times* that he had hired one of California's top criminal attorneys to represent his sister. After her lengthy confession to Alistair, loaded with admissions of premeditation, Nan knew April would need all the legal help she could get. It would wipe out her whole freedom fund, assuming the IRS didn't get it first.

She had just enough time to run a brush through her hair before Jonathan arrived at her door. She was starting to get used to the idea that he was out of her life, understood there was no way they could hope to go on together. Even so, she wasn't prepared for the dull ache that she felt when she saw him standing in the hall.

"I should have called," he told her, "but I wasn't sure until I got here if I could face you." He didn't meet her eyes.

"I understand," she told him gently. "Why don't you come in?"

He perched awkwardly on the edge of the sofa, and she remembered making love with him on the floor in front of that same sofa. He was tense and rigid and when he tried to smile, it didn't quite work.

"I can tell you I'm sorry," he said, "but that doesn't

seem . . . Oh hell, Nan. I knew this was a rotten idea. I shouldn't have come."

"I'm glad you did," she said. "Really. It wasn't your fault, Jonathan, any of it."

He shook his head. "I should have known. I should have realized how sick she was, how much she hated me, hated all of us." He looked at Nan then for the first time, and there was pain and confusion all over his face. "The only good thing is our parents aren't alive to see this."

At that moment Nan wanted more than anything to take him into her arms and comfort him. But she knew that she wouldn't, and that he wouldn't want her to.

"You couldn't have known," she said. "There was no way."

Her reassurance didn't sound very convincing, not even to herself.

Should he have known? Could he have? She had found herself wondering, these past few days, if perhaps he *hadn't* known something. Was it possible that he was so far removed from the operation of his own business that his sister could steal it out from underneath him?

Certainly he must have guessed what happened when Nan's brakes were sabotaged, must have remembered the hours April had spent working in the Henley family garage back in Rocky Glen, Wyoming. Nan recalled how haunted and haggard he had seemed, visiting her in the hospital.

"I'm going to the Midwest next week," she went on. "I'll spend a few days with my mother and then go to South Bend and see Debra's mother. I want to try to explain things to her."

"That's good of you," he said formally.

"I don't know about that," she demurred. "But you know, Debra was really a lovely, caring woman. And there were so many unpleasant, unflattering things that we all focused on about her. Her awful relationships with men, the places she hung out, her offbeat spiritual beliefs, her bad marriage. And then it turned out that none of that had anything to do with what happened to her at all. She got killed because she did her job too well, because she found something that didn't make sense and tried to figure it out. It's crazy to think of killing somebody for being too good a secretary, but in a way that's what happened."

"I suppose you're right."

Well, he could hardly deny it. Nobody said he had to sound enthusiastic.

Nan went on. "My other reason for going back and seeing Mrs. LaRoche is selfish, really. I'm hoping if I can see her and tell her everything, maybe that will ... kind of close things for me. You know, a resolution. Not terribly tidy, maybe, but it's all I've got."

"That makes sense," he said. "And here's another resolution for you. I've arranged to replace your car."

"I wasn't expecting—" she protested, truly surprised.

"Of course you weren't, and that's part of the reason I want to do it."

"I have to testify, you realize."

He stood up, suddenly angry, paced toward the window and turned to glare at her. "I'm not trying to bribe you, for God's sake, Nan! You had a neat little car and it got totaled and I want to get you another one."

"But—"

"Listen, horrible things have happened all around me and maybe they're my fault or maybe they're not, but either way, I want to be able to *do something.* I've never felt so impotent in my entire life. I can't heal your broken arm and I can't bring anybody back to life. I can't cure Alistair's AIDS and I can't fix whatever's wrong with my sister's mind. But I can goddamned well buy a car and I don't want you trying to talk me out of it."

"But my insurance—"

"Will triple if you let your carrier take care of this. And you won't get what it was worth anyway. They don't care that it was a classic Mustang. As far as they're concerned, it was just an old Ford."

Nan sighed and smiled. "All right. I won't try to argue you out of it. Thank you, Jonathan. Very much."

"I'll have them get in touch with you directly," he said, raising his voice slightly to compete with a screaming baby passing by in the hall outside. He smiled for the first time. "Did you ever make your mind up about the house in Venice?"

She smiled back. "Almost. Well, yeah. I'm gonna do it, Jonathan. I'm ready for a change."

He might have been that change, she realized as she spoke, and she could see in his eyes that he realized it too.

"So are we all," he answered obliquely, pacing back and forth around the room. "I'm closing down the PLI, Nan. It's a mess up there. The IRS are all over me, and the district attorney's office. I don't have any idea what was going on, what she did. I . . . I always thought I was a good judge of character, that I could tell someone who was fundamentally good. That's why I was so willing to take on people like Carleen and Bartholomew even with their backgrounds, because they struck me as decent people. That's why . . . that's why I was so attracted to you."

The past tense hung hard and cold between them. There was silence now, and it wasn't the companionable silence of earlier times. It was painful and uncomfortable, the silence of broken dreams and might-have-beens.

"What will you do?" Nan asked him finally.

"I don't have any idea," he admitted. "I can't stay in LA, I know that. Of course I can't leave yet, either, with everything about the PLI so totally unresolved. Everything is in limbo. I'd . . . I'd ask you to . . . take up with me again, Nan, but I just can't . . . somehow, it would seem . . ."

"You don't need to explain," she told him. "Maybe you'd better just go."

And he did.